John Vernon

Simon & Schuster

NEW YORK LONDON TORONTO SYDNEY TOKYO SINGAPORE

All
FOR LOVE
Baby Doe and Silver Dollar

SIMON & SCHUSTER
Rockefeller Center
1230 Avenue of the Americas
New York, NY 10020

This book is a work of fiction. Names, characters, places, and incidents either are products of the author's imagination or are used fictitiously. Any resemblance to actual events or locales or persons, living or dead, is entirely coincidental.

SIMON & SCHUSTER and colophon are registered trademarks
of Simon & Schuster Inc.

Designed by Crowded House

Manufactured in the United States of America

10 9 8 7 6 5 4 3 2 1

Library of Congress Cataloging-in-Publication Data
Vernon, John, date.
    All for love : Baby Doe and Silver Dollar / John Vernon.
        p. cm.
    1. Baby Doe, d. 1935—Fiction.   2. Silver mines and mining—Colorado—
Leadville—Fiction.   3. Industrialists' spouses—Colorado—Leadville—Fiction.
4. Tabor, Silver Dollar, 1889–1925—Fiction.   5. Colorado—History—1876–1950
—Fiction.   I. Title.
PS3572.E76A74   1995
813'.54—dc20   95-9617
                                                                                          CIP

ISBN 0-684-80371-2

In memory of Richard Vernon and Laurie Litchford

I am the moon up in the heavens
Isis is the moon Lily yes it is!

so said Honeymaid

Dear Virgin I will give to 6 poor mothers furnished
homes and I ask your aid in getting me the 3500, to day.

so said mamma

I go right up in heaven on stepladders and bring my
beautiful papa down with a mustache on and he can have
lunch with us and everything

so said Honeymaid

Papa used to tell Cupid that the moon was sick when
it was a half moon and she would say "moon go to the
Chinese doctors and get well"

so said Cupid

socky kiss so said Honeymaid

mamma mamma Oh! Oh!

If papa goes away I hope he wont change his looking

so said Honeymaid

I love you more than the heavens
my own darling angle mother

so said Honeymaid

—written by Silver Dollar Tabor, age ten, June 8, 1899, and pasted into
a scrapbook by her mother, Baby Doe

Contents

Part I　Firkytoodling

Part II　So Said Honeymaid

Part One

Firkytoodling

1. Oshkosh, Wisconsin 1872

"No grunt no ginger."

Earnest fake straining. Ginger was Baby McCourt's favorite taste.

"You finished, then?"

"Mamma, you don't have to stand there no more. I'm perfectly capable of going by myself. I'm fourteen years old."

"You'll just sit there all night and piddle and gas."

"I won't!"

"First you don't care to go, then you don't care to leave." Mamma's voice buttered the privy door. Baby pictured her pockets, one full of mousetraps, one stuffed with ginger. I never did pick the wrong one, she thought.

"Nnrrrrrunh." Her eyes popped. She slapped her soft knees. She did like the sweet smell of pine oil, true enough. Quicklime, pine oil, kerosene from the lamp, fresh yellow pine of the new privy walls. The air in Oshkosh always smelled of yellow pine. Homeowners built new privies each year from slabwood and mill ends, wood being plentiful. Baby had once dearly wanted a playhouse big enough to sleep in, but Mamma said no. She liked fresh wood, strong tastes and smells, liver, ginger, clots of bubbling liquid. In the darkness below, she touched her little nockhole. Firkytoodling, Mamma called it. Fooling with holes. It's what happened when you just piddled around.

"I'm going, then. I'll send your Da later to come fish you out."

"Can I still have the ginger?"

Her footsteps were gone. Mamma was amply warm but a worryguts. "Mother and child," in the carol "Silent Night," used to mean Mamma and her child, Baby. Baby's given name was Elizabeth, but the general wish to cuddle her had never abated once she grew older, so she stayed Baby. When everyone sang "Shepherds quake at the sight," it was she their voices had smuggled into Bethlehem, her sight they quaked at. She perversely clung to such half-deliberate errors because they made sense. The fire brigade came to set your room on fire, and this conviction filled her with terror whenever she heard the bells ring and dogs bark. The doctor called to make you sick, that's what doctors were for, it worked every time.

Her address was Ten Street, not 10 Algoma Street.

Christmas carols were best, their clay was softest. In "The First Noel," for years she'd assumed the third verse referred specifically to her:

> *This star drew nigh Elizabeth*
> *O'er Bethlehem it took its rest.*

She bellowed the words and everyone laughed. Then Aunt Maggie offered her the snapdragons in their flaming dish, and Baby folded back. She'd been set apart by their sparkling eyes. A beam of pure joy broke out of her throat. It felt like those times she'd pictured herself floating above the congregation during Mass at St. Peter's, still in kneeling position. She pictured it now, seated on the hole. She'd been singled out, chosen! She showered down. . . .

By the time she realized her mistake about the song it didn't matter anymore. One day Daddy acted disgusted. "Is it Baby said that?" Then Nealie told her where the star really drew nigh: in the Northwest. I always knew, she thought. I think I did. The knowledge flowed back and eddied through cracks and filled little crannies. It set. The world hardened.

The first time Mamma led her to the jakes she stood there all night urging Baby to finish, never realizing it was her very presence that prolonged her daughter's stay. Thus, a habit was formed. When at last she did finish, Mamma had to help. Mrs. McCourt's children-in-training were obliged to shout "Wipe me!" when ready, but Baby didn't shout, she screamed out each word, she rattled windows nearby, causing Mamma to rush in waving corncobs in each hand. "Glory be, Baby, you're yelling so loud every Paul Pry in town'll know your private business, is *that* what you want?"

Later, Baby took her rosaries to the outhouse till Mamma found out and forbade it absolutely. Each round black seed planted prayers in her fingers. Firkytoodling on the seat, she prayed for the North to win the Civil War. *Civil:* courteous, polite, gallant. Clearly some words lied. Crack their hard shells, tongue out the meat. Oshkosh meant something noble in Indian, she wasn't sure what, but sounded like staving in rotten pumpkins. Comics made fun of it at the Harding Opera House.

Oshkosh. Fog and nine-month winters. Tree stumps and slash piles. "Volcano of the hemisphere, pincer of space..." You could put words together where they didn't belong. "Trenchant cow. Baby's whiskers...whiskey...ashcash..."

Once Baby saw a man on the street outside a saloon dancing in a wool skirt. Hair on his face, black hair on his legs. He boasted out loud he hadn't changed his clothes in seven long years. They must have been long! Daddy said he was a Molly Maguire, but Mamma averred as he was just drunk.

"Charlie dogbreath, sheer lard, Sultana..." No moths assaulted the lantern tonight. "Pope's nose. Ecstasy." She thought she heard breathing. The evening felt cold and dogs barked somewhere.

She unbuttoned one sleeve and carefully rolled it as far back toward the shoulder as possible. Despite the cold, the inner flesh of her elbow felt damp. She dearly kissed it. Harvey Doe had pronounced her that very day to be the most beautiful girl he'd ever seen, and said he'd go to hell and back for her. She flattened her tongue against the bare forearm and ran her rosebud mouth up and down, wrist to elbow, elbow to wrist. She practiced moans. Inflated the muscles and felt them hard against her teeth. A match blossomed somewhere—in her heart, she assumed. She confessed her sins, committed them again, confessed them again, longing for more.

When Katherine O'Neill danced the transformation dance at the Harding Opera House, first she marched around in military drill, hoisting, unshouldering, and spinning a gun. She kicked high on fat legs and fired blanks at the audience. Then an unseen angel pulled a strip string backstage and her uniform flew off and she became a washerwoman. The gun became a paddle swirling in the washtub. She danced an Irish jig and sang "Throw 'im Down McCloskey." Then that dress flew backstage and she stood there with a spade and a French maid's short skirts with heart-shaped bib. She mimed digging holes while hopping about, rolling her eyes, leering and winking.

Her forehead looked like a nest of seething veins, but her face was all suggestive pronouncements. She wasn't singing now but mouthing silent words. Eye strings on the strain. Legomania! The band thumped and scraped. High stepping forward, she bent at the waist as though eager to plunge into everyone's lap. Baby couldn't erase from her mind the lewd mouth, the tongue worming out, the mock infant innocence. Crooking one knee, she straightened up, thrust back her shoulders, lowered her chin, and licked her own thumb as though it were a lollypop. Daddy cheered wildly when the curtain dropped, but commodious Mamma with furrowed brow was herding her ducks out the theater already. Nealie, Peter, Philip, James, Willard, Claudia, and Baby, all raucously slaphappy. They plucked each other's tails. They felt light as air.

Mamma and Daddy took Baby and her siblings to every new bill at the Harding Opera House. Among the better lives she imagined for herself, dancing on stage was the most angelic. She'd wear feathers and sing. How tedious to be told all your life you were pretty as a picture if no one ever saw you!

She cobbed her bottom and dropped the cob in, jumped to her feet, snatched up her drawers, pooched out her skirt. She fingered the sore grooves left by the seat on the backs of her legs. They weren't sore until she stood. Something thumped outside. "Who's there? Claudia? I'll scratch out your eyes!" A rock struck the outhouse. Giggles unleashed. She unbolted the door and rushed into the darkness behind the privy, but tripped and fell. Two shapes ran up the alley.

The cold earth felt hard. Out here you could see the light from her lantern gullying cracks in the privy wall. Overhead, the moon. "The moon's a silver dollar . . ." Leaves on the oaks scratched like paper in the breeze. Was it Claudia and Nealie or someone else? They sounded like boys. Feast your greedy eyes!

The ashpits had all been rained on that day and smelled like raw fog, lungs filled with dirt. The moon had a rash. She lay there smiling. She'd scratched her cheek. Good. It would last as long as the full moon lasted, not a second longer.

Harvey Doe returned the next day on his way home from school, having made a circuit around Main Street to longingly walk up Baby's alley. He tried not to stare too much at her back porch, and averted his eyes entirely from the privy. The mayor's son couldn't be a pokenose. Last night he'd braved raspberry thorns to catch a glimpse of Baby McCourt kissing her own arm. The sight made him prickle. Some nocturnal rite of the shanty Irish? He rushed straight home to strangle the goose after swearing to Will that he'd seen her private parts.

What color was they?

Red, guessed Harvey.

In persuading Will, he'd converted himself. Folds parted in memory, revealing more folds. Every corner of the afternoon rhymed with dark secrets. Walking down alleys was like peering backstage. He'd often dreamed of sailing through alleys on slow massive ships half submerged in earth. The backs of his neighbors' lives opened up, those parts even they couldn't see. Could they see themselves in nightshirts

All for Love

dashing through ankle-high grass to make water? Burning caterpillar nests, draping washed bloomers over privets to dry... cursing fouled wicks on the back porch at dusk?

Most people allowed the weeds and briars to grow behind their privies, to create a zone of privacy. Porcupines and rats made themselves at home there.

What was it this afternoon that dredged up pictures from dreams Harvey'd long ago forgotten? Behind one house, in a bower of unpruned lilacs and hawthorns, stood a low storage shed whose back wall consisted entirely of windows. They swelled with frames askew, reflecting the sky. He couldn't see inside. As in his dreams, this shed was low and unplumb, a place to be prone in. Moss grew on the roof. Nothing happened in the dreams. It was where he lived away from his parents with rooms full of girls. Usually there were several buildings clustered near an alley, mazed by pathways of grass. Rooms opened into rooms with old iron cots and low slanted ceilings held up by posts and struts. He mostly slept and, inside his dream, experienced happy dreams without content. The sense of a blessed and secret refuge dimly glowing with ordinary warmth and sunlight on the floor is what he remembered. It makes more sense than anything I've heard concerning salvation at Sunday School, Mommy! He gawked at the shed. The place seemed to call him. Thick grass surrounded it. Actually, he'd likely glimpsed this very backyard and shed long ago, and it triggered those dreams in the first place. Of course.

If he were a ghost in a dream, he could sneak—no, walk boldly— into Baby's house and watch her talk with her parents and brush her long hair and undress for bed and climb under the covers. He could watch her kiss her arm.

The air in the alley was blue and dusty and smelled of sawdust. If Oshkosh grew bigger, as his father predicted, it would do so by alleys dividing and swelling until the town mushroomed. Every street had an alley behind it, its shadow. He emerged onto Irving Street and followed it to Main.

Cameron and McCourt was Baby's father's shop. Peter McCourt made suits for Harvey's father. From here, Main Street declined toward the river, where smoke rose from sawmills, shingle mills, and planing mills. The blue sweep of the lake ran east behind buildings, below the horizon.

Chubby Harvey whistled. Enormous rafts of logs floated offshore beyond the river's mouth. Stacks of lumber ten and twenty feet high covered the piers and spilled up Main Street. As the logs got milled they were squeezed into new stacks between the old ones. The very timber from which the boards had been sliced had floated through town not long ago, down the Fox River, some on barges built from the same trees, some floating freely in jammed-together rafts. Harvey liked the wood best in heavy stacks. You could travel on the train between Oshkosh and Milwaukee and see nothing but stumps left from the Cutover. New houses and farms had gathered in hollows like seedlings blown there. He liked to imagine their house paint unpeeling, nails popping out, boards coming unstuck, running wounds closed, sap sucked back in, balloon frames collapsing. He ran it backwards in his mind but always stopped at the stacks, not the trees. The stacks were more striking, his father owned half of them. Barns, churches, and schools caved in, also fences, wagons, railroad ties, sidewalks, rafts, and slabwood cut up for burning. All folded themselves back into stacks, the gulched boards unshrunk and split corners tidied, then were loaded on barges and shipped back here and piled to the sky without a single gap, without one drop of light to trickle between them.

The buggy outside his house meant company. In the parlor, Papa introduced a man he called Senator Stephens. Cigar smoke filled the room. Will smoked cigars—he'd smoked one last night, in Baby's alley —but they made Harvey sick.

"'Oiling the wheelbarrow,' he says," said the senator. Elbows on knees, he leaned forward. He sat on the Does' brown damask sofa, while Harvey's father filled a stiff armchair. When Harvey Senior shifted his weight the room seemed to adjust. His son lingered near the door. He'd interrupted a story. " 'Leave it alone,' says the boss, 'what the hell do you know about machinery?' "

"Ha ha. Pat says to Mike," said Harvey Senior, " 'What would you do with a million dollars?' "

"I heard that one, Mr. Mayor. 'Put six inches more on my pick handle,' right?"

Mayor Doe turned to his son. "The senator here's trying to sell us a gold mine."

"Where?"

"Out to Colorado." He lowered his voice. "Don't tell your mother yet."

"You got the future right here in Oshkosh," said the senator. "Let the money you make here work for you there."

"That's what I figger."

"I had two prosperous mines in Central City myself. Partnership in a twenty-stamp quartz mill, a miner's boarding house, mines on Quartz Hill. I got more claims there too."

"What about injuns?"

"They'll be gone by the time you're a grandpa," he said. He glanced at Harvey Junior. "Maybe sooner," he added. This senator looked like a lumberjack to Harvey. He had the logger's pox, made when one lumberjack stomps another's face with his hobnails. His cheeks were sunk in.

"You ever jack trees?" asked the boy.

"In my younger days."

"We're all lumbermen here," said the mayor.

"But what do you do when there's no more trees?" The senator furrowed his prominent brow. He looked concerned.

"Centuries won't exhaust the pineries above us!" Harvey's father gestured vaguely north. "If you and I planned it like this, sir, we couldn't have come up with anything sweeter. Settling the West means you turn to the northern forests for lumber. But say we do cut them all. Even if that happens—which it won't, I'm saying, but even if it

John Vernon

22

does—so much the better. Our forests, like the savages they spawned, are only fit to be exterminated. That's what I say. They hinder the plow and block the sunlight. When Wisconsin becomes one vast planted field of grain, then we lumbermen all shall be farmers, I say, and amen to that."

"Or gold miners."

"Told! You can't have the West and its riches without you got a supply of lumber, upriver no less, to make it livable for Christians. Right here in Oshkosh, we're right at the crux. All the forces of nature intersect here. We're the bees that make the honey. The advantages of nature draw populations in, the populations draw in the raw materials from the tributary countryside, and the resulting spontaneous growth bodies forth the metropolis, see? What happened in Chicago will be dwarfed by Oshkosh in decades to come."

"Never thought of it that way."

"We'll surpass them soon enough." The rings of fat around Mayor Doe's eyes glowed with faith. His son wasn't listening, he'd heard it all before. He'd been born on the frontier. That meant the forests of his childhood were just obscure green clouds now. All his life, all seventeen years, trees had surrendered their wood to people. Holes in the earth surrendering minerals at least had a whiff of novelty about it.

"What say you, son?"

"Who's Pat and Mike?"

The older men laughed. Harvey, swimming in smoke, looked down. His stomach sloshed back and forth like water in a bucket. He waved the smoke from his nose and conjured a picture of Baby McCourt with hair red and curly, nose tip-tilted, round and soft mouth. It unclenched his bowels. Her blue eyes sat further apart in her face than any other girl's he'd ever met, giving her a look of overflowing generosity just this side of lunacy. Her father possessed that same look too, but tamed it with precision. Constructing loose clothes took more architecture than nailing houses together, Harvey decided. He conceived of a sudden desire to be a tailor. He could apprentice himself to Baby's father.

"What's so funny, son?"

If Papa only knew. If he knew whose daughter his son was in love with!

Winter came early, as always in Oshkosh. The first snow powdered brown leaves on the oak trees. At home Baby never did chores, being precious. Her hands were too soft. She sat in the parlor and thumbed through a photo album. One picture showed Daddy outside his old store next to Mr. Cameron, hands behind his back. Last year the store'd been destroyed in a fire, but he rebuilt it larger than ever. It was prosperous times, he announced at home. They bought new furniture, made new dresses, hired a maid fresh from Norway. Mamma'd taught the maid to make snapdragons, and Hilde set the pan on the parlor stove now. Baby curled up on her folded legs. As the oldest girl, she sat next to Daddy, furthest from the stove, while he read the paper. Mamma didn't want her to burn her pretty fingers on the flaming raisins, or to dry out her skin in the heat from the fire.

But the same Mamma raised no objection when the youngest, Nealie, plucked a raisin from the pan and rushed with the pale blue flame to her sister. "Take it, quick!"

"You'll burn yourself, Nealie," Baby cautioned. Nealie put it inside her own nose and held her breath. She squeezed out a slow squeal. She seemed to turn red.

"Will you for God's sake stop the nonsense!" cried Daddy. He didn't say "By the pipers!" or "Great cripes almighty!" because, Baby knew, he was practicing control. He'd been born in Ireland, as he bragged to his children, but more often these days he spoke of the Irish as though they were a foreign race. I'm a Catholic, he once said on a Friday, but I've a Protestant stomach. I could eat a plate of beef.

Mrs. McCourt patiently explained that one man from County Cork who'd done just that had choked to death in a New York restaurant only last week, but Daddy shook his head. His laugh was more splutter

than laughter. "Next you'll be saying that Protestant men have to pray standing up, whereas their women are required to lie down."

"Peter!"

A sideboard overflowed with figurines and curios. Red tassels hung from the curtains on the windows. Peter Junior sat at the piano and stared at the snow falling outside. Because he couldn't play, he was drawn to the piano as though to lithos of French cathedrals or women's corsets. One finger on the high keys tried to imitate the snow.

Mamma sat sewing. Her husband was a tailor, but Baby knew he wouldn't ask whose green skirt that was in Mamma's lap being shortened and hemmed with a narrow band of fur. Our secret, she thought, is safe inside this parlor, land of the incurious.

"I know something, Daddy!" Nealie had pulled the raisin from her nose and swallowed it whole. She and Claudia stood at the stove, snapping up the flaming raisins. "Ida Shelley's entry hall windows are made out of sugar."

"She's an angel now," said Claudia.

"No, she's a Congregationalist."

"Where does the child get such ideas?" Daddy seemed on edge.

"It's all my eye," said Mamma.

"I've never heard such foolishness."

"It's true!"

"Was the house warm when she was waked?"

Nealie shouted yes.

"Was there fires in the fireplace?" asked Daddy.

"Yes, there was!"

"The windows would have melted, then."

"They look just like glass."

Maybe Daddy knew what the skirt was for and didn't give a fig. He'd decided to allow his favorite daughter and her mother their little conspiracy, that's it. No. Hardly likely. The skirt only barely came down to her knees! Half of Daddy's customer's were Congregationalists, including Harvey's father. They lit their cigars entering his store, where the smoke got mixed with smells of broadcloth and varnish rising from the new counters. The smoke didn't make Baby dizzy, like her sisters. Heavens, she was stronger than even most boys. For example, she could skate until she dropped. She fell asleep at night by composing a surface of virgin ice in her mind, hard and smooth, and running it out through a forest of waist-high stumps in the snow. Then she skated from Oshkosh on powerful thighs, with a lullaby rhythm, as she'd often in fact skated up the Fox River, escaping the buzzing and whining saws, the piney smells, the smoke and sawdust. *Come back, Baby!*

But she was gone.

They'll have to come down off their high horses and kiss my bright forehead and shake my soft hand and pin me a medal when I win, she thought. Won't that be nice. Everyone in town will view my extremities. The thought made her glow. She felt like a powerful stranger come to town, the object of envy and admiration. Girls would hate her, boys fall in love, adults pretend shock. Would Mr. Cameron ever invite her to sit on his lap again? Would he dare?

A merchant had once come into the store and asked her daddy if he wasn't afraid someone would steal such a beautiful daughter. Over my dead body, he gallantly answered.

She'd learned to flirt at the ice cream shops. The boys wondered out loud would she measure them for new clothes? Mouthy Alice Hunt called her a green nigger; it was well known that the Irish bathed once a year regardless of whether they needed to or not.

The long weeks ran into the skating contest like the river whose length she nightly skated into sleep. Even practicing in secret was a form of dreaming. Her mother sat on the lake bank and coached her. Baby pictured herself spinning on a music box until the figure she imagined unspooled into flesh. Her legs seemed to hatch out of membranes of thought. She skimmed and twirled in widening circles crossing the edge of her mind and crossing back. Each time she leapt the world's shell cracked open. The secret nested in her skating was its pattern. Even Mamma didn't know what that was. Baby'd sketched it on paper back at home. The banks of Winnebago Lake made a natural amphitheater, and astute observers might figure it out, those looking down from above. But not likely.

The banks swarmed with people, on blankets, around fires. Judges included Mr. James Clark, the manufacturer of matches. She'd registered under E. McCourt, since they couldn't ban Papists, and a female name might raise eyebrows. It was generally understood that a skating contest sponsored by the Congregational Church was for men only. When her name was called and she threw off the lap robe in which Mamma had wrapped her, she never heard the gasp. She was already at the edge of the lake, where the ice had trapped bubbles and black stems and grass. Her bare legs felt gloriously cold, they were humming like engines. She took dozens of running steps on her points, then pushed off sailing. She could cross the whole lake! It had been Mamma's idea to include the mink muff, which matched the trim on her green wool skirt. Keeping her forearms inside it raised problems of balance, of course, but decanted the judges' attention to her legs. She wore a cute little fur cap too.

As though peering through a dream, she spotted Harvey and his father, each seated on a tree stump. The cracked wet sack of Harvey's mouth hung open. Her own father was there, and the rest of her family, watching the whole town watch her bare legs. Daddy wouldn't mind. He was proud of his daughter. But her brothers lewdly giggled. Can you read, she wondered? She was skating a sentence in florid cursive, making the ice hiss. Its surface, full of shavings, was too scarred and shot to hold the words with any clarity. You'd have to, like Baby, engrave it on your mind. Even then it might only be barely decipherable. The *O* foliated with flowers and tendrils, the *S* scrolled with roses. When the words had finished pulling through her limbs like needle and yarn through one of Mamma's samplers, she threw off the muff, bent to one knee, lowered her chin, and licked her white thumb with a wonderful pout. She flaunted the message no one could read: *Oshkosh Go To Hell.* But she knew they felt it. She'd inscribed it on their brains. She sweetly smiled.

Cheers and bravos erupted. Mamma ran out sliding on the ice and wrapped her Baby in the lap robe from their buggy. She couldn't stop hugging her, and the two almost crashed to the ice like circus clowns. Ten minutes later, the announcement came: "First prize goes to Miss McCourt." She skated out to receive her blue ribbon and box of candy from the mayor himself, whose weight on the ice was a test of winter's progress. Back on the lake bank, his son sat sheepishly stunned on his stump.

Oshkosh did go to hell two years later. Everyone on 10 Algoma Street was home for dinner, Daddy included. A lumberman on a horse galloped up the road shouting that Morgan's Mill was on fire and all able-bodied men were needed on Main Street. Baby's whole family piled into their buggy. Already, the smoke filled the sky. Daddy shouted, "We're done for in this wind," and he was right. By the time they arrived half of Main Street was burning and people were throwing their furniture out of second-floor windows in hopes of sparing it the flames. Instead, it got smashed.

Ashes filled the air. Smoke blocked the sun but the fire gave off light, doggedly eating its way up Main Street. When the first wall of heat struck the McCourts, Daddy and Pete had to jump from the carriage and drag the horses by their bridles. Merchants in lines emptied out stores, but further down the street scattered piles of goods had caught fire already. Beneath the eaves of Dart and Williams, snakes of smoke blew out as though from the lid of a boiling pot. Then the roof exploded, and a cyclone of fire rose into the sky, showering sparks.

To Baby it seemed like a picturesque dream. It lit up the street with pitiless clarity but didn't belong, like a full moon in daylight. Daddy'd said they should have rebuilt with brick after the last time, and of course he was right. This fire looked worse. Why not save themselves the trouble, why not burn all the forests before they got cut. . . .

Somewhere down Main Street kegs of pitch exploded. She tried not to smile. Eruptions of power made her feel happy. Uncontrollable blasts of ruin and pain—goodness, what frenzy—what a cure for the mulligrubs! Sidewalks burned from one end to the other faster than people could manage to walk. The clapboard siding of one carriage warehouse had all been consumed, leaving its trellis of beams serenely burning. Crowds of men ran back and forth shouting orders, and barrels of whiskey had been rolled into the street from saloons not yet burned, and broken open.

The McCourts made a line and filled their buggy with bolts of cloth from Daddy's store. Dust and smoke blew everywhere. Tides of fire passed over Main Street, sucking air from their lungs. Daddy had to hold on to the horses, who stood frozen in the street, ears back, eyes wild. Pigeons circled up into the air, got drawn into the fire, and popped as though shot. Baby noticed that Harvey Doe was helping them. He carried ready-mades packed in tissue out of the store and threw them in the buggy. Soon it was full. Pete Junior drove it off, Daddy ran up Main Street looking for another wagon, the rest of the family stood around getting hotter. Harvey told Baby that several merchants out of desperation had driven their wagons into the river, and they burst into flames even though half sunk.

Looking down Main Street, they couldn't see the river. Mountains of black and red smoke billowed up. The roar of the fire swallowed other sounds. Everything grew quiet. Brick walls fell silently into the flames. Fire entered the east end of Mead and Company and in seconds appeared at the west doors and windows.

"I heard Parson Moody grabbed his Bible and run." Harvey's voice seemed to have risen an octave. He and Baby's family were scooting up Main Street. Tendrils of flame had already begun climbing the wooden front of Daddy's store, and across the road two stores separated by an alley had simultaneously burst into flames. Then a crazed horse ran by and knocked Baby over. Harvey yanked her to her feet and they ran up the hill. Baby glanced down and saw his pant cuffs were on fire. They beat them out with their hands. "He had six thousand books in his library," said Harvey. "What one shall I take, he asked himself? It was the Bible."

For the past year or so on every Friday night Harvey'd visited the McCourts and played their Clementi piano and sung. He'd billowed with song, but that close to Baby his heart unravelled, his boyish grin hurt. Sometimes their voices braided for duets, what intricate bliss! His father had resigned himself to the thought that his own flesh and blood might hear Irish music and see Irish beer drunk by mustachioed laborers . . . but not his mother. She warned him of priests writing his name in secret ledgers, for subsequent conversion. Irish women, she said, snatched babies from their carriages and smuggled them into church to be baptized. Now the churches were burning. At least, Harvey thought, we'll have a clean slate soon. Could we start over, please, neither Catholic nor Protestant?

Then Baby and I could attend the same church.

They passed an angular mound of picture frames tossed into the street. The fire was everywhere. Copper nails in the steeple of the Congregational Church glowed bright red from the heat inside it. "Daddy says we ought to move west," Harvey shouted. "They don't have these fires in the mountains of the West."

"Nothing to burn but rocks," said Baby.

A bug-eyed horse raced up Main Street toward them, pulling a wagon filled with burning couches. The faster he ran the more they burned.

The most heartbreaking sight to Baby was watching the Harding Opera House go up. It was brick, but a firestorm erupted inside it. First the balcony on the Temple of Honor across the street flared up and disappeared. Then the Opera House roof peeled completely off, and several cones of flame shot into the sky. It felt like her childhood was being consumed. All the minstrel shows she'd seen, all the Dutch comics, the singers with arms outstretched on balconies. An Italian man had draped odds and ends on volunteers from the audience and made lovely dresses right there onstage. He'd made a wedding gown! Soon the walls collapsed. She couldn't help crying. Every opera house in America went up in flames, every dream and gasp. Baby felt queer.

Spires of churches keeled over. Trees became charred twigs. Curling volumes of black smoke rose above the town, and Baby, exhausted, realized those domes of smoke were Wisconsin. Their milled and stacked lives were being consumed and offered up as spectacle. Acres of light eddied this way and that. The fire made its own wind to speed its own ships. She felt drained of blood, scraped clean with a knife. Emptied out and cauterized. Her head ached something awful. She'd thought they were standing pretty far above the fire, but an oak tree across from them burst into flames. They continued up Main Street.

Her family was here. Wagons and buggies had pulled into a field and crowds of people stood around. Merchants and their children guarded barrels of vinegar, piles of mattresses, bedsteads, wagon wheels, shoes, crates of dishes. They walked through the crowds. Harvey sprayed her with words. He couldn't stop talking. His face was red and he rambled on about everything and nothing—plans for the future, questions, regrets—like a man consumed with fever. He was thinking out loud. Would he himself have thought to take his Bible? Gosh, he wouldn't feel right if he saved all his own things while everyone else's were being burned up. What if this fire spread to consume what was left of the northern forests? His father owned gold mines; he'd given one to Harvey. Why not make a lot of money? There was nothing left here.

Suddenly Baby realized what he wanted. He was asking her to marry him.

2. Central City, Colorado 1879

Harvey's eyes flew open and sucked in darkness. Sharp edges pressed. Smell of sulphur and nitrate, moldy wool, gold-laced piss. His thoughts sparked and died as though, in his brain, a knife were being sharpened: Baby's winning voice.... Jake Sandelowsky kneading her back.... The wicked lend money, the rest of us, what.... Jake's gold tooth.... He was Harvey's friend!

That did it, the sadness returned, a crushing sadness. He closed his eyes. Hell, open or shut it didn't matter, the darkness was the same. That's why he'd come here. In a mine shaft only sounds have an outline. Hard rocks knuckling his shoulder and hip felt miles apart. The distant thudding of a stamp mill broadcast underground through rock containing who knows how much gold seemed actually to come from the base of Harvey's skull as though he himself, Harvey, stretched out supine, were lifting and swinging his own head back as hard as he could against the rock....

He was doing that. It felt good for a while. When he stopped, the muffled shock of a blast arrived through the cradling earth like a shrug. Something was scratching. Cockroaches, Harvey?

Harvey Doe Junior wondered if he'd always be a Junior, even when his father died. Not that he prayed for Papa's untimely demise, but does the son assume the father's title when it happens?

Harvey disliked the smell of piss, but he'd brought it on himself, and now even two blankets wrapped around him couldn't shut it out. Indeed, they'd absorbed it. What other animal fouls his own burrow, then passes out in it? It was for a good cause. He needed to salt his mine, to make a quick sale, to pay off his debts, to get out of the hole he'd dug for himself—to leave everything behind—and therefore he'd taken to excess of drink, not to mention gained weight, solely in order to punish his kidneys, for which druggists nowadays sold a medication containing gold chloride—superior to Dr. Sherman's Prickly Ash Bitters—which, if you voided it in the right place, improved your health and your lode at the same time.

Harvey Doe climbed Quartz Hill every night at dusk to piss into his mine. It seemed to be working. The last half cord of ore he'd mucked out yielded at the rate of two ounces a cord when run under the stamps, a small improvement.

Harvey enjoyed watching the yellow rope of his piss pulled down into the mine, it was such a relief. Prospective buyers nowadays brought their own dynamite when blasting for samples, so you couldn't very well dip the ends of the sticks in gold dust first.

Harvey's little cubby was five feet of drift at the bottom of the shaft, like the toe of a shoe. It meant that he couldn't just piss from the top, he also had to come right down here and aim directly onto the face of the lode. As to why he'd passed out, it was necessary to consume enough nose paint to produce a good yellow stream and clean out the kidneys. He'd relieved himself once from the shaft collar above, then descended the ladder to wait for his tanks to fill up again. Once there, he'd wrapped the blankets around him and lay on the wet ground, and lo, mother earth took him unto her bosom. Then to maul the rising chorus of sadness, he smashed the back of his head on the ground. In this fashion, he fell asleep.

Harvey wondered what the scratching was. He couldn't get warm. Harvey, who liked to whistle and hum to make people think he was amiable and winsome, realized he was doing so now. And to whom was he providing evidence of his happiness?

Harvey's father must have known this mine was *borrasca* when he leased Benoni Waterman's half interest, then deeded his own half to his son on condition that he make it pay. Why, Papa even found him the very carpenter to shore up Harvey's botched timbering job, for four hundred and eighty-five dollars, it turned out. To pay this debt he'd tried to borrow from the bank, but he owed the First National five hundred already—for the Cousin Jacks who'd sunk the shaft deeper —so now Peter Richardson, the carpenter, followed him everywhere, even paid for a notice printed in the paper to announce to one and all that Harvey was a deadbeat.

Harvey whistled and hummed.

The first samples assayed were worthless, so what do you do, you keep digging. Then it blossomed a little, enough to buy boots while he prayed for the source, the pay streak, a blowout—the true fissure fault lode. Meanwhile, Papa leased the Troy Mine to Baby, and now Harvey's thoughts spiraled out of control. Baby in felt hat, union drawers, brogans, and trouser cuffs tied below the knees. He and Jake Sandelowsky had buried her wild bird that died in its cage. He sat bolt upright. From balconies in his heart came the weeping sound again, from the cells in his blood came a rising hiss, and there sat poor Harvey trying to hum and whistle and drown it all out. Also, his face hurt. She'd mucked in the Troy, in the Fourth of July, even shat like the men in a candle box down here. He wished the darkness would suck him right out through the neck, as the moles do to worms, then hang up the skin. That way he could feel sorry for himself but not have to cry. . . .

Harvey Doe tried to spit, but nothing came out. He hummed "If You've Only Got a Mustache," but it didn't drown the funny scratching sound. He wished it would stop. One thing he liked to feel down here: that the world outside had nothing to do with him, it spun like a slip clutch with no fixed connection. This gave him comfort. He was in the hole, and he was the hole. The shaft was his throat. He sat in the earth, head thrown back, enormous. No one could see him, humped up and waiting. . . .

From somewhere in the mine came the sounds of collapse. He'd dug and blasted the shaft without care, knew beans about timbering, hastily worked the ore, hated the place, wrote it off a dozen times, so now no wonder rocks and pebbles were sliding down the walls and curtains of dirt sifting through timbers. And that scratching! Getting closer, certain. Maybe some animal had fallen down the shaft, a dog for example. A ferocious dog with powerful jaws, dragging himself in Harvey's direction by seizing a chunk of stone with his mouth and pulling his broken body forward while drooling and bleeding, yes, that sounded good. That made him smile. A horrible dog coming to tear at Harvey's throat with razor-sharp teeth, that made him want to piss again. The entire bottom half of his body loosened, and a thread of golden pee shot down his leg. Too precious to waste!

Harvey stood up to water the wall. A light popped behind his eyes and flowered.

"Harvey Doe?"

Candle in hand, the man was climbing down the shaft, but his bulk blocked the flame.

He resembled a bell swinging softly side to side in flaring skirts; it seemed he wore a nightgown. He filled the shaft, yet when he arrived he'd shrunk to a pipsqueak, only came to Harvey's nipples! Just standing there, he appeared to be bustling, full of spunk but neckless and toylike, looking up at Harvey. He wore a nightcap. Face like an upright flatiron with smallish features painted on. Here was a person perpetually startled, who woke instantly from sleep, and never harbored secrets. "Billy Bush wants to speak to you." He held out a bottle.

"What's this?" As though he didn't know.

"Popskull." The man's shrill voice contained the anonymous optimism of a monkey shriek. Billy Bush had aroused this little man to find and lure him with drink. Well . . . it might work. He seized and uncorked the bottle with rage, and greedily drank. When he finished, the small man snatched it back. "Harold Leighton." An introduction, Harvey realized.

"Harvey Junior." Like a tin of smoked ham opened with a key, a broad grin rolled across Harvey's face. "Just the man I want to see. Harold," he said, "have you ever thought about owning your own mine?"

Stumbling down Quartz Hill in the dark, Harvey savored the gloom. Somewhere behind, Harold tried to keep up on his stubby little legs. A salesman himself, he'd turned out not to be interested in mines. What did he sell?

Wallpaper.

The night wasn't so advanced that you couldn't see smoke spewed from the mills, dark spun from darkness. The sun had set maybe two hours ago, judging from the faint light smeared above the mountains. Below, Central City lay in a tailspin under folded whorls of earth from which light leaked up. Hammer of stamp mills, shriek of steam hoists, steady beat of Cornish pumps. Steam and grease. Smell of lumber in stacks wet from the evening rain, which had slicked the hill too, a drunk man needed caution. Raw flowers of sewage opening left and right. Tree stumps, mud, board shacks, smashed roads, abandoned boilers, tin roofs. Even in June, the night air went cool once the sun slammed its door. "Wallpaper *here?*"

"Mines mean miners. Miners mean boardinghouses, stores, saloons, tonsorial parlors, dance halls. Suchlike means walls. Walls mean wallpaper."

"Not boardinghouses, gawd!" Harvey had bounced from one boardinghouse to another after Baby kicked him out, and none had a single wall worth papering. It would be like painting dirt.

"Not yet. Give it time. Think of the snuggeries in this town papered to the gills. My company has judged the outlook to be good for a most wonderful improvement of the western settlements, due to feminine influence."

"Baggage and crib girls."

"I can't tell you what it feels like to see unpapered walls. What an itch it gives me! I could sing you some beautiful stories of folks falling out of windows to break their collard bones, of the beautiful broken heads I've seen, all for lack of a papered wall to frame the window so's you could tell it was there. People are just one large mess of bones and ashes, and liable to fall apart any minute, you wouldn't poke 'em with a fork, filthy as Turks, without they have some comfort and pretty things in their lives and commit to memory the good advice their mother give them underneath the wallpaper. You have a child with rickets, let's say, and what do you do with it, drop it in scalding lard and fry until done like a doughnut, Harvey? *I* say paper its walls with something modeled on a shrubbery blight, mostly yellow, and let it sleep in a brass bed and grow healthy teeth and climb mountains and eat lavish meals cooked on a range that looks like a narrow-gauge locomotive and not complain about liver ailments and some type of heart failure and never drink out of someone else's cup because life ain't easy no matter which way you cut it, and we need some civilizing influences, don't we. . . ."

Down here near the cemetery you had to be careful, the steep cutbanks began without warning. It was best to walk directly through the cemetery, but someone had sunk a new shaft below it, just grazing the graves. Maybe Harvey could lead Harold Leighton past the hole? Startle him at the proper moment? Harvey pictured the man lacing on his boots under his nightshirt when Billy Bush summoned him. Now he was jawing on about cockroaches, even speeding up didn't help. He was at Harvey's heel. Mix some plaster of Paris with three or four parts of flour in a saucer. When the plaster sets it clogs the creature's innards—with fatal effect. . . .

"Cockroaches live off wallpaper," said Harvey. "They like the glue-paste."

"That's a bald-faced lie!"

On Spruce Street, where civilization began, a man walked up to Harvey Junior and asked, "Is there anything the matter with me?"

"Yes, your face is covered with blood."

"Oh." He wiped it with his shirttail and walked off.

Music, boot stomping, laughter, and shouts came from three or four places at once. On Pine Street, a whore walked directly into Harvey and before he knew it he'd knocked her off the wooden sidewalk into the mud.

"Nose-bag! Stick-wipe!"

"Bushel-cunt!"

"Gut-bucket, can't you see?"

"It's true I can't tell shit from honey."

"You can't see your own feet." Well, *that's* an exaggeration, thought Harvey. His *panza* hung out a little, sure, but on tall folks like him it looked worse than it was.

They were outside the Bucket of Blood, and patrons had swarmed out to stir up the brew. The woman just sat in the mud, skirts flared. "Where's it from?" someone asked. "Wind blowed it in!" Harold Leighton tugged on Harvey's trousers. What an annoying little pinch bug he was!

One man chased another through the mud, stomping on his heels from behind. This brought the latter to his knees, but he kept stubbing forward due to momentum, until the other base fellow viciously kicked the small of his back. His boot must have been spiked because blood-stains bloomed on the victim's shirt. Slowly, he rose, flushed all over, and—Harvey never saw where he got it—swung a shovel at the first man's head, then exclaimed, "I do dislike you!" For some minutes, they hugged and pummeled each other, and when one went down the other followed, smashing his nose with his fist all the way. Even from the sidewalk, this fist looked unusually large, then its owner winced and dropped a roll of coins. "Don't stop! Don't stop!" he shouted pretty loud. At whom, Harvey wondered? The man on the bottom gouged his thumb in the eye of the man on top. The man on top shoved mud up the nostrils of the man on bottom. Then both were on their sides, and one seized the other's hand and bit down so hard on a finger the poor fellow fainted. The victor spit something out and exclaimed, jumping to his feet, "Am I good, or what? Am I good?"

The other man lay in the road and didn't stir. Harvey realized he'd never even heard them apply harsh epithets to each other. Fighting was nothing if not infectious. Knock a whore in the ditch and soon there's a riot. If the man in the road died, what would happen? The coroner would issue his usual verdict of deranged suicide and bury him out of sight.

Someone spun Harvey around. "Don't I know you, you bastard?"

"Keep your hat on."

"Why, you're just a big piece of sugar candy. I'll eat you up."

Harvey backpedaled through the crowd. Behind this large gump the woman he'd knocked into the road was waving her fist and gnashing her teeth. "Hump it," said Harvey, who realized he'd said this to Harold Leighton, still clinging to his pants.

"Not so pissen fast!" cried Harold.

In the Hurdy Gurdy, Harvey bolted two Guckenheimers, then spotted Billy Bush waving from a table. He ordered two more. Ain't no back out in me. Some get drunk to avoid their duty, but Harvey was more responsible than that, he drank to *do* his. Of course, Papa thought Harvey was scared of his own shadow—had told him so, plenty—but Papa was always overstuffed with meat, and no trace of human weakness ever clung to him. Even after he'd gone back to Oshkosh, his influence rippled biblically everywhere, and one of his angels was now summoning Harvey here in Central City.

The wallpaper salesman was nowhere to be seen. At the altar, the bar-dog, with white shirt and red vest—a geranium and sprig of fern wrapped in silver paper pinned on his lapel—turned and told Harvey, "Keep your nose pits open."

What a kind friend! "I shall."

Sand on the floor annoyed Harvey's feet. Fiddles and squeeze-boxes played up on stage, and four dolly-mops sang over and over, "Merry Little Birds Are We." Billy Bush nodded Harvey into a free chair; beside him, his lady friend seemed to be swallowing her own spit repeatedly. She looked like someone forced to suck lemons. Black, precise lips sliced with a razor, flaming red hair. Something funny happened. Harvey, who really liked women, really did, seemed to attract this one's absolute enmity, the way some dogs get chased even by cats. "Nominate your poison," said Billy Bush.

"Old Towse."

When Billy Bush gestured, jugs appeared magically. "Man I know," he said, "drank a pint of this licker, ran home and stole one of his own horses. Hid it in the woods all tied up, and next day didn't know where it was. So he had to get drunk again to find it."

"Ha ha."

"Here. Your Poppa said to give this to you." Beneath Harvey's nose, he waved a wad of bills.

Harvey counted one hundred dollars. "What's he want me to do?"

"Nothing. It's yours. He thought you might need it. Just remember that he's thinking about you. Keep yourself tidy, work hard, save money. Every person in this country has the same and equal chance with everyone else, and them that fail got no one to blame but themselves, you know that. Your father never told me to say this, but you want my advice, sell the Fourth of July and move to Leadville. Leadville's the place."

"Sell it, I'd love to. Find me a buyer."

"Also, your Poppa told me to tell you to go back to Baby."

More Old Towse! Harvey felt as though someone had kicked him in the lungs. The face of Billy Bush was a zoological specimen, glasses and all; his smile looked taxidermic. Why couldn't Harvey grow a mustache like those flapping rat tails? Billy Bush always said one thing and winked another, his small face had dozens of secret codes. Red face, black hair, stony gaze, careful hands. Harvey pictured a toad squatting on his heart. He couldn't have been that much older than Harvey, but he'd paid for his savvy with dark, sunken eyes wrinkled like prunes. Small nose, thin sly smile. A self-conceited man. And women found him attractive! Why, Baby had once danced every dance with Billy down at the Shoo-Fly, while Harvey looked on. . . . "You come here from Leadville today?" Harvey asked.

"Yesterday."

"Why'd you leave a good job managing the Teller House?"

"For a better one managing the Clarendon Hotel."

"They say the ore in Leadville's low grade. Nothing but black, dirty rocks."

"Well, it ain't gold, any fool could see that. It's carbonate of lead with plenty of silver."

"How much?"

"One assay on the Keystone ran nine hundred and thirty-four ounces of silver to the ton, and not only that, it was forty-two percent lead, Harvey. You can't hardly squat to pee in Leadville. Paper says the population tripled in a year. The road there's choked with freight wagons, prairie schooners, stages, buggies—Chicago bankers, New York stock men, Denver engineers—you name it. For the privilege of lying on a dirty mattress in a boarding tent or maybe a saloon, the lower grade of folks pay a dollar. Your wealthier types, every man jack, pay ten bucks a night to sleep at the Clarendon. There's other hotels, but none up to our snuff."

"Billy, I want you to thank my father for his, for his—paternal extravagance." Harvey held up the bills.

"You thank him yourself. Write him a note."

"Papa and I never—correspond."

"He's a good father."

"The very best! Only problem, how would I possibly spend such a fortune? Should I buy a silver mine?"

"You'd best look to selling your gold mine first."

"You do it for me, Billy." Harvey thrust his wad of bills into Billy's small hands, then fished in his pockets. "Ah. Here it is." He unfolded a ledger-sized sheet of paper. "You know the mining reporter for the

Call. Give him my father's money, give him this, and my trials will be over."

Billy Bush squinted at Harvey's meek scrawl. "You write a woman's hand, Harv." He cleared his throat. " 'Rumors have recently been ripe' —You mean *rife,* don't you, son?—'of the striking of another big bonanza. It is the Fourth of July Mine on Quartz Hill and much excitement has recently prevailed over it. Rumor has it that its owner, Harvey Doe Junior, was a short time ago offered four thousand dollars for it, and a few days afterward, seven thousand. Mineral in goodly quantities assaying as high as four hundred and eighty-seven dollars to the ton has been found' "—Billy Bush's laugh sounded like steak sizzle—" 'and everything pertaining to it is very encouraging. Prospects are daily looming brighter and brighter.' " Wipe that smirk off your face, Billy! "That's beautiful, Harvey. That's a pure work of art. I suppose you been salting the mine as well?"

Harvey sulked. Had to piss.

Billy pushed the note and money back across the table, then leaned toward Harvey. "She's your wife. That's a fact. She's pregnant. Fact again."

"Not with my child."

"I don't misdoubt it. But what can you do short of ripping her guts, and Harvey, you're not the man enough for that. Besides, what she likes, she likes a good spanking. That's all you got to do, and she'll take you back. Why, Harvey, she likes most to squeal like a puppy when you pinch a few soft spots, then fix it with kisses. She was never one for gentlemen fitting parts of theirselves never meant to by nature into orifices only intended as egresses, not entrances, *I* know. Her kisses alone scale the walls of chastity." But Harvey couldn't hear. He was slapping his own ears. Billy pulled down Harvey's hands and held them. "Jake's with her now. You go there, Harvey. You rescue her from that Jew, and there's another hundred dollars waiting for you here. Your Pop wants it for you to patch it up with her. We all got to reap what we sowed, Harvey Doe. You made the bed, lie in it. She's your wife. You may rest assured that we ain't that much higher than the lowest of animals unless we can clean up the messes we made. Your Poppa don't want no more of this scandal, and he don't want it that Jake Sandelowsky should be with your wife for the blessed event, no matter who seeded it. Them Jews want to see us Christians wallow in our own filth. Why, Harvey—they try to get Christian women to drink their own monthly blood!"

"What on earth for?"

Billy Bush shrugged, and glanced at the woman seated beside him. She cocked an eyebrow. "Hair of the dog that bit them? Something."

Baby Doe lifted her head, then let it flop. Her dead baby lay on one arm, neither warm nor cold, just dead. "Lay down, Chris."

"Oh, Honey." Jake's face lowered, filling her pupils, so close there were two. He'd make a beautiful woman if he didn't have a beard. Dark, like a gypsy.

"Wasn't talking to you, talking to Chris. Sit down."

"Oh, Baby."

"I decided to call him Chris, Jake darling. My baby boy Chris has dark, dark hair, very curly, and large blue eyes."

"How do you feel?"

"Like the whole bottom half of my body got blown up. Lift the sheets and see if I'm still there. It's a bloody mess, ain't it? Oh Jake, did I say awful things when it happened, I mean when he was coming out? I remember singing, I'm going to have a *baaaaaaby*, I'm going to have a *baaaaaaaby*. Why is it I never get hysterical? Instead I sing a song. I sang, Harvey, you'll *paaaaaay*, Jake go a*waaaaaaay*, but I did it in a fit of passion, Jake, no one can blame me. I've never felt such horrible pain in my life."

"Honey, he's dead. The baby's dead."

"I know, I'm coming to that. That's not the main thing. It ain't nothing the doctors can't fix, and you can't say it's my fault. Maybe just the tiniest, littlest bit is my fault, the rest I don't know. That's not what I mean. . . ." Jake's face grew smaller, and the haze descended. Her eyes hummed shut, tendrils of pain broke out of her middle and shot around the room, then slowly sank. Her bottom half felt like a large excavation collapsing at the edges, a dark bruised rose floating in a bowl. Shapes she couldn't comprehend floated past. A shadow embraced her insides, squeezing blood. Something flushed through her body top to bottom. From everywhere at once came a whistling sound. Mamma, Daddy, I lost all my buttons down the root cellar, rats ate my fingers. . . .

Here's a dollar to buy us a ham, Baby honey, hurry up, we're hungry! The nice butcher tied the ham to her side so she wouldn't drop it. But she couldn't climb out. Each step up that loose slope frayed and collapsed. Her shoes filled with dirt. She was losing the ham! As the fat ham sank, pulled down by its own weight, loop by loop the rope slackened. Everything slid. Cold sweat, panic, rapid sharp panting, screeches like long wires pulled through her lungs. . . .

She lay on her back and let herself slide.

"Honey? Baby? It's Jake, it's me. I'm gonna take this away now. I'll just take it out, honey."

"All right, Jake. That's fine. How is he?"

"The little tyke's dead."

"Well then, take him away. It ain't my fault he's dead. That's the way he was born, imagine. That's not it, Jake, can you call Mrs. Collins? She could clean him up nice, put a nice shirt on him with a bow and some nice socks. Put a bonnet on his head. She could apply some bloom of roses to his cheeks, if it's not too much trouble, Jacob. Don't he look like a doll? Why can't I cry, Jake? He hurt me so much. I'll die if this keeps up, or I'll run away or shoot myself, or something like that."

"Well, you got to let go. He'll be all squoze."

"In my trunk, Jake? Just open up the top, I got his baby clothes laid out. You get them and have Mrs. Collins clean him up and dress him up nice. Do that, Jake."

She lay back and relaxed and felt Jake lift something from her side. Then she heard him at the foot of the bed opening the trunk, but kept her eyes closed. "Jake honey, you could fetch Mr. Glascott. He could bring his apparatus. Ask Mrs. Collins if she's got some eyeblack and bloom of roses. . . ."

When he'd gone, Baby opened her eyes. Why wasn't she crying? Cry now, Baby Doe, before Mrs. Collins makes up your face! Jake had left the trunk open. Its ribbed top lay propped on the bed's foot rails, blocking her view of the things inside. Jake better have taken the blue linen shirt, it was right on top, the very same one she'd worn as a newborn, according to Mamma. Her wedding dress was in that trunk too, her porcelain doll, her silver tea set, still unpacked. Trinkets and gewgaws. Hair nets, hairpins, back combs, corsets, plumed hats, mink muffs, a little fur tippet. Her skates and the green skirt she'd worn for the contest sponsored by Harvey's priggish church, when he first glimpsed her legs.

That did it, her face burst and flooded. The outbreak jerked her innards so hard she opened her mouth to scream and nothing happened, she nearly swooned instead. She thought of Oshkosh. She'd tied on her skates, she was racing away in long smooth strokes with her powerful legs, up the Fox River. Come back, Baby! First one leg then the other, each bursting with strength.

The voice shouting Come back was Harvey's, of course. She threw a chunk of ore at his face. He'd lured her to Colorado on a promise of riches. Central City consisted of tree stumps too, but there the resemblance to Oshkosh stopped. Here, if you weren't dead drunk you were gophering rocks, smashing everything in sight to make smaller and smaller pieces of matter, then suck out its cheesy wealth. She'd done it too—mucked with a pick, pushed the ore cart herself, driven wagons overflowing with ore to the mill. The *Call* had even written her up, to Harvey's dismay. "This is the first instance where a lady, and such she is, has managed a mining property. The mine is doing well, and produces some rich ore." After that, Harvey became a laughingstock. Well, too bad, Podge. Gut-pudding. Gum-suck.

She threw another chunk at poor Harvey. The man who'd failed her in every worldly respect. It was just Baby's luck that Harvey had managed to stiffen his spine and summon up spunk and defy his parents only once in his life, for his marriage to her. The effort must have exhausted his supply.

She could take him back, that would thicken Jake's mettle. Maybe Jake would carry her away to Chicago, maybe New York. Jake was by far the wealthier of the two, being owner of a store, and Harvey's presence greased Jake's pump when Baby wanted presents. Jake would probably say to himself, She's taking him back, he must of straightened out. He must of struck blossom rock, it's all over, quite possibly his father gave him money . . . lots of it for a change. A fine kettle of fish. Well, Jake was absolutely the last person on earth to lie down and die when a challenge came his way. His kisses were hard and sweet, like apples. He'd bought her three diamonds, three gold puff bracelets, one solid gold cross, total one thousand four hundred and eighty-five dollars. A cross from a Jew? Did the Jews have a hell? He thinks I kicked Harvey out because he neglected me, but really, let's face it, Harvey threw himself at my feet, he was always there. I could have used some neglect, for relief. Gentle, kind Harvey. I'll never never find a better friend than old dog Harvey.

And Jake and Harvey had been friends themselves, when they first met. She'd flirted with Jake right in front of her husband—sat on his lap and nuzzled his beard—Harvey never made a peep. Jake fucked like Harvey slept, long, hard, and deep. Harvey's little mosquito pecker. . . . She wouldn't put it past him to sneak in at night and rip all her dresses right up the middle, after first sniffing them.

If her baby was dead was she a dead mother? Hail Mary, full of

All for Love

grace. . . . Roses wide around her tomb gently wave and sweetly bloom. They'd weep out their guts if they thought I was dead. 'Tis the grave of Baby Doe, née Elizabeth McCourt. Elizabeth, Baby, Bessie, Lizzie, Lizard. Green, with thick skin. Baby fat Doe. Thank God she wasn't pregnant anymore. At least now she could lie on her back. When her belly was swollen she lay on her side, but that made her ankles puff up something awful. Bloated, large and slow, how perfectly disgusting. It hurt so much too, still hurt and itched now, she wanted to scratch the whole thing out, uproot it to the backbone. Her fingers shot down there, how soft, wet and sore, how steaming hot, what a pile of slimy towels. . . .

All those times when Jake came and lay by her side and rubbed her back with his long and large hands. . . . Even hard, his dibble pointed down. Jake, darling, wilt thou be gone, gone love from me? Stay—'tis the nightingale that sings in yonder tree. 'Tis the lark, Baby, 'tis not the nightingale, I must be gone. List! 'Tis the nightingale, simpleton, stay! Hell no, 'tis the lark that sings in yonder pomegranate tree. 'Tis the nightingale, lummox. 'Tis the lark, slut, I got to hump it home, lemme go. Stay, 'tis the nightingale, you bucket of spit. Lark, tart! Nightingale, rum-sucker! Wait. . . . 'Tis Harvey. "Harvey," she hissed. . . .

Her eyes flew open. Disheveled and crying, hat crushed in hands, her husband stood there by the bed. She closed them again.

"Where's the baby?"

"Dead." This time she barely cracked her eyelids, and peeked circumspectly. Still there. He was sweating like a horse, lathered all over. So was she, she realized. Slowly, the pain filmed over and crusted. From sore she went to dull ache, from dull ache to numb. Her flesh turned to slag. She held out her arm. "Oh Harvey."

"Baby." He dropped to his knees, crying like a girl.

"It's all Jake's fault, he never loved me, Harvey."

"I know, I know." He buried his face in her bosom, convulsed, and she stroked his head. He stunk so of liquor the fumes made her woozy. Every few minutes she passed out and came to, still stroking his head.

"Hold that pose! Don't move." Baby's eyes flew open, but she obeyed. She felt Harvey stiffen, but he didn't move either, he always did what he was told.

She realized from the sound—the sensitized plate being inserted, the dark slide pulled out—that precisely this moment, externally viewed, would be placed in her album in just a few days. By then she'd feel better. The air seemed to crackle, shot through with scratches. "Beautiful! Very moving. Now, Mrs. Collins, the child, if you will." Baby sat up and saw them all: Peter Glascott, the photographer; Mrs. Collins with a wicker bassinet cradled in her arms; tall handsome Jake now in coat and tie. Her heart flew out to him. Mrs. Collins approached, but Baby wouldn't look in the bassinet. That was over now. It would soon be a picture.

"Ain't he beautiful?" the midwife asked.

"Yes."

"I picked the flowers fresh. That's the bonnet you wanted, I hope, Mrs. Doe. The doll in his arms was Mr. Glascott's idea. Says I, he's a boy; says he, that don't matter. Without so much as a by-your-leave he thrusts the doll in the poor lad's arm. But you can remove it, if you so choose."

Baby signaled with her eyes for Jake to approach. Harvey stood on one side of the bed beside a fluted column. Before him, on a table, books were strewn. None of these things had been there before. He'd tucked in his shirt, brushed off his coat, and someone had placed a top hat on his head. Mr. Glascott and his assistant, a young boy with large ears, stood behind the camera. Mrs. Collins arranged the bolster and pillows behind Baby Doe. With a wet rag, she wiped Baby's face, then applied eyeblack and rouge. She began brushing her hair, but Baby wouldn't have it, she seized the brush and handed it to Jake. "He does it better."

"Let's have the father wistfully peering out the window, side to the camera, hands clasped behind." Harvey and Jake glanced at each other from either side of the bed. Harvey shrugged and tried to smile.

"Jake, you go over there with Harvey," Baby said. "Both of you do it."

The dead child, in a blue shirt, bonnet, and bow, flowers in one arm, a doll in the other, lay in the bassinet propped next to Baby in a pose of restful sleep. "Mrs. Doe, look at the child." The photographer ducked beneath the cloth. "Mrs. Doe, turn your head. Wipe a tear if you wish." Mournfully, Baby forced her shy face toward the dead child. But she so blurred her eyes with fluttering lashes that nothing was visible. She smelled oil of roses.

Harvey clasped his hands behind his back and stared at the window drape inches from his face. To make room for Jake, they'd had to move the furniture. The column and table now stood behind Harvey, Jake had squeezed between Harvey and the bed, and they posed at the window gazing out upon nothing, tall men with long faces. Upright on the bed between Jake and Baby Doe was the bassinet and child, tipped toward the light. Mrs. Collins had stepped behind the camera to watch.

"Hold that pose," said Mr. Glascott. He folded the cloth on top of the camera, replaced the lens cap, and inserted the plate holder. "Don't move." He pulled out the dark slide and thumbed off the lens cap. Those who still could breathe held their breath. Glascott consulted his pocket watch.

Inside the camera, crevices of light struck the silver bromide coating the dry plate. Fissured by light percolated with shadows, the salts of the silver commenced to sizzle, their atoms snapped and decomposed, and errant electrons attracted silver ions and formed silver atoms, real metallic silver! In this way, a latent image no one could see of some human rite no one understood formed on the plate in mere seconds. Mr. Glascott then pushed in the sliding door, and the light was replaced by the idea of light, by expressions flung gravely into the future, by the sentiment of death, queer feelings of jealousy, betrayal, grief, lack of moral fiber, all sucked into the camera. And none of it existed.

The Troy and Fourth of July mines were neighbors on Quartz Hill, but on different roads.

The Troy Mine contained several drifts embracing a stope, also rails and one ore cart. All this had been excavated then abandoned long before Harvey and Baby arrived. One could argue that Harvey's Fourth of July held more promise. The rock had barely been scratched, the drifts just begun. Whoever quit the Troy must have concluded the lode they'd stoped out wouldn't pay, but only after several years' of digging around it. With the machinery in disrepair, including steam hoist and bucket, Baby had to climb down the shaft by ladder—just like Harvey in *his* mine. Healthy again, she spent her weekends mucking ore with a quartz pick by candlelight, while balanced high on crossbeams underneath the stope. From it, chunks of rock fell toward a crude chute below. Every hour or so she had to climb down and, balancing one leg on the cart's edge, elbows flared out, reach up with her shovel and pull the rock from the chute. Nothing had changed. She still lived in rooms over Jake's store, Harvey still begged her to come back. Billy Bush wanted her to move to Leadville, and when in Central City entertained her with such tales of wealth that she'd been tempted. Just one more load to the mill, darling Billy. The mineral salts on that ore looked promising.

Baby Doe was pretty as a bird, Billy told her. She wouldn't have to grub in the mines in Leadville, certain. Leadville was the place to mine *people,* Baby.

She rode back to town on the huge ore wagons making the rounds; they all knew Baby. She showered in the basement of the Teller House at fifty cents a pop. She emerged in stays, a scarlet dress, black bands around her skirt, thick hair piled in clouds on her head—bright as a picture in the broad sunlight. One day, on Spruce Street, filled with vague longings, she noticed, looking up, that dusk had come. Bits of fluff floated in the air. A tall man walked toward her holding something in his arms. The wooden sidewalks, the brick buildings, the mud, the plate glass windows, all hazy and rich in the evening light, broke apart into rain silently falling. Music came from somewhere. Ghosts playing pianos. Smells of garbage and mud. Harvey emerged from a door in an alley across the street, a notorious parlor house. Harvey? In a brothel?

She was suddenly blank. Someone was running. A jolt, a shock to her brain, a shiver, a sense that the handle of the parasol in her hand was a foreign object with a strangely empty curl. Harvey sheepishly glanced across the street and stopped for a moment, in the rash of dusk. Things cross-sectioned. It felt like a guillotine crashing down, the blade sliced the moment, the moment peeled off and slowly faded. Harvey, it seemed, was debating whether to cross and confront her, but finally walked off, hands in his pockets, shoulders humped, like a contemptible person. The noise of traffic returned. Horse carts, hand trucks, dogs and boys, eminent citizens, miners, crib girls, all sped past Baby now in a blur.

The next morning, having locked her door, Baby Doe could have fun with Billy Bush and simply ignore Jake when he knocked. "He wants that you should open the door."

"At this precise moment?" Straddling Billy, she nuzzled and tongued his nose and mouth, contorting her face. She bit his hair. She still felt a little sore below, but couldn't stop now, bore down and bore down while Billy just smiled. What a long thingy he had, he was pulling it through her, making it curl. . . .

She gave one hoarse involuntary shout, and soaring, spread out like a parachute. She was still floating down when Billy said "Finished?" and thrust up hard, making her wince. Something spit deep inside her. Then they lay there like sacks dumped upon each other.

She noticed a letter pushed under the door, and, dripping spunk, hopped out to retrieve it. Running back to bed, she couldn't help herself, she spread her arms and legs, making a bare *X*. She pinched her own nipples then playfully licked one with her tongue. Back under the covers, Billy seized her shoulders and swung her on top. That was the only way they did it, because of his length. She fit them together and slid down his sickle-shaped ding-dong, "Wheeee!"

They lay on their backs half awake staring up. "I want babies, rooms full of babies, Billy. Babies in flowerpots lining the walls. I'll water them every morning and evening."

"Come to Leadville, we got everything else. Might as well have babies."

"Whiskey bottles, ropes, whips, enemas, corsets, pincers, needles, stuffed bunnies."

"What's that a list of?"

"Things in Leadville."

"Add silver sponge, mountains of silver. You going to open that letter?"

"It's from Harvey," she said. "Here, you." He tore it open.

My Darling Babe,

Let me tell you what happened I hope you won't blame me. I am heart broke about it I shal go crazey it was not my fault that I went in that parlor house. There is a man in this town whose trying to sell my mine for me. I had been looking all over town for a man who said he could sell it so we hunted all over for him. So this man said let us look in Lizzie Preston's for him. I told him I did not go into such places as that. Well he says if you want to sell your mine to this man we have got to find him right now for he is going away in the morning so I told him if he would not stay in there I would go right in and right out again.

So I went in and came out and who should be a cross the

street but you when I came out of there. Just as I was coming out you caught me and I no you did act like a perfect lady and conducted yourself as if you never saw a thing.

Now darling Babe do not blame me. I went in there on business of great importance to me I can assure you. I was so hard up I did not have any money nor nothing to eat in the house and I thought if I could find this man I might get money from him to help me out. I did not go in that place with any bad intentions no no I love my darling wife to much to ever disgrace her in that manner. I have been as true to you as any man could be to his wife so I went into that parlor house thinking I might get some money to help us along in the world.

Even my own father has worked against me and wherever he could hinder me from making money he has done so. I hope and sincerely pray dear Babe you will not blame me and do try and come back to me. I could sell your mine to and we could get some money and try to live normal lives and do things the right way and stay out of trouble. Oh Babe will you come back. You are all I have got in this world. Will you come back please will you please dear Babe.

Your Loving Husband,
Harvey

As Billy Bush read, his voice stayed flat, neither maudlin nor sardonic. He folded the letter, handed it back, and pulled on his pants under the covers.

Baby's heart swelled. Poor Harvey! She felt like a worm, with a worm's narrow outlook—the spirit gone blind that eats dirt. She could take Harvey back, start over again. They could move back to Oshkosh, work in Daddy's store, or maybe move to Chicago, it was such a gay place. . . .

John Vernon

"You're not listening to me."

"Yes I am."

"These are grounds for divorce in this state. That's all you require. It's there in your hand."

"Oh Billy. I couldn't."

"Suit yourself." He climbed out of bed, snatched his shirt, wiped his face with it, put it on. He sweated a lot for such a short man, whose skin had no give. Short and compact. Like Jake he was bearded, but Billy's facial hair was black and smart, the mustache quite thin, every hair in place. Jake's was a long streak of rust, it tempted you to pull it. Billy's was trim, just like the man. Dark, sunken eyes; small, handsome face. He never laughed much, and his smile was something not meant for other people. Billy Bush talked the same way he fucked, methodical and tireless. Generally metallic. If everyone else was dancing he'd sit, if they were sitting he'd dance. "Nothing's so common in Western cities as wives divorcing their husbands, see. They been doing the like since we become a state. Why do you think he wrote that letter?"

"Why?"

"He knows what you'll do with it."

"What will I do with it?"

"Take it to a judge in Denver."

"Oh, I will, will I? You sound like you know what you're talking about."

"That I do."

She watched him dress. Divorce poor Harvey? Might as well shoot him. It would tear him up so. Mommy and Daddy in Oshkosh wouldn't like it. She could be excommunicated! She'd keep his stereo viewer though, he'd given her that. Problem was, Harvey couldn't support her, and she'd had to take a job in Jake's store, then muck in the Troy mine on weekends hoping to strike it rich, and to what end? So Harvey could drink up the little money she earned? Once a tosspot you can't do much about it, that's the way you were born, you're a kitten in catnip. Before she kicked him out, he'd actually sold two of her dresses to purchase liquor. How was it that someone who always cried poor still managed to gain so much weight in one year? She couldn't stand the jiggling collops of flesh that circled Harvey's middle. He was growing into his father's body. Would it even be possible to see the man naked, ever again, let alone let him touch her? He didn't have a mouth so much as a muzzle, the slack lower lip of a pampered horse. For a wedding gift he'd given her a played-out mine, compliments of his father. She wrapped his name around her nose. *Haaarvey.* She lay there looking up at the ceiling and realized Billy Bush was watching. Fully dressed. He looked so flash! "Which judge?"

Six months later Baby rode the stage to Leadville, her small hands inside a brand-new mink muff, compliments of Billy. The funny little man seated beside her kept her in stitches the whole eight-hour trip. An employee of Billy's, he'd been given the job of repapering the Clarendon, the very place Baby Doe was to stop at. "Man in Kansas City I know—businessman like me—invented a walking machine?" Baby couldn't help it, his little head was so bald she found her fingertips upon it rubbing its smooth skin. It was smooth and tight but thickly furrowed on top and behind the ears. It almost seemed to rise in her hand! "Runs on gas," he said. "Walks one million miles in one million five-minute periods of time, and drinks nothing but sherry wine. No doubt somewhat faster than this here coach."

"It's criminal slow, Harold."

"Which?"

"Our stage."

"Well, this walking machine? It makes its own gas. With the help of the politicians and reporters. The stride is regulated to suit the different tastes of all the critics. My friend says he knows this machine will just fit the bill. Hundreds of pedestrians and pedestriennes may then take a rest, for their arduous labors will no longer be required."

She couldn't stop laughing, even though she'd produced it. "Oh, Harold. . . ." He smiled up into her face. Outside, scrub oak and pine trees rolled past. Patches of snow, steep slopes, frozen mud. Blankets of ozone suspended in air a foot above the earth.

3. Leadville, Colorado 1882

The night Oscar Wilde lectured in Leadville, Baby Doe had a tissick. Her little fist wrung the cough by its neck beneath her heavy veil. Oscar, on stage, never looked up. *Osc, osc.*

Everyone else looked. Rustle of dirty necks in collars. They all knew she was there alone in her box, hair piled in the style of the Second Empire, though it felt to her like a foreign object, shredded string on a scalp. Her blood-red velvet gown brought up beneath her breasts by a diamond-studded girdle clasped with a cameo set in pearls rubbed across the rigid corset when she breathed. The dress had no tucker, and exposed soft immensities of skin, still cratered where Horace had placed his sooty fingers earlier, at dinner. Even now, everyone saw it, she felt. Horace slouched in his own box across the stage, and she sat in hers, but everyone saw his great mustache on her neck, she knew that's what he wanted. He wanted to observe her across the theater which bore his name, and he wanted to watch the audience stealing glances, wondering just how beautiful she was, imagining the two of them in bed, then clucking their tongues.

They couldn't sit in the same box, of course. With Mrs. Tabor back in Denver, what the papers would say! His affair with Baby Doe was Colorado's open secret, but as long as they maintained a theater between them, observers subscribed to the fiction of rectitude. Her veil was their contract with social cornstarch.

At the Tabor Opera House, a red, white, gold, and sky-blue expanse of satin plush, columns, drapery, thick carpets, and gas lighting in polished fixtures, with a hat rack beneath every seat, Baby sat inside Horace's name. It felt like being in a novel. There was no outside-the-name-of-Tabor, everyone sat in it, glad-handers, tinhorn aristocrats, even Horace himself slurping champagne and carrying on next to Billy Bush, his paymaster, factotum, drumbeater, and go-between.

Only Oscar Wilde was spared. He'd told Baby at dinner that "Tabor" sounded like a condiment from India. On the stage, the famous aesthete, reading his lecture, dragged his voice through the English language, accenting every fourth syllable without once glancing up. With his flabby colorless wide flat face resembling an overripe fruit, he looked to Baby like the sort of large man who likes to climb hills and then be rolled down them. His head inclined toward the one leg thrust forward. Parted down the equator, his hair reached his shoulders. A Prince Albert coat, knee breeches, silk stockings, low shoes with bright bows...yellow silk handkerchief flowing from one hand...frills of lace at the wrists and collar....

Rough surroundings need not roughen hearts any more than a gilded cage makes a palace, and Leadville bent a courteous ear to Oscar's lecture, trying to decipher its precise operations by which consonants became vowels and vowels displayed an inclination to billow. He'd pitched his voice at about middle C and varied the tone only when tired nature asserted itself and compelled a rising inflection by means of an intake of breath. Baby thought this might have compromised his message; when he should have been swelling like a mountain, he was sinking like a gulch. "Think of those things that inspired Botticelli. He saw brilliantly lighted palaces, arches and pillars of marble and porphyry. He saw noble knights with glorious mantles flowing over their mail riding along in the sunlight. He saw groves of oranges and pomegranates, and through these groves he saw the most beautiful women that the world has ever known, pure as lilies, faithful, noble, innocent."

First get rich, then be innocent, thought Baby. Smart people want money so they'll never have to want anything else. They want not to want.

She raised her beautiful glacé gloved hands and caught the tissick at her veil. Then the door to her box opened, and a footman appeared with a glass of champagne and a folded note on a silver tray. She had to lift the veil a smitch to drink the champagne, which caused the audience below to squirm with a collective rustle, trying to steal a peek. The people of Leadville watched Baby nod to Horace and Horace blow a kiss. She opened the note.

> I'll come to you at midnight it seems like ages since dinner. I love you to death and I am yours from hair to toes and back again. I must return to Denver in the morning, it would be much pleasanter if I could be with you always and be under the sweet influence of your smiles and loving self. I love you I love you Kiss Kiss for ever and ever.
>
> E.G.Y.P.T.

Baby scribbled at the bottom, "Come at one," and handed it back. She could write to Billy too, but that wouldn't be necessary, he knew by instinct when to come and go.

"Art must no longer be the luxury of the rich or the amusement of the idle, it must enter into the everyday life of the hardworking masses of the people." The foot on stage previously thrust forward now was retracted, and another took its place. Shifting toward that side, Oscar raised his head and sipped from a glass, then departed from his text, or so it seemed to Baby. His words grew more thick and he glared at the audience through heavy-lidded eyes. He worried and frayed his poor little suffixes. "When I entah a room in Americah, what do I see, I see a carpet of vulgah pattern . . . a cracked plate upon the wall with a peacock feathah stuck behind it. I sit down upon a badly glued machine-made chaah that creaks upon being touched, I see a gaudy gilt horror in the shape of a mirrah and a cast-iron monstrosity for a chandeleah. All that I see was made to *sell.*" He sighed. "I turn to look for the beauties of natchyah in vain, for I behold only muddy streets and ugly buildings. Everything looks second-class. By second-class I mean that which constantly *decreases in value*. The old Gothic cathedral is firmah and strongah and moah beautiful *now* than it was long ago. There is one thing worse than *no* art and that is *bad* art." He surveyed the theater, waving one hand fitfully. "Don't paper your walls, but have them wainscoted, or provided with a dado. Don't hang them with pictures. Have some definite idea of *colah*. . . ."

Baby yawned beneath her veil. She wrinkled her nose, retracted her lips, and grimaced, biting the nub of her tongue. Across the stage, Billy Bush lit a cigar and Horace popped another cork. When he'd built his other opera house, the one in Denver, he'd reported to Baby how the architect had asked what he wanted it to look like. In answer, he'd peeled off four crisp one-thousand-dollar bills and ordered him to go see the great opera houses of Europe. But don't pattern my place after those chicken coops, he'd said—just pick up any good ideas they've got laying around.

And he did. He picked up miles of Belgian carpets and French tapestries, French silk to line the boxes, not to mention cherry wood from Japan, mahogany from Honduras, and Italian marble for the pilasters and lintels. Talk about beauty! The style was modified Egyptian Moorish, with a crystal chandelier thirty feet wide and a curtain depicting ancient ruins with lions padding through fallen pillars. A portrait of Shakespeare hung in the green room until Horace replaced it with one of himself.

He was immense, Horace—large as a mine. Like Oscar Wilde, he shambled when he walked, though not with that disagreeable motion of back and hips displayed by the apostle of beauty. Horace's big feet were turned inward, and he wore a monstrous diamond on his dirty right hand. His face was often blotched; Baby liked to pull it to hers by means of the ends of his bushy mustache, like a flop dog's big ears. So what if he seemed uncouth and awkward? He was also helpless in love, the big walrus. No one knew his exact worth, not even himself. When he walked the streets of Denver or Leadville, curious people threw coins in his path, having bet as to whether he'd pick them up.

Why, everything he touched turned to silver! Railroads, stage lines, real estate, newspapers, mines, and more mines. . . .

Since 1879, he'd been lieutenant governor of Colorado. The newspapers called him "Governor" for short, except when he came up for reelection, then they said he had two wives and called him a Mormon and charged him with importing cheap Chinese labor to the exclusion of the pioneer miners. But how could he employ Chinamen, thought Baby, when such were banned from Leadville? The first thing cruel people felt the urge to do with Horace was to fling mud at the large target he presented.

Not Baby, though—she wanted to marry him.

"One of the most absurd things I ever saw was the young ladies painting moonlights on a bureau and sunlights on dinner plates. The decorator should not wish to disguise the article or change its purpose but merely add to its beauty. Love the beautiful and good, hate the evil and ugly. When you find anything ugly, it was made by a bad workman. But the beautiful is everywhere. Wherever in your fields you find men driving cattle or women drawing water, there you will find models of beauty. If an eminent sculptor should ask me where he could find models for his art, I would show him men at the mine shafts in Colorado, waiting to descend." Confused applause. He'd said something good about miners, sure, but to call them . . . beautiful? Leadville wasn't certain.

Baby glanced down. Every man wore a frock coat, and some ladies wore furs. It was just like church, and Oscar was the priest. During dinner at the Saddle Rock he'd blessed the wines, before remarking that his temperament was so delicate that just to look at those delicious bottles plunged him into a drunken frenzy. Now, on stage, his voice pitched upward, approaching the steep slope of his final sentences. A low rumble rose from the men below reaching for their hats.

She could lift her veil and expose herself to the multitude, she could run over there and sit on Horace's lap. . . . But not while he was gunning for the U.S. Senate. That meant stumping across the state for sympathetic legislators who, in the fall, would choose the new senator to succeed Henry Teller, and he couldn't do that with Baby on his arm. In the upcoming campaign she'd have to stay out of sight, but it wasn't any fun to drink champagne veiled. It wasn't any fun to eat baked horny-toad, broiled Gila monsters, rice with tarantula sauce, and scorpion salad with a few poached wood lice on the side, while Augusta Tabor sipped consommé in the comfort of her mansion in Denver. . . .

At least Horace had taken the first step and moved out. Now he was trying to quietly divorce her. But how could he do so without sullying the name which Baby could only take if he . . . sullied it?

And he wanted her to look pretty and respectable!

"The reason we love the lily and sunflower, in spite of what Mr. Gilbert may tell you, is not for any vegetable fashion. It is because these two lovely flowers are in England the most perfect models of design, the most naturally adapted for decorative art. Surround your evenings and your mornings with flowers, and you may sort through all the ugly black chunks of rock that you wish. We spend our days looking for the secret of life. Well! The secret of life"—he looked up—"is *ahhht.*" Without even a bow, Oscar stuffed his remarks back into their morocco case, and strode offstage with the gait of a lumberjack.

"Well, here's the beans. What you said about pictures was good, but about wallpaper was bad. What you said about moonbeams on plates, now that was hunky-dory, but who in blue blazes is this Botticelli fella and why in hell didn't you bring him with you?"

Oscar sighed, then passed a vinaigrette box under his nose, breathing deeply. He looked down at this little man with no teeth. "My dear fellow, you musn't say this was good and that was bad. Good and bad are not terms to be used by you. You may say 'I like this' or 'I don't like that' and be within your rights. Now have a whiskey, you're sure to like that. As for Botticelli, he is dead."

"Who shot him?"

Oscar's laugh was convulsive, louder than Haw's. A crescendo of tinkling glass, tipsy laughter, squeals, and toots from distant brass bands—curses, shouts, shuffling feet, bubbling horses, faro games, chuck-a-luck—caught the laugh and reduced it to noise. A piano hammered clinks to the walls. Kerosene lamps swung from the ceiling, stirring eddies in smoke. Sin! thought Oscar. Let's have some. . . .

Oscar and Horace were the tallest men there. Once they'd tipped a few glasses together, Billy Bush had returned to the Clarendon. Standing at the bar with Haw, surrounded by little men in their woollies, Oscar noted a sign above the piano: *'Please do not shoot the pianist. He is doing his best.* But no shootings had occurred that night—none that he'd heard—and he wondered why. Hadn't his host told him how murders were so common in Leadville that when one particular fellow died from drink, his daddy back in Maine was overjoiced to learn his son had expired through natural causes?

What's a mining town, thought Oscar, without the rough element? Granted, the men here *looked* the part—dirty faces, rotten teeth, black hair shingled to their scalps, thumbnail-sized scabs on their necks and brows—but tonight all their talk was about . . . bugger me, interior decoration! What hath I wrought?

Above the long-sleeved wool underwear, they wore breeches with bibs and straps; the poorer sort sported boots split open and tied with ropes. Oscar himself had changed after the lecture into canvas trousers, corduroy coat, and slouch hat. "General Tabor," he said.

"Governor."

"Governor. With the influence you wield in this town, I should like to request that you empty the jails. I miss the sheer excitement of the American boomtown, the roaring, fast, glorious, magical, adventurous furor that gets into your blood—"

"Or spills it."

"Yes, of course. You didn't by any chance clear the streets of riffraff before I came?"

"See that critter by the door?"

"The one with the eye patch?"

"That's him. His job is to trip people up when they walk in, and start a fight."

"He never tripped me."

"You were in my company."

Tabor's frock coat was smudged, and his push-broom mustache flecked to capacity with foam and debris. He seemed fifty or so, old enough to be Oscar's father. His large umber smell wasn't unpleasant, just a bit strong. He'd made reference several times to his enemies, but to Oscar the man wasn't clever enough to have enemies. His volume recommended him, but were size and volume—buttered by wealth, of course—sufficient qualifications for the U.S. Senate? "Mr. Tabor—"

"Call me Haw."

"Haw." Oscar tasted the name. "Where are the women of the street?"

"Home in bed."

"The women in bed, the men in jail. Where will it all end? In New York, the men all carried fans. They should do so here."

"What sort of fans is that?"

"Ostrich-plume."

Haw seemed to be weighing the pros and cons. "I been sticking up for you, Mr. Wilde. I said you was a regular fella, but I don't know about ostrich-plume fans."

"And I've been sticking up for you, Haw. In Denver, one of your enemies asserted you weren't fit to guzzle pig's guts, and I assured him you were."

"Why..." He looked at Oscar with half-lidded eyes, his face completely blank. Then a beefsteak laugh flew out of his mouth and he slapped the poet's back. "I was right. You *are* regular!"

"Regular as a woman."

"If you want the rough element, they're underground," said Horace.

"At this time of night?"

"We put troublemakers on the night shift, Mr. Wilde, the Irish and such."

"Would you listen to the man? I'm Irish meself."

"You don't sound like no Mick."

"Does he think I was born in a pot? Bejazus!"

"Mr. Wilde, in this town, when your Irish miner finishes his shift, he finds a Cousin Jack and together they march to a seedy café and order pistols for two and coffee for one."

Oscar felt his jowls twitch. Was that a little moue of discontent he'd detected on Haw's face? I've underestimated the man. . . . "I should dreadfully like to find the same café and spend some time there."

"I've arranged something better for us, so far as sitting to supper is concerned. You'll be swimming in Irish."

"Where?"

"Down the Matchless."

"The Matchless?"

"My most faithful mine! For constancy, she beats any mistress to hell. Why, one shipment of ore last summer gave returns of ten thousand ounces of silver to the ton. She averages two thousand dollars a day, Mr. Wilde, and she can't be exhausted, even by those work-plugs, your fellow countrymen. I got it set up to celebrate there, since today, tomorrow—it's almost tomorrow, damn this watch, anyhow—that's the fourth anniversary of my first strike, I mean to say. The one that made me filthy rich!"

Blossoms of mineral salts painted on a ledge caused palpitations in a prospector's heart. First you searched for float, then dry washed, panned, and placered it out, digging like a gopher all the while, scattering test pits in the earth left and right. Work upward on the slopes, find a mineralized lode at what seemed to be an apex, break off some chunks, moisten your tongue and lick off the dust, then pulverize the good-looking pieces, pan off the gangue, and sprinkle the dark float on a hot shovel. . . .

The trouble with the drag in California Gulch south of Leadville, where Horace once panned, was all the bothersome black sand from which Augusta had to cull their meager gold. Poor Augusta . . . such tedium. . . . Later they found out the black sand was silver. More test pits! Pick- and shovel-work to break out rotten quartz and chlorides, two or three drill holes to expose the virgin rock. Then find some Cousin Jacks—Cornishmen—to drive the shaft, hire joiners to timber the drifts and crib the stopes, pay Irish to drill and blast out the adits, dig up any young grunts to muck out the ore and load the buggies and haul them to shaft heads in buckets, and dump. Mere children outside could sort the ore for pennies, thus keeping idle fingers busy that might have been blown off by playing with blasting caps. It took some big gorillas, though, to load up the wagons and haul them to the mill with the help of mules and meat-eating horses. With their sledges, crushermen worked it down to fist size, then shoveled it in chutes, where it got washed over vibrating tables. Or smelters cooked it and spewed through their stacks the sulphur dioxide, carbon monoxide, tellurium, and arsenic which hung over Leadville in black and yellow clouds and made the air smell like pillows that were died on. Old men skimmed off the slag and dumped it. Meanwhile, narrow-gauge trains hauled in more headframes, more buckets, boilers, Cornish pumps, cages, drills, jaw crushers, stamps, mullers, and separators, not to mention more coke, iron, and limestone flux, for more mines and smelters, all so Horace and Oscar could warm their drunken fingers by jiggling silver coins in their pockets in a rattling carriage on their way to the Matchless.

Uphill in the dark, past shapes of humming smelters glowing yellow at their windows, past squealing headframes, mills stamping in place like petulant golems, miners with lanterns sagging home. . . . Across from Oscar and Horace sat two men, a reporter named McDonald who never said a thing, and Lou Leonard, manager of the Matchless, whom they'd roused from sleep for this midnight romp. Liquor didn't fuzz up Oscar's mind, it organized his thoughts; he was only twenty-seven. He spoke with consummate precision about the most rational form of art criticism ever devised, the notion that horrid pianists might be shot. "I am never wrong, my dear fellow," he told Horace.

"Go on, twist my arm."

"Simply put, bad art shall be punishable by death. I admit that this means it is better to be beautiful than good. On the other hand, wanting a choice, one should always be good instead of ugly."

"Don't I know it."

"If the aesthetic application of the revolver were already admitted in the case of music, my apostolic task in the decorative arts would be much simplified."

"Objection sustained."

"And think of its application for the stage! You may use, not blanks, but real bullets. When the villain overacts, shoot him. Suppose you were to produce *Macbeth*. Surely, there are plenty of female poisoners you might release from prison to play Lady Macbeth."

"You got something there," said Horace. "But excuse me. Wouldn't such business exhaust the supply of actors?"

"Posh. Actors are like bunnies, sir, the more you shoot them the more they multiply. They're like money, the more you spend the more there is. . . ."

"Ain't that the truth."

Lou Leonard began naming the mines they were passing. The Kit Carson, the Lickscumdidrick, the Chrysolite, ah. . . . "There it is, the Little Pittsburg." He waved his hand at the darkness and began reciting sacred lore. A divine afflatus overtook him; Oscar felt he ought to bless himself. "When Horace Tabor first come to Leadville, he owned a simple grocery store. After years of extending credit to miners, two prospectors came to his store requesting to be grubstaked. You're familiar with the term, Mr. Wilde?"

"Grubstake? Punishment for heterodox larvae?"

"Tell him this was four years ago, exactly, to this day." Haw could never listen to this story without spatchcocking it.

All for Love

"Four glorious years! Unto Horace Tabor came August Rische and George Hook. Grubstake us, they cried. That's when a merchant extends supplies to prospectors in return for an equal interest in their claim. Horace Tabor may have been gruff, but he was the poor man's friend, and he never failed to dig deep into his pockets for old miners down on their luck. He advanced them coffee, lard, flour, frying pans, blankets, shovels, gads, drills, hammers—"

"And a bottle of whiskey."

"And a bottle of whiskey. And they came to Fryer Hill and sat under a tree and drank of the whiskey, and finding it was good, decided that was the very spot to dig. And they dug, and behold, at twenty-seven feet they struck carbonate ore running two hundred ounces of silver to the ton. Soon the mine was producing twenty thousand dollars' worth of silver a month. Hook sold out to Rische and Horace Tabor, and Rische finally sold his half interest to David Moffat and . . . Horace Tabor. After that, Horace Tabor bought the Chrysolite from William Lovell, who'd salted it with ore stealed from the Little Pittsburg. What derision was heaped upon Horace Tabor's shoulders, having boughten a mine salted with his own ore! But Horace Tabor dug a mere eight feet deeper and struck a vein of silver which soon was producing one hundred thousand dollars a month. He capitalized the Chrysolite for ten million dollars. After that, he bought the Matchless, and the rest is history."

The smell of sulfur in the air now seemed comforting. In April, Leadville's night air was cold, well below freezing, and their carriage was open, but Haw had thoughtfully provided blankets, one for him and one for Oscar. The horses had slowed to a labored walk. "Remember poor Rische when we bought him out, Lou? He'd never seen so much money in his life." Horace spit into the dark. "So he scoots off to Denver, and he goes to a bank, the First National."

"Of which Horace Tabor is now the vice president," added Lou.

"And he deposits his money except some he wants to spend, and he tells Sam Wood that he, August Rische, plans to sample the town and see if it holds up. He's gonna tear the roof off from hell and fall down inside it. By tomorrow morning, he says, I'll be broke, and I'll come to you for my money, see? But you don't let me have it. I'll say, Who in hell's money is it, damn your soul! And you say, It don't make no difference, you shan't have it. Then I'll say, You give me my money you son of a bitch or I'll make it rain blood in this here bank. And when I say that, you go call the janitor and tell him to throw me out and say, Go to hell, Rische, you shan't have your money. If you don't do that, he says—I'll take my business elsewhere."

At the Matchless, Oscar was wrapped in a rubber suit, one of Horace's spares. The two men were about the same height, but the pantaloon legs in Oscar's toga had lost their shape and flopped about. "I suppose their purpose is to keep us clean? You Americans are so wonderfully practical."

"Sweat like a pig inside this thing, though."

"You need some storks embroidered on the flaps . . . Haw . . . with ferns and swamp flowers along the edges."

Bells sounded, then a hiss and metal squeal. Oscar looked up. The great wheel on the headframe shuddered and turned, casting rippled shadows on the metal roof. The hoist shack trembled, and a cable rose up through a hole in the floor. Kerosene lamps rocked beneath their shades. Someone shouted from below. More bells. The cable stopped, then hung there vibrating. Oscar followed it up over the wheel through a stanchioned opening into another shack, where it seemed to be yoked to a modern centaur: top of man, bottom of machine, snorting left and right. Its levers and handles jerked the man's arms. The cable rose again, and a barrel of iron emerged from the hole, caught a metal bar and tipped all its rubble into a chute running through the shack's wall. Clouds of dust rose.

Oscar's foot hurt. Already he'd begun to sweat, and he pictured his bothersome left heel decaying like a piece of cheese, the bone working through the chalky flesh rotted by fungal threads. . . . "Mr. Wilde, Charles Pishon, the superintendent."

"Charmed."

"Howdy."

"Mr. Pishon will take you down," said Haw.

"By what route?"

They all looked at each other. "Why, in the bucket."

The filthy barrel came up to Oscar's waist, but twisted and turned in the narrow shaft, causing him to grab the cable for all he was worth. All in all, it felt intestinal. As he sank, the spirochete in his spine, contracted years before from a syphilitic whore, inched its way upward toward his meninges, beginning its journey of twenty-two years. . . .

"Now this here rock, you can tell it's good ore from the black patchy parts, and see how it gets osterish on the back? Sort of blue in the creases? Very rich chlorides and carbonates, Mr. Wilde, muxed up with galena." They were in a crosscut, slogging through puddles. Oscar had to walk slightly bent over. Pishon's voice echoed in such a way that it sounded like the echo, not the voice. "If it shades brown or red, like that down there, it ain't worth pissing on, maybe hematite or some such. Grey, it's just gangue. See that over there, that's where the lode pinched out. We had to drift left, with the lode, in this direction."

"Show me your most valuable piece of rubbish."

"We don't take the value out, we put it in. One stone ain't worth much, it's the aggregate. I always say, it takes a gold mine to run a silver lode, Mr. Wilde. What I mean by that is the cost of extraction is partly what makes the stuff so damn precious. Are you enjoying this?"

"My dear man, it's the finest sight in the world."

Miners surrounded him, offered him whiskey. "A smahan, Mr. Wilde?"

"I'm a devil for drink, by the holy God. A Dublin man."

"Tell us about beauty, Oscar."

"You won't find it killing hogs in Cincinnati. The minerals you extract from this earth are beautiful, but they must be worked. The beauty lies in the value you place upon your work. But the most beautiful thing on earth, my dear lads . . . is a cottage in Ireland . . . dear old mother in her rocking chair. . . ."

Their black faces grinned, showing black and white teeth.

After Oscar was invited to begin a new drift with a silver drill, Lou and Horace showed up. They decided to name this one "The Oscar," and Horace predicted it would produce millions. "Then you must offer me shares in it, Haw."

Horace laughed.

"In your grand simple fashion, you name it after me. But in your untutored avarice, you keep it to yourself."

No one said a thing.

They sat to a banquet in a large tunnel, where a table was laid with a long white cloth, white napkins, gold china, and silver service. Silver candlesticks held spermaceti candles, whose weak yellow flames tugged at the rock ceiling. In black ties and tails, waiters offered covered dishes: warm biscuits, fried turnips, beefsteak, plum pudding. Lima beans and stewed tomatoes. A large fried pie made from dried peaches, with a dab of butter still melting on top. . . .

Oscar lit a cigar. He couldn't prevent himself from baiting Haw. When the wealthy clod loudly cracked his knuckles, Oscar pursed his lips and drilled smoke. "I suppose you must be forgiven, my dear fellow. The feeling of deficiency in the joint is overwhelming, I daresay." When Horace popped a nut in his mouth, Oscar clucked his tongue. "Kindly refrain from opening the nuts between your teeth, Mr. Tabor. You should use the silver instrument provided for that purpose. And what has become of your crackers, my good man?"

"I ate them in my soup." Horace looked abashed. Bells rang somewhere, and several miners stood up. Oscar took the opportunity to slip two silver forks and a knife and spoon inside his rubber suit, in the pocket of his trousers.

· · ·

All for Love

At the knock on the door, Baby cooed, *"Entrez."*

Billy Bush walked in. "Who taught you that?"

"Miss Gaddis-Rose, in Oshkosh."

"In French, or Parlor Gallantries?"

"The way I remember it, in fifth grade everything got sort of smashed together. That's why I can't tell Leadville from Paris. Miss Gaddis-Rose used to say, Close your eyes. Where do you want to go? What do you want to be? I very highly admired her."

"I can see why. Did she teach you French larking as well?"

"Billy, go ram a needle up your ass." Baby's suite at the Clarendon consisted of two rooms, a boudoir and bedroom. To match the green, black, and yellow paper of the boudoir—fronds and lilies at night—she'd put on her black velvet dressing gown lined with green fur. Billy was diked out in frock coat, stand-up collar, and worsted trousers. How they'd both gone from worm to butterfly! He stood by the door sucking a cigar, and Baby lay half uprooted on her settee. "Where is he?" she asked.

"He went off with the lah-de-dah. They were planning to go to Alice Morgan's for an orgy."

"I hate it when you say such things."

"Fine, he's cutting his corns with a razor. Alice always said he was vulgar and dirty, even after he got rich. Why are Haw's nails black, she says. Because he scratches himself! The only way she can stand him is to get blind drunk. See, when you're in Denver, he comes up to Leadville on business and commits debauchery feats. Then when you're in Leadville, he goes to Denver and ditto. This is the man you love."

"He said he'd come at one."

"Two or three's more like it."

"I told him one."

"Don't count on it."

He gave her a look that said I know whereof I speak, then swaggered right up and stood before her. Bend down and tie my shoes, said his eyes. But what was he thinking? Everything he told her had two or three meanings, each expressing a different motive. He reached down and thumbed her ear, but she turned away. "Not tonight."

He tugged up his trousers by the knees and squatted down. "I got some news."

His nails were clean and trim. She settled back to listen. She crossed her legs and pendulumed one foot.

"Augusta has sued for support. She wants the house and fifty thousand a year of what she calls alimony, even though she declines a divorce."

"But the court granted Haw's decree!"

"That's just it. Even Lou Rockwell says it ain't legal."

"Why?"

"Neither of them never lived in Durango, except Horace did briefly when he bought some mines there. He got to know the judge, and that's his excuse for leaving ten thousand dollars in his feed bag. Also, how can he sue for divorce if he's the one that left her? Besides, the complaint is full of lies. I suspicion that's why the court never gave her the chance to answer it. He accuses Augusta of every crime, except drunkenness and treason. The main charge is adultery."

"Augusta? In bed with a man?"

"Guess who we named as corespondent? Me!"

"What you won't do for Horace, Billy. I'm surprised you didn't charge her with rape. You always say one thing and do another, that's what bothers me. Why am I so calm, I should be screaming. Haw told me the court granted his decree and you served her the summons!"

Billy stood up. "Between you and me, I informed him I served it, but I never did. It's just so much bumwad. It ain't worth the paper. What I did was wave it in her face. I said this is the sort of slander she could expect if she didn't grant her husband a divorce. I figure she won't budge unless she's scared. But she says, I'm just a broken-hearted wife and I want him back."

"Then she'll never divorce him! And it's all your fault!"

"Will you listen to me? Says I, you don't grant your husband a divorce and he'll cut you off without a cent. You won't have nothing to lay against the wet days. Says she, I don't want his money, I want him back. Says I, He's got no intention of returning, Horace Tabor won't be budged. Oh Pappy, she cries, clasping her hands and casting her orbs to the mahogany ceiling, It will be your ruin! Let's bury the past, she sobs. I tell her to get herself a good attorney, so what does she do, she gets Amos Steck, and he comes up with this cockeyed notion of filing a bill of complaint asking for alimony and proper maintenance but no divorce. She wants the convenience without the scandal. She begrudges you the carcass, I suppose. Under Colorado law, there's no provision for alimony and separate maintenance except in cases of divorce, so her piece of paper is just more humbug. But it's a step in the right direction, and if you'll keep your trap shut and lie low and behave, you'll get what you want. I'll harass her to death."

He stood right above her, cigar in mouth. "Don't fall off that thing, Billy. What will Horace say when he smells cigar smoke?"

"He's too blowed to smell. He disposed of two bottles of champagne during the lecture, then at Pap Wyman's he started on whiskey. Oscar Wilde matched him glass for glass. That's when I left. What's Egypt?"

"What?"

"Haw signed his note to you 'Egypt.' What's that?"

"None of your beeswax." Whose side was Billy on? He stood above her, one hand in his pocket rattling something. His eyes looked dead, but that was the quaint way desire spoke within him. Baby went moist below, flush above. She could rake him over the coals if she wanted. What claim did he think he had upon her? He'd hooked her up with Horace, sure, he'd once carried notes back and forth between them, he'd even stepped in to keep her warm when Horace passed out on his way to Baby's bed. Since coming to Leadville then moving to Denver, Billy'd married and kept his wife under wraps. They'd hatched a little Billy to bounce off the walls. His life had always been a maze of alliances, but add to that Horace's finances and building schemes, foreclosed mortgages, court cases, bribes—well, it honeycombed Bil-

John Vernon

ly's dark side. Actually, it made him...alluring. Like a rat, a little plug of solid gristle, he scurried here and there, he was always on a drainpipe, up some alley. Fact was, he knew everything. The only way to keep him in line was not to tell him something. "Egypt is a secret between Haw and me."

"Oh, it is?"

She pictured her little hand reaching up to find out what he had in his pocket. "It's a term of endearment with a special meaning. Get that shit-stick out of my face, it stinks."

Billy held the cigar for a second between them, then turned and walked off. When he swaggered out the door she opened her robe, for ventilation. Then she threw it off and stood there in her negligee, thin as a veil.

One o'clock came, then two. Baby still wore just her negligee. She was someone else, stretched out on the settee, nodding off but never quite plunging into sleep. She was free! She could stroll out the door and leave Baby Doe lying there....

Haw was the slow kind that couldn't adjust. Everyone joked about Tabor time. He could never anticipate, nor attend to more things than one at a time. How could such a lump divorce his wife? In bed, his routine was earnest but clumsy, also long and endless, like unskilled labor. Each lurch of his hips was just like the one before, with no mounting frenzy. He went on and on forever most times without finishing, instead he merely popped out and rolled over, already asleep.

How nice it would be to lie down in bed, but she couldn't. She couldn't go into her bedroom, not yet....

When Haw finally lumbered down the hallway, with its flocked red walls and gaslights turned low, he paused for a minute before knocking on her door.... Now, do I want to do this?

The brief moment of reflection surged and inverted him, wrongside out. He kicked instead of knocked.

"She's not here, go away. She went back to Denver."

"Oh Babe, open up."

"I'm not your 'Babe,' I'm the porter. She's gone home."

Funny, the way she'd deepened her voice. Made him think of holding a child's head underwater. "Let me in, Baby. I'm sorry I'm late."

"Who is it?"

"Egypt!"

"Embalmed, I bet." The door swung open and she stood there in her dressing gown. Horace reached out, but she turned and walked in. "I think I turned into a mummy waiting. That would fix your hash, Haw. How's that for a scandal? What's Egypt?"

"Come again?"

"What does Egypt mean?" She sank to the settee, crossed her legs, and leaned back.

"I thought you knew that one."

"What is it?"

"You know."

"Tell me what it is."

"Everyone knows."

"I want to hear you say it."

"You know . . . Egypt." Horace couldn't help grinning. "Eager To Grab Your Pretty Titties."

Baby sat up. "You vulgar man! How dare you say such a coarse thing to me!"

"Everyone knows it. You can't say you didn't."

"Don't touch me." Stumbling, Horace backed off. "Sit there." Horace slumped into a boudoir chair that only came up to the small of his back. "Look at you, you're a mess. Where have you been? There's food in your mustache!"

"You sound just like Augusta."

"Then go back to her! Don't come to me stinking like a sewer, three hours late. If I'm just like Augusta, how come you're here?"

Haw combed his mustache with his fingers.

"Would Augusta wait up for you this late? Is she pretty? Does she smell good like I do?"

He smiled. "Oh Babe . . ."

"Don't Oh Babe me. Wipe that smile off your face! Would Augusta do this?" From the folds of her dressing gown, she plucked a fan. How fiercely she snapped it open and shut!

"I don't get it."

"You get it, Horace, everyone does. You can't say you don't. It means you're cruel. Would she do this?" She twirled the fan in her left hand.

"What's that mean?"

" 'I wish to get rid of you.' What about this?" She lay the fan on her right cheek. Horace just stared. "Would Augusta do that?"

"What is it?"

"It's a Yes, you big oaf. Lummox."

He sat up straight, as though called to attention. Now Babe held the fan in her left hand, loosely hefting it.

"This?"

He shrugged.

"It means 'I am satisfied.' "

Haw began to relax.

"You can't tell me women haven't signaled you with their fans. Or their gloves, or handkerchiefs. I bet Augusta did it when you courted her. They bat their green eyes, they twirl their parasols, they whine goodness gracious, how cruelly you treat me. 'I've sacrificed my happiness just for you, Horace Tabor.' Have they said that to you? 'I've sacrificed my virtue, but I'm not to blame, you took advantage of me'?"

Horace shrugged.

"Go now. Leave. I was raised to honor God. It's getting harder to explain in my letters back home just what my relationship to you *is*, Horace. I'm a Catholic, in case you forgot. I don't parade my religion, but I do go to church. I'm devout, in my own unostentatious way. I remember my First Communion in Oshkosh as though it was yesterday! You should have seen my white dress! I ask myself, what would my mother say? Imagine, her daughter, Elizabeth, divorced ... and now ... a kept woman. ..."

Horace felt his blood rise. Baby stood and paced, wringing her hands. Her soul seemed to pour from her beautiful face!

"Since the store burned down, they hardly write me anyway, I don't know why. They can't afford the stamps. But I know I'm in their thoughts, I'm their only hope. Between you and me, Haw, I've been sending them money. Anonymously. They'd send it right back if they knew who did it. That's not the main thing, the main thing is, they don't know what I've become! I'm careful to send just enough to get by on, but not so much that they could hop on a train and come here and visit. I'd die if they saw me. I'd be so ashamed! Anyway, there's no danger of that, I've stopped it completely."

"Stopped what?"

"Sending money."

"Why?"

"Why, isn't it obvious. ... Why! I've sent all I have! There's no more to send. ..." From her bosom, Baby produced a little hanky, and holding it to one eye, discreetly turned her back.

"How much do you need?"

"How about a million dollars? No, two million. That's not it, give me everything you own. Every last cent! You mutton-head! Looby! Can't you see I've been acting? You can't tell me women haven't practiced such tricks on you." She turned and approached him, glowing like a queen. "Their weapons are handkerchiefs, gloves, fans, parasols, and above all, tears. Sit there and say with a straight face that Augusta hasn't used devices like that. I'm sure she's a better actress than I am, she's convinced you that she's as pious as a saint."

Horace squirmed in his chair. "Well ..."

"See? She weeps, she touches her hanky to her cheek. What she wants is your money, like all the other coquettes. Like every other woman in the woodworks, tugging at your sleeve. They're all the same."

"But you're not, I suppose. You're not like them."

Her eyebrows arched, and she smiled and grimaced, both. Her eyes exploded! "I'm not like anyone."

Well, of course she wasn't, that much was true. But he didn't deserve this, Haw decided. He'd rushed from a good meal, surrounded by good ore.... Sure, Baby was sharp but.... Her skin was so milk soft you'd never think it possible she could bite so hard. Well, he could go back to Augusta, why not. It was all a green fog, Augusta, Baby Doe. Billy'd once told him he could become President! He was rich enough, powerful, but first....

Something in his head had congealed behind the eyes. It seemed they'd swollen in his sockets something horrid....

"Oh Christ," he erupted, "I love you so much it hurts all over. Don't do this to me, Baby, I love you something awful. Let's go to bed."

"Not tonight."

"What?"

"Take me with you tomorrow, on the train. We can ride on the same train at least, for God's sake."

"Not while things are at this... delicate stage." He paused for a long time, grinding his teeth. What the hell, he could get angry too. He felt conscious of his face. "Look, this divorce. We have to keep it quiet, understand? Billy served the decree, and when things calm down we can go to St. Louis on the sly, how's that? We can get married there, that's what you want."

"He never served it."

"Of course he did. Sure."

"He didn't. He told me. He waved it in her face."

"He informed me he did."

"Well, he's your lackey, not mine. But he didn't. Go ask him yourself. You're no more divorced now than a week ago. And here you are in another woman's room!"

"She sued for support!"

"Without conceding a divorce."

So he *could* go back to her.... As soon as the idea swelled up, it drained out. He thought of Augusta, straight as a post. When they'd first come to Colorado, prospecting in the mountains, there were nights their camp was so steep they were forced to drive stakes into the ground, roll a log against them, and sleep nearly upright, a feat which Augusta accomplished with ease. More than twenty years ago! She used to wash shirts for fifty cents a pop in the mining camps. There was a time when their total worth was a pick, a shovel, and a dog that had to lean its head against a rock to bark. Now she was even more down on him rich than when he was poor.

He saw Augusta in his dreams, pursing her lips, scaly limbs grinding squeals in his ear, a cricket in the stovepipe. . . . It wasn't so much her plug-ugliness, no, but the way she flaunted it. See what you deserve, she seemed to be saying. You did this to me. You treated me like dirt.

Don't a man deserve a little fun now and then after spending his life gophering and coyoting?

". . . go back to her, then." Baby's face was like a flower! Her lips were so perfect, her little chin just like the toe of a slipper. "I suppose you prefer it. Let her scold you and lie there in bed like a statue and order more iron deer for the lawn and peacocks for the roof and blackboards for the schoolhouse. Go back to your schoolmarm, let her ruler your knuckles. She keeps your nose sharp! I'm tired as a dog. . . ."

"Look," he hissed, "I don't have to take this."

"No, you don't."

"How does a fellow rid himself of a wife unwilling to divorce? Tell me that."

"You tell me. You're the pasha."

"Oh, Babe . . ."

He found himself in the hallway, confused. The wealthiest man in Colorado—in the West!—felt like a child whose toys had been snatched away. She said she was flying the red flag tonight, but he sensed she was lying. Baby, oh Babe. . . .

Horace had his own office in the Clarendon, attached to a suite with a bedroom and parlor. He unlocked the door, lit the gas, and stared at his desk strewn crazily with papers. Inkstands, ledgers, paperweights, pens, a knuckle-sized gold nugget mounted on a stand. The mustache wax he never used, but hell, if he really wanted to be respectable. . . . He opened the tin and smelled the yellow grease.

In his bedroom, he lifted the pitcher from its washstand and drank half the contents. The red curtains howled. Nothing looked familiar. He noticed the thick knobby legs of the bed and wondered why some-one had made them so ugly. Who made them, how on earth did they get here, who killed the ox whose blood, mixed with buttermilk, was still, after decades, sinking into the grain? He felt like someone re-turned from the dead who couldn't recognize a thing.

With a spasmodic lunge he flung out his hand, big fingers splayed, ridding himself of all handshakes, past and future. He kissed the fingertips. I'll marry her, he thought, despite what Billy says. She's no coquette. . . .

At last, in her bedroom, Baby woke her little man. Harold Leighton yawned and stretched. Since coming to Leadville, he'd grown wealthy selling wallpaper. Folks trusted his taste. "Harry want some water?"

"Waa waa!" His hands shot under her robe and started pinching her. She wrapped the sheet and coverlet around him, pinning his arms, then reached for the glass of water on the nightstand. "Have some water, Harry."

He lay there unmoving while she poured the whole thing into his grinning mouth, where it overflowed and ran down his neck and soaked the bed. "Waa waa!"

"Harry want some milk?" She flung off her robe, lifted her negligee, ripped off his covers. He pounded his fists on the bed, completely naked. This was going to be good, she could see that already. Harold was laughing to beat the band, squirming like an infant, kicking his heels. He reached up for mamma.

She lowered herself across his hairless body.

All for Love

"You smile? I amuse you? Don't hesitate, my fellow, get on with it."

"I can't help it, you look so . . . wicked respectable."

"Young man, you must never apply that epithet to me. Only trades-people are respectable. I am above respectability."

"Well, shit. I don't know. I shot a horse once. I got drunk and slapped a whore."

"Ah, very good. I shall never forgive you, silly boy. Did he die?"

"Who?"

"The horse."

" 'Course he did. His brains was full of worms."

"Get yourself another drink." The other boys at Oscar's table waited their turn. At this late hour, even the Odeon was quiet, that is, the band was reduced to one fiddle and a piano, and no threats had been heard in a good twenty minutes. The place was half empty. Outside, the wind screamed. No, it's a banshee. . . .

Oscar thought of his mother. He and she had once decided to form a society for the suppression of virtue. Should you live to my advanced age, she'd told him, you will know there is only one thing really worth living for, and that is sin. Dante was her ancestor! One of her uncles wrote *Melmoth the Wanderer,* and a Dublin poet had praised Lady Wilde for the great capacious ocean of her soul. . . .

Two more boys sat at the table. Bejabers, the word traveled quickly. When the men passed out, the boys woke up, having pockets to go through, trysts to carry out. One of the new ones was so filthy ugly Oscar couldn't help squealing. His teeth were rotten, squats marked his face, his chin held a fresh scab. He leered through eye slits resembling stab wounds. "Oh, here's a beast, an animal, I daresay. Nothing of the human left. Well, this is consoling. I should hate to see a rude person with a noble face. And what have you done?"

"I burned down a church."

"Splendid! Splendid! And you?"

John Vernon

"I stole some money an old lady hid in her cookstove once. I threw a Chinaman down a well."

"How naughty. Go on."

"I blew Doc Holliday."

"I boxed a nun's ears."

"One at a time! The pair of you, here, buy yourselves a drink. I wish to talk with this young man. How old are you, child?"

"Twelve." Half this boy's hair had been burned off his head, but his nose had never been broken apparently, unlike the others'. It was covered with freckles.

"Tell me something dreadful."

"Huh?"

"Your worst deeds. The bad things you've done."

He scratched his ear and opened his mouth. His head began to bob. A stutterer? Dear me. "I. . . . Oncet, I found a pair of bloody trousers."

"Where?"

"In a cabin."

"Whose were they?"

He shrugged.

"Go on. Proceed. Have you cheated at bowls? Disobeyed your mother?"

"This boy I knew about? He was eleven. He drowned his little brother in a horse trough."

"How loathsome. Did you watch it happen?"

"No."

"Was he a friend?"

"No, someone told me."

Oscar stared at the boy through bleary eyes. The world seemed to sink. "You produce no effect in me whatsoever, poor child. You neither injure nor delight me. Leave at once."

"What did I do!"

Dawn. Patches of snow making profiles. Dull thuds in the air, ubiquitous hammering, crippled by one unmodulated roar. The wooden sidewalks were so up and down, Oscar walked in the street on the hardened mud. At the doors to saloons, men swept out sawdust, and boys sifted through it looking for coins. Wafting in eddies then drifting away—depending on the street, it seemed—a disagreeable odor of burnt rubber came and went. Train whistle! No, the damn banshees again. . . .

Mother, I'm coming. Stocious Melmoth. The world had gone raw, its face torn off. Then a beer-colored light seemed to pour through Leadville. Smoke from the forests of stacks above town oozed out, flowed down, and spilled across roofs. It was every noxious color, red, brown, and yellow.

4. Washington, D.C. 1883

All her life Baby'd been told she was pretty, but not by a President of the United States. "I've never seen a more beautiful bride." First to walk the reception line, Chester Arthur bent over her hand, and she noted the perfectly combed silver hair, shingled and kinked. He straightened up, smiling. Burnside whiskers scudded his jowls and ran up and over his mouth, unwaxed. She nudged Haw, hoping he'd notice that none of the gentlemen here waxed their facial hair. . . . Blue gentle eyes, baggy and moist, big nose, fat cheeks. President Arthur resembled a gopher with manicured paws. His Chesterfield manners billowed with pity at the absence of senators' wives in the room. He was too well-bred to remark upon it, but not enough to prevent effusive kindness from rubbing extra spit on his polish. Kindness . . . or lust. "May I —beg a rose from that lovely bouquet?"

Down on your knees, she thought. She made herself blush, removed a white rose, handed the bouquet to Haw, then stood on her toes to pin the pretty flower on King Arthur's lapel, pressing her bosom against his large belly. He looked as though he might faint. . . .

There was no Mrs. Arthur next in line, she'd died of pneumonia three years before, never having shared her husband's rise from boodleman to President when Guiteau shot Garfield. Instead, Arthur's sister served as First Lady, but she wasn't here. Even Billy Bush's wife hadn't come, and he was best man! It made Baby feel strange, it steeled her bitter triumph. She'd laugh in all their faces. . . . Demure, sweet, attractive, alluring, she pictured herself fettered by her corset as though chained to a wall, with a cute little slouch to the naked shoulders. Her white satin gown with plunging décolletage ruched with tulle had cost Haw one thousand five hundred dollars. Take that, Washington! White gloves lapped her elbows, exposing the beautiful upper arms, which ran into the shoulders and bosom unsheathed. Her diamond necklace was worth ninety thousand dollars, but Haw'd refused to state the cost of the pearls. He'd sent Billy Bush to New York to buy them from a Lebanese Jew, and Billy had returned breathlessly flourishing a certificate which guaranteed this choker to be made from the very pearls Isabella had sold to finance Columbus's first expedition. In other words, they were priceless.

They felt like teeth around her throat.

At last the president turned to Senator Tabor, who proceeded to lobby him about the price of silver. He'd only be senator two more days, he'd never have another chance like this. Having lost the big prize—the permanent seat—Haw had been given the one month left in Henry Teller's term as a consolation. This was Arthur's doing; he'd made Teller his Secretary of the Interior effective thirty days before his term expired. Was it the appearance Augusta had created of being dragged bodily to court which had cost him the full senate term? Bet your boots, thought Baby. The mansion and a quarter-million dollars had been forced down her throat, the poor spurned woman. At the end, Augusta had asked the judge what her name was now.

Tabor, he said.

I'll keep it until I die, she declared.

Well, so will I, thought Baby. She felt unreal. Names were like jewels, loosely strung and expensive. Baby Elizabeth Bonduel McCourt Doe Tabor stood at the head of her own reception line trying not to gasp for air. After the president came Secretary Teller, the slimy hypocrite. He'd been quoted in the papers as saying thank God Tabor wasn't elected for six years, thirty days is nearly killing us. He took her two fingers, she sweetly smiled and turned to the next man, Tom Bowen. They all waited their turn, those that were here, in other words Colorado's delegation to Congress. Invitations to other senators and congressmen had been returned, one torn in two and stuffed back in its envelope. Washington didn't cotton to divorcers, especially them that wore diamond stickpins.

Next to Horace stood Baby's family: Daddy, Mamma, Pete Junior, Philip, Claudia in silk, Nealie with a baby in her arms and another in the oven. James and Willard hadn't come, being friends of Harvey Doe, but assorted cousins and uncles from Oshkosh compensated for their absence.

Hurry up, Haw! He was still bending the President's ear, forcing Teller to linger awkwardly at her elbow and stare at her teeth. "The miner of silver here, that has got silver, could take it to the mint and get his silver dollars for it, you understand, but not if you let a foreign government fix the price, sir. . . . That old muley country over there to set a price! Pretty near all to admire over there is old tumble down buildings, Mr. President."

"These are policy matters, Senator, and I don't discuss policy at a wedding reception."

"Well, let's you and I have a drink on the side. . . ."

Five minutes later Chester Arthur was gone.

Poor Haw hadn't known it was his responsibility to provide flowers for the bridesmaids—Baby's cousins—and cufflinks for the ushers, her two brothers. So she'd done it. She'd bargained with God all month about this wedding, especially after Haw's first appearance in the Senate was ridiculed by the foul Denver *Tribune,* before she came to Washington. Eugene Field described Senator Tabor as passing down the aisle clutching a patent leather gripsack and wearing a superb trousseau of broadcloth and jewels, which consisted of polished boots, a gold watch, gold buttons, pearl and diamond stickpins, diamond rings on his fingers, diamond cuff links large as postage stamps . . . a diamond in his navel. "Great God!" exclaimed a senator amid the general hush. Strong men wept like babies, and several ladies, most notably the wife of the Spanish ambassador, were borne from the gallery in a swooning condition.

Make them come, Baby'd prayed. Let our invitations be like the seed that fell on good soil and yielded a hundredfold. I'll offer up six novenas, God, I'll give ten thousand dollars to the nuns in Leadville. . . .

If no one had come, would the wedding have occurred? Or would she have turned into one of those people to whom things never happened because persons of importance never witnessed them? Well, *she* was a person of importance now; she was Mrs. Horace Tabor. At least the President had shown up, but he was a Stalwart, not a Half-Breed, and Republicans like him needed sources of funding. The priest who'd abbreviated the nuptial Mass had collected his two hundred dollars and left. You could come to Washington, stay at the Willard Hotel, get married in its ballroom, and meet the President of the United States himself without once having to walk outside. It made her think of close things, like Haw's fecal smell, caskets and beds. . . . Bloody claws and teeth amid the lovely flowers. . . .

At its center, the banquet table held a huge wedding bell of white roses surmounted by a Cupid's bow of heliotropes whose arrow had pierced a heart made of violets. Below was a structure the papers later referred to as the Swinging Garden of Babylon, a floral piece six feet long and two feet high made of red and white carnations, honeysuckle, and roses, topped with clusters of rare blossoms from the national hothouses. Crystal compotes and cut glass decanters stood beside the flowers. At each plate was a boutonniere, and each dish of dainty viands was circumscribed by flowers. Both ends of the table held large four-leaf clovers made from red and white roses, camelias, and violets, garlanded with smilax. The smell made her dizzy, soprano and bass smells. . . .

The Marine band performed operatic selections.

The wedding cake sat on a separate table devoted to its sole support. Chaste in design, it represented the Capitol building with bride and groom standing on the steps. Above it hung a canopy of flowers with trailing foliage.

The whole thing was a failure, but no one would admit it. At least she was beautiful. She assumed the posture of someone admired, someone hourglassed by her clothes, whose soul drained through a little pinched hole suspended in her hips. Some kind of obstruction was backing it up. . . . The room broke apart into bulges of color, ridges of shadows, and she floated through them. She felt moist inside. She was only twenty-six! Glowing, exposed, squeezed into her skin. . . . She couldn't squat to pee even if she had to. Could satin *drink* you?

You can't be snubbed if you refuse to notice it. Every color and smell in this room was corseted, every smile frozen. Naked flowers grew dry as sparrow bones. She pictured entrails packed in crates beneath the tables, each a little root cellar. Don't slip in the offal, Papa wouldn't like it. . . .

Her father stood before her. "Baby."

"Papa!"

They embraced too long, then he held her at arm's length and looked her in the face, grinning broadly. He'd been drinking, she smelled it. He'd taken to drink the second time the store burned down and the bank wouldn't loan him any more money. The poor man had lost every penny, their house and every stick of furniture. Mr. Cameron'd hired him on as a salaried tailor. He sewed her lips shut with a kiss right now. "I'm so happy for you, Baby."

"Me too, Papa. Did you pay Father Chapelle? Did you tell him there were no . . . impediments?"

"I told him so."

Mamma embraced her quickly then jumped back so as not to crush her three skirts of white silk flowing with ribbons and hooped up with roses, shamrocks, and lilies, all topped off by a hideous headdress. She turned away sniveling. Then Peter, Philip, Claudia, and finally Nealie, the only one who understood her. "Nealie, help, what have I done?" Squirming on her shoulder, Nealie's little baby began to cry.

"You've become filthy rich."

"Rescue me, Nealie. Come and get me tonight. We'll run away and join a convent. . . ."

That night in their suite she railed at Haw. "Where was Senator and

Mrs. Hill? Ain't he on that committee you're on? Pensions and claims? What about Sherman and Morrill, you told me they'd come. Even Roscoe Conkling never showed up, and you stayed at his house. I thought I'd die. Where was Billy's wife?"

"Indisposed." Haw had changed into his silk and lace nightshirt with gold buttons, the very gewgaw he'd made the mistake of showing to reporters on the train to Washington. Now the papers called him Senator Nightshirt. "You were beautiful, Baby. They don't know what they missed."

Had he even washed his hands before the wedding? "One forgets that one is human," she mumbled. Somewhere, real people were doing real things, using real knives and forks to carve bloody joints. . . .

Haw had rearranged the furniture in the suite so as to clear the route between the bathroom and their canopied bed; he'd even thrown some chairs into the hallway. He'd had a few drinks, she could tell, his face glowed. He was fifty-two, making this the only year he'd be twice her age. From now on the gap would gradually shrink. . . . "What do you even care about them birds?" he asked.

"You should have left your diamonds in the hotel safe."

"Does the pope hide his jewels under the mattress? Does he wear his tiara or just admire it?"

"He don't wear it to bed." From each of his hands she removed a large diamond and dropped it in her bosom. Baby's chemise of virginal silk threw sparks when she brushed it. "Come to bed, Haw. I'll whisper dirty words in your ear. You can listen to my heart. I'll tell you my secrets. . . ." She pulled him by his mustache. He had the slow staggers. Clots of wax hung from the hairs of the mustache, she had to let go and wipe her fingers on his shirt. The black dye in his thinning hair had streaked his scalp where he'd run his hands through it. Pads of his fingers were smudged with black too. "Wash those hands, you big gallomph. I don't like dirty hands."

"You're so . . . classy, Babe." He fell to his knees when she sat on the bed, and rubbed his oiled head into her bosom, opening the chemise. He came up with two diamond rings in his mouth. His thick hairy body inspired disgust, but disgust made Baby . . . amorously inclined. In his dirty ear she whispered atrocities. She thought of the smell inside his pants. She thought of her parents' soft bed back in Oshkosh—the unmade, soiled sheets; the close, fetid odor—and felt comforted and nauseous, ready to buck her hips and die.

Once she'd overheard her father in the store use a strange word: "rantallion." Peter told her that was a man whose oysters were so big and relaxed as to hang down below his member. Snatch-blatch, rantallion, muddywort, hair pie. Piss flaps, gutstick, lollypop, hisssss. . . . Horace was hairy, and never cut his toenails. The yellow claws curled down under his feet.

When they climbed on the bed, he stiffened, closed his mouth, and looked the other way. She rubbed up against him, thinking what a sham Washington society had proven. Gilt-edged invitations. . . . He rolled away. "What's wrong, Haw?" Her promiscuous tongue fooled his earlobe. Should she feel proud or ashamed of the wedding? Good lord, why piss on convention at all if it made you so stupidly supplicatory? To spend all your life sucking crystal and china, lapping eggy fluids. . . .

She felt him relaxing. Rubbing bosom and thighs against his hairy back helped. She reached over and mucked around with his taffy. After a while he rolled over to face her. She lay back. He climbed on top.

Well, the President had come. His upholstered body had pressed against hers. She'd pinned him a rose!

"Oh, Baby . . ."

"Haw!"

He was scaling a mountain, he had to keep checking his burrowing packrat. He clenched his teeth and hissed, "Don't move." Baby wished she were the worm that once ate the rose that grew in the slippery crack in the garden. It was hard to imagine why she existed. Why was she doing this? Why not. . . .

His desire fermented, he released his fetid breath, she could swear what came out of his fat little sausage wasn't hot grease but a mere dribble of urination, drops gathered in his bladder like rainwater in a cup. . . .

"I like it when you wrap your legs around me."

"Oh, Haw. You should of said so." They'd have to do it again, then. Let's see, there were secrets she still hadn't told him. The gold nugget she'd once stolen and hidden in her poozle. Orgies she'd dreamed up with aunts and uncles . . . with Mamma and Daddy! Eating pig's nuts, which tasted like headcheese. . . .

Haw met Billy Bush for breakfast downstairs while Baby slept late the next morning. After steak, eggs, and biscuits soaked in gravy, then coffee, mints, and candied fruit . . . a morning cigar . . . it was almost time for lunch. Activity at the Senate would commence in an hour with a meeting of Haw's subcommittee on epidemic diseases, but Bush was Horace's business agent, and business had backed up during the wedding preparations, during the meetings with politicians and codfish aristocrats . . . the snubs of senators' wives. Haw liked to say that people think mining's a crapshoot but it's not, it's a business; and business is business.

Still, it was hard to keep his mind on such matters as Nicholas Atkinson's suit against Sam Bruckman regarding Haw's purchase of the Tam O'Shanter mine, then Tabor's countersuit, and Atkinson's appeal, based on the argument that Horace Tabor scorned us small fry now that he wasn't one, and we're getting nothing but peanuts in this deal because we're poor and he's rich and powerful. . . . It was hard for a bridegroom on the morning after to wipe the grin off his face, to shut down the invisible electric fluid given off by his sheer animal magnetism, even if Baby *had* been his mistress for more than two years now. It's different when you're married.

John Vernon

"Here's a letter, Haw. From a Josie C. Abel in Cape Girardeau, Missouri. States that a fortune-teller predicted that she would marry a foreign gentleman by name of H. A. W. Tabor. Inquires whether such a person exists. Now I wonder why she wrote you?"

"Well, what do you think, is she stringing me on?" Haw felt enormous but elastic—in a state of suspended mollescence. He looked around the restaurant with its fern trees and beveled mirrors reflecting fern trees. Outside, even now, buds on the cherry trees thickened and swelled.

"I'll write back and recommend pink pills for pale people."

"People get so one-idea'd."

"Hell, Jesus Christ was one-idea'd himself. Now this here's an offer from something called the Illinois Indemnity Corporation to trade fifty thousand dollars of their stock for sixty-three thousand preferred stock of yours in the Calumet, Chicago Canal and Dock Company."

"I wouldn't want to let go of Calumet at present prices. Write Marshall Field and ask him if he knows them birds."

"Take a look at this one, Haw. Nellie J. Bemis of Morris, Minnesota, requests that you and your bride each send her a silk handkerchief. They'll be auctioned off for the benefit of charity."

"Which charity does it say?"

"It don't. . . . This scrawl's hard to figure. Looks like a boardinghouse for ruptured lumberjacks."

"Baby comes from logging country, show it to her, she's got plenty of hankies."

"She's . . ."

"Upstairs. In bed."

"What about you, you got plenty of hankies?"

This talk of hankies made Horace grin broadly, he didn't know why. The feel of silk on one's skin? Hell, steak grease and egg yolk congealed on a plate made him grin too, though it was a sad sight. Even Nathaniel P. Hill's scumdrum wife, seated across the restaurant, couldn't spoil his day. It was she who'd torn up her invitation to the wedding and sent it back in an envelope. She wouldn't look in his direction. "Billy, there's that shit-pail of Hill's."

"Ignore her."

"I'd like to sit on her face."

"What about them pledges on the post office lot? Do you want to pursue that?"

Horace sucked his teeth. "What's the status of that?"

"Well, John Evans and his son still owe you five thousand."

"Tell Lou to sue."

"For five thousand dollars?"

"They pledged it because they wanted the post office built on my lot, and now that it's going to be built there, if everything pans out, I mean to say, and their lots are more valuable—which is the result they wanted, ain't it?—now the bastards think they got no call to pay."

"I told Duff if the government would not accept your property they can stick their post office and you'll build a first-class brothel on the site."

"That's the ticket, Billy."

Near the entrance, the simpering maître d' had been seized by a fit of scraping and bowing. Haw watched with interest. Waiting to be seated were Treasury Secretary Folger and his wife, who just last week had regretted their inability to attend Senator Tabor's wedding, having planned a trip around the world. Tinkles of silver and china flew about. Hard crystal, soft lips. How faintly the waiter's black shoes trod the carpets. . . .

On either side of his plate Horace spread his fingers. He regarded the diamonds large as berries. "Say, Billy. You think I'm a showboat? Too flash?"

Billy turned around to see what his boss had seen, then turned back and shrugged.

"What's the papers say today, William?"

"They say, 'Senator Tabor Marries an Oshkosh Lady.'"

Horace looked away.

Billy sighed. "It ain't you, Haw, it's *her*. Meaning no disrespect to your wife, these people here don't want to meet *her*. They know the story. They consider you was married once proper, she was too, and they don't brook divorce, in a woman particular. For a man, well, they'll wink. But it stirs up slanderous tongues for a woman. Me and you, see, we know it's just . . . malicious gossip, but they say Baby was a loose woman before you met her."

"How come your Ellen didn't come?"

"I told you, she's sick."

"Where is she now?"

"Sick in bed."

"What's the papers say about Baby?"

"Well, they recount her history in Oshkosh. They talk about her marriage to no-count Harvey Doe, who had no especial promise, as they put it. They talk about the dispute regarding her brother's creditors over the diamonds you gave her, which she gave him."

"They don't say she divorced Harvey, do they?"

"They don't mention that either way. He could be dead. You would naturally think so."

"What else?"

"Ain't that enough? They rave about she's beautiful and bewitching, and a devotee of fashion. Not a blessed word about Jake Sandelowsky, Haw." Billy seemed to be snorting. His words came out chewed. His eyes had narrowed, staring at Haw's face. His trim little mustache twitched as he spoke, and his mouth barely rippled, involuntarily it seemed, less a smile than a spasm or wink. "Nothing about her life in Central City, that's what's eating you. Not a word about threesomes, foursomes, whatnot. Baby dressed in a little maid's apron without no pants on, playing the skin flute. Shit, Haw. Grow up. You knew what you was buying before you bought it."

"Her past . . . may have left something to be desired."

"It left a lot to be desired, you knew that."

"She's changed. She loves me so much it really don't matter what she used to be."

"*I* say, Golly Gee. I raise my left eyebrow. She ain't the town pump no more, you're saying? Pull yourself together. You made the bed, lie in it."

"You're going too far, Billy. This is my wife."

"I know, I know."

"I can prove she's changed."

"Then fine. Hunky-dory."

"She loves me."

"I don't doubt it."

"She's Mrs. Horace Tabor now. Go to her, Billy. Try to debauch her. See where it gets you."

"Sure, Haw. Simmer down."

"I'm serious. It's an order."

"What is?"

"You heard me." Horace never trembled, not when he'd gained the upper hand. He felt large and generous, strong as a mountain. The proof was in Billy's shifting eyes, his sudden slouch, as though someone'd cut his strings. "Go to her now. Address her, Billy. Woo her . . . spark it. You don't have to go the whole hog, you shan't be able to anyway. She'll throw you out on your ear, you'll see."

"Haw, I've worked for you five years now. You got no call to humbug me this way."

"It's no humbug. She'll throw you out on your ear."

"Well, I won't do it. You can fire me, I don't care."

"I got no intention of firing you, Billy. Sometimes you're too much mouth, though, I'll say that."

"I been your flunky, I won't be your pimp."

"You ain't my flunky, you're my business associate."

"Are we done? You got your committee to go to."

"No, we're not done. What about that hanky?"

"What hanky?"

"The two silk handkerchiefs for charity."

"What about it?" snapped Billy.

"Well. You better go get one from Baby."

"Oh? Shall I do that?"

"Sure thing."

"Fine. I will. They wanted one from each of you."

"Gee, all I got is this here in my pocket, I can't really spare it. Can I borrow yours?" With a rolling motion, Haw heaved himself up, thigh by thigh. Standing on his trunks, he reached across the table and snatched Billy's handkerchief out of his coat. It was folded so nicely!

"They want one with your own monogram, Horace."

"I'll monogram it." Horace shook out the hanky, took a deep breath, then blew his big nose in it, trumpeting the deed for the whole restaurant. The patrons all looked, startled by the sound. He tossed it on the table and lumbered out of the restaurant, on his way to discharge his senatorial burdens.

Ten minutes later Billy knocked on Baby's door. A voice inside said, "Go away."

"C'mon, Baby."

"I'm not your Baby, I'm the maid. I'm busy, go away." She'd altered her voice. Strained it through cheesecloth.

"You owe me. Pay up."

"What a buck ignoramus! I'm just the poor Irish maid making up the beds. Baby went out shopping."

"Are you going to open up?"

Each time she spoke the voice seemed further off. He pictured her huddled beneath the covers shouting with lopsided precision, all innocence and venom. "It's against the rules, gobshite."

He bent down to the keyhole. "Cunt. You'll be sorry."

Baby and Haw slept late the next morning, and might have lingered until evening in lethargic bliss if a reporter hadn't learned where their room was and snuck past the desk. At the knock, Haw climbed out of bed in his nightshirt. Through the open door she heard him slinging bunkum. She heard the blustering tone, not the words. He came back and told her the newspapers had learned about their secret marriage in St. Louis seven months ago. The reporter wanted to know if that marriage had also ended in divorce.

"Also? They're not digging up our divorces?"

"Well . . . that part's in today's editions."

Baby dressed without a corset and ran downstairs to purchase a *Post*. She brought it back and spread it on the bed. "Who told them?" she cried.

They looked at each other like guilty children.

SENATOR TABOR'S MARRIAGE

The Priest Who Officiated Complains That He Was Deceived

The Rev. Dr. P. L. Chapelle, Pastor of St. Matthew's Roman Catholic Church, is deeply grieved because he was induced to violate unintentionally the rules of the Church by uniting in marriage Senator Tabor, of Colorado, and Miss McCourt. He did not know until today that either had taken part in divorce proceedings, and he was astonished when he learned that the first wife of Senator Tabor and the first husband of Miss McCourt are living. He declares that when he was requested to perform the ceremony he asked the customary questions and was told by Miss McCourt's father, a Roman Catholic well acquainted with the rule of the Church in such cases, that no impediment existed. He also questioned the senator, but owing to the assurances of the bride's father it did not occur to him that it could be necessary to ask whether or not he had gone through a divorce court. He says he supposes that Mr. and Mrs. Tabor are married in the

eyes of the law, but that there was no real marriage from the point of view of the Roman Catholic Church. Dr. Chapelle says that a business associate of the senator called upon him this morning and represented the senator's views on the matter and acknowledged the senator had greatly erred in concealing the facts, albeit unintentionally. Upon receipt of the news, the outraged Dr. Chapelle returned the senator's $200 wedding fee through the same emissary. The prominence and great wealth of the bridegroom, the fact that President Arthur was present during the ceremony, and the character of the congregation of St. Matthew's Church have made this matter one of the great sensations of the day in Washington.

"Where's Ellen?"

"Engaged."

"Where?"

"With the President's sister."

"I thought she was indisposed."

"She was. She's disposed now. Miss Arthur suggested an afternoon tea."

"And little Billy? Where's he?"

"Out with his nurse."

"This room is certainly more splendid than ours."

"There's four of us here."

"Four?"

"Three plus the nurse."

"Who pays for all this?"

"Your husband does."

Baby glanced around with contempt. Her hat, cloak, and parasol, her overskirt and bustle, meant she'd been out. Her royal blue dress with its chaste white collar held in place by a cameo brooch, hung with becoming slackness on architecture, for she'd laced her corset as tight as a boot to sustain an impression of elevation. She felt taller than Billy, but then everyone did, it was wasted effort. She stood as though poured there, held in a gasp.

Plush chairs, lacquered tables, thick Belgian carpets. Through a door she spotted a canopied bed. Rose-colored curtains curdled the light. The walls looked creamy banana yellow.

"Did you tell the papers about my divorce?"

"Well, they kept asking where's Mr. Doe."

"I'm surprised you didn't produce him."

"Say! I like that."

"And Haw's divorce too?"

"It was public knowledge."

"Our marriage in Saint Louis?"

"See, I lost the marriage license. A reporter found it."

"Haw wants his two hundred dollars back."

"Tell him to sue me. A Roman Catholic priest threw it in my face. He seemed to blame me."

Baby grew a few inches. She was squeezing rage. Cold and dizzy, she felt herself sway, then gave into the motion, even nudged it along. The little scumbag in his dressing gown grinned. She felt pale as death. Somewhere a girl on a swing popped her stitches. Queens drank poison, cocked pistols tossed into vats of acid spent themselves firing. She saw bullets whizzing through barrels boiled off and swallowed by nothing . . . triggers dissolving . . . To faint in this corset would be a feat of engineering—unless Billy caught her. Well, she'd planned it this way. A sob ballooned up and choked for lack of air. She felt herself rise, but knew she was falling. Billy, you slut, you better loosen my stays. . . .

Her eyes flew open. She lay on her back. Billy's face swam in the air above her. "Call off your dogs." She felt the words slur.

"Lock up your bitches."

"Haw loves me, Billy. He feels awful about what the papers said. You had no call to tell them those things. We're man and wife now."

John Vernon

102

"Two dickey birds."

"What can I do to make you stop?"

"Gee, I don't know. Kiss my bright forehead?"

The white and blue carpet felt soft as a bed. He crouched down beside her. With quick fingers he unbuttoned her overskirt and gently divested her of the bustle, now she could stretch out. She stiffened; turned her head and summoned tears. The royal blue dress had been carefully chosen, as it buttoned down the front. The buttons were beads and there were hundreds, thousands. She pushed away his hands and with trembling fingers unpinned her brooch, removed the collar, and started on the buttons herself. She worked from the top, he from the bottom. "Remove your filthy fingers," she sobbed.

She lay stiff as a board, cold and withdrawn. The tears flowed nonstop. She unbuttoned the dress with measured progress, as though crossing a steppe. You're such a piece of shit, Billy Bush. His hands squeezed her breasts where they bulged above canvas. He couldn't hurt her any more than the corset, which felt like a saddle. He made fish noises. He sucked at her skin. He rolled her over and, with his pen knife, cut the strings of the corset instead of untying them. Her body flowed out, pinguescent. "Now what'll I do," she sighed, meaning the corset. She refused to help him. The sobs came fast and thick. "I knew it was you that blabbed to the papers. I asked myself, should I beg him to stop? We used to be friends. That don't matter, you were never very passionate, Billy Bush. You heartless little snake, you're disgusting. I hate you. I can't believe you'd do this to a woman. If Haw ever found out he'd pinch your head off. He loves me and I love him. I'm doing this for love. I'd rip out my heart for Horace Tabor, if you want to know the truth. You don't have an ounce of pity, you pig. How can you do this and get away with it and not feel a thing or care what I feel? I came here planning to offer myself to make you shut up, but I never thought you'd do it. I never thought you'd take me up on such a sordid bargain. What's over is over. No one can blame me. What kind of gentleman would do a thing like this? Does it make you feel good to force yourself on me? Just like an animal, like a dirty animal. I'll shoot myself, you bastard, you'll see. I'll get Haw's gun, he always takes a six-shooter with him in his grip. Just in case. I'll run away and shoot myself. Don't get any ideas, I'm doing this for love. Love for Horace Tabor."

"Shut up."

"Why should I?"

He'd entered from behind and was grinding away. On her elbows and knees, she tried not to help him. They used to do it with her on top because of his length, but he didn't feel long now, he'd shrunk a few inches. He never was very long, she decided. "Loosen up," he said. She was dry as a bone. Every time he thrust she jerked ahead a few inches. "This is no good." He pulled out and turned her over.

She lay on her back, crying with eyes closed. He stuffed himself in, only half erect. He tried to find a rhythm but she wouldn't help.

All at once she stopped crying. She felt in control. Cold and withdrawn, she raised her head with open mouth. He sucked in his breath and got her tongue instead. He couldn't help himself, she knew, she felt him go thick for an instant and quiver. But he still wouldn't stop. The more he thrust the more he dissolved. She felt moist now but knew it was him. Her head fell back and she smiled for the first time. His eyes were half closed. He didn't seem to be quite sure he'd come. His eyes were still rolling up into his head, he kept trying to thrust but dissolving instead. . . . The flesh of his face, normally tight, hung like a bag of feed around the nose.

What a sucker, she thought. I've got him.

The anticlimax came when Ellen Bush screamed, having unlocked the door and walked in. Billy was up on his hands and knees, bare-assed and dripping. Baby Doe lay in a storm of piled clothes, one brown nipple floating up. Her mound of pubic hair was red as a carrot.

Well, it could have been worse, Billy thought. Little Billy could have shown up instead.

The open door seemed to make everything shrink. Billy realized how

fully exposed they were on the floor, where the gas light pooled. "Animals!" screamed his wife. "Filthy dogs!" She became hysterical. Her black hair collapsed on one side of her neck, she'd gone pale with red patches. Her upturned nose, flaring, resembled a death's head's. "A pair of dogs, that's what you are! Spitzes!" She waved a piece of paper in his face. Billy couldn't make it out.

Baby could, though. She knew the look of anonymous letters, especially this one, having sent it herself.

When they all returned to Denver, Haw fired Billy for gross mismanagement of the Tabor affairs, and at his wife's urging replaced him with her brother Peter. He brought charges against his former factotum for embezzling funds from the Tabor Grand Opera House, for defaulting on loans, and for pocketing the $200 wedding fee returned by the outraged Father Chapelle.

Billy sued and Horace countersued. Billy sued for the $5,000 it cost him to help Haw become senator for one month, for the $10,000 he'd spent to search out testimony against Augusta in Haw's divorce, and for $75,000 in damages due to malicious prosecution. Horace countersued for recompense regarding Billy's incompetent supervision of the Opera House—for example, booking *Uncle Tom's Cabin* to death, six times in two years.

In court, the celebrated actor Lawrence Barrett testified that Billy was a woefully underpaid impresario. He only earned $75 a week. Horace told the judge that time and again he'd staked William Bush in games of poker and was never paid back. Once he slipped him $1,000 to call his opponent, and Billy won, but kept Haw's stake.

Billy's suit was thrown out, Haw's countersuit won a judgment for $19,958, Billy promptly appealed, but the appeal died a slow death. It got swallowed in briefs and deferred court proceedings. Billy ran out of funds. He sank for a while, then found his niche managing a playhouse uptown, far from the busy scenes on Sixteenth Street. It was rumored that miscreants in his employ shipped ore across the border into Mexico for milling into fandango dollars, which were then shipped back to Billy, to manure his finances.

To the Tabors, Billy Bush never stopped representing malicious forces right there in your backyard, where you least expected them. He gave them a new verb. Say a chimney collapsed at the opera house, or one of Haw's mills in Leadville burned down, or Baby's invitations were returned unopened, they could claim they'd been Bushed. With a name, bad luck wouldn't mean things were senseless. It was part of the plan.

5. Denver 1886

"Bushed again." Haw snorted. Baby crushed her face against the glass. Steam from their horses glowed due to gaslights on California Street, electric lights on Sixteenth. Shavings of light crannied darkness all around, held there by the cold. Stuck, like them. The police in the street, blue and helpless, exhibited their usual detergent influence. They tugged on bridles and shouted at coachmen, as though that would untangle the opulent mess. The performance had already begun, of course, they were fashionably late, though such fine points hardly mattered, thought Baby. She leaned back against her husband. If they never showed up would they be all the rage?

"Huhnng?"

"This might be a good time to find my earring."

Haw rapped. The panel slid open. The sound of it always rippled Baby's heart, recalling as it did confessionals at church. But this wasn't church, it was the brown victoria with red and yellow trim and silver harnesses and mahogany paneling from the Honduran forests and white satin upholstery matching her ermine opera cloak, what a lark!

The first time they'd been Bushed that evening occurred when, having just left, she felt an earring missing. Haw was too large and she too corsetted to bend down and search, so Haw now ordered their coachman to do so. The panel slid shut, the landau tipped, then cold air rushed in. Baby didn't look. Icy hands fussed too close to her feet, and soon the familiar halfspray of diamonds was pressed into her palm. Shouts came from outside; the traffic was moving. Raymond, their coachman, rushed back to his perch, having closed the door on Haw and Baby Doe. She bolted on the earring and felt reconstructed.

It matched her evening gown of white and silver tulle with tight-fitting bodice, ordered from Paris.

At the Tabor Grand Opera House on Sixteenth and Curtis—far grander than the Tabor Opera House in Leadville—footmen clamored to open their door and hand Baby down and succumb to her shy smile. The Silver King and Queen dodged other carriages approaching the expansive portals of cut stone, and Haw couldn't help himself, he lumbered ahead. Always, he swaggered and took enormous steps, he imperceptibly drifted to the side, creating a vacuum that dragged his wife along. She tried to catch up, on stubby little legs awash in the ermine that hung to her ankles, and leaned to one side too, hands clasped together. She also drifted. Men greeted Haw, Haw greeted men, and the latter tipped their hats at Baby.

Was Haw on a leash or she on a towline? Just watching his back made her heart swell. Horace Tabor, she knew, had never lowered himself for anyone or -thing in the world, but he'd kiss Baby's feet at the drop of a hat. He'd crawl like a worm and throw dirt on his head and look up her dress and beg for affection. Not her, though. She'd never be common. She disdained vulgarity now that she was rich, but stayed loyal to Haw's coarse manners in defiance of the world. It made her feel proud. The rugged men of the West who'd once mucked in mines were preferable to the perfumed and brandy-soaked gallants of society, she declared to whoever would listen.

Through the marble foyer they marched straight for their box. The Tabors were never required to wait for interludes; a boy in livery held the door open.

And there, beyond the curved railing of the box, there—marbled, fringed, paneled, carpeted, columned, and painted—unfolded their temple, just now heaving with music. It was the mad scene from *Lucia di Lammermoor.* On the stage to their left, in moonlight and fog, stood Amy Abbot, whose specialty was screams and high C's shattered by ghostly sprechgesang. She was to precede the Boston Howard Atheneum Specialty Company singing Christmas songs and novelties, including the ever-popular "Down Went McGinty."

Fifteen hundred people turned to look, in boxes, tiers, and stalls, when the Tabors walked in. Baby and Haw shed their overgarments. The populace raised their lorgnettes and opera glasses and studied every detail of her costume. They took mental notes. Later that week their own cut-rate dressmakers would copy it down to each buttonhole, she knew.

The interior of the theater scrolled around the stage in huge operatic chasms. Japanese columns stood at either wing, and the aisles were covered with thick Wilton carpets. Above the proscenium arch was a painting of Hector arming for battle. In coves and niches, lining walls of the boxes, were ornaments and scrollwork of gold, blue, and black. Electric lights secreted in nooks behind oyster shells made a counterfeit twilight. The entire theater glowed. Should one bend one's neck back, one could see the evening sky with Colorado clouds painted on the ceiling and, inside the spandrels, gold harps and laurel.

Their box was filled with lilies and champagne. Haw popped a cork. Amy Abbot stole a glance.

The large silver plate engraved *TABOR* in their box was Baby's idea. Eighteen months ago their daughter was born, Elizabeth Bonduel Lily Cupid Tabor. What better way to honor the occasion than pass out gold medals and mount silver plates and thus sow the name of Tabor on good soil? They'd often brought Cupid to this box, and endured the contempt of Edwin Booth and Madame Modjeska, who'd each halted performances to glare and stamp their feet at the squawling nursery hung above the stage.

In the orchestra below, Baby spotted Augusta. The first Mrs. Tabor was looking right at her. Baby's chin sagged with fat. Her soul felt exposed, love flooded out, her love for Horace Tabor filled the whole theater. Augusta often came to the Tabor Grand, having been granted a pass by her former husband. Her face looked haunted; Baby saw it everywhere. Augusta was contagious, it seemed. They had the same name, they'd shared the same body. For the past three years Baby'd found herself pursuing references to Augusta Tabor in the *Rocky Mountain News*. When Haw wasn't home, she scoured his private papers for old letters or recipes, whatever she could find. She imagined Augusta telling intimate stories about her early life as a pioneer with Haw. Why not meet her at Joslin's and instruct her in the latest Paris fashions, Baby thought? They'd be secret friends. Baby had actually referred a former maid to Augusta's household, unbeknownst to Haw. She could advise her on investments, help her with her spelling, send her venison and pheasants, order her carriage to be made available in case Augusta needed an airing. Did Augusta have la grippe? She could dispatch her doctor. . . .

Sudden applause. Amy Abbot bowed. The curtain fell, a target for flowers, then Amy marched out and scooped them up, flinging kisses at the audience. When all the flowers were in her arms, Baby stood, leaned out, and launched a lily. Amy genuflected and, bowing still lower, plucked it off the boards with her teeth. The applause decayed, and Amy looked puzzled. She walked off stage. Baby sat down.

The Howard Atheneum was a popular favorite. They sang Christmas songs and Stephen Foster selections. After their final tableau—a Christmas parlor with Mamma and Poppa and all the little children and a huge Christmas tree and a fire in the fireplace and mustachioed neighbors singing "While the Bowl Goes Round"—the theater swelled with the thunder of departure. Baby and Haw waited for it to empty. Soon a footman informed them that the reception had begun.

The main reception hall was swimming with flowers, both tropical flowering plants and cut lilies. Behind Baby a wag shouted, "Here's the Silver Queen!" She spun around, clutching lilies to her bosom, then crouched, gliding forward, and swung her free arm, fingers bunched together like a striking cobra. She sputtered, "You, Peter," collapsing into laughter. Everyone watched. Her brother poured her some champagne. With his eyes he directed her gaze toward the buffet. Mrs.

Senator Teller had come! Baby didn't dare greet her, not yet. And with her were the Honorable and Mrs. J. B. Grant, and Mrs. Charles Ballin of the Woman's Home Club. She could run over there and kiss insipid fingers, or she could stab them with a knife, which would it be? The knife plunged in, something popped, blood fountained. . . . The sudden picture frightened her. She stood there in a daze.

Haw and Pete always planned these receptions, but they were known to be Baby's. She was the hostess. Her husband and brother had induced a few doyennes to take a chance they never would have hazarded by calling at her house. A first step! She felt panicky, happy. She flung a lily at Peter.

She made herself stately. Erect and commanding, she approached the buffet. Around her hovered gold brocade and green velvet petticoats with demi-trains of old pink, orchids crossing white satin bodices and drooping over breadths of cream-tinted tulle trimmed in gold and black passementerie, not bad. She glided past them, fastening her attention upon the shrimp salads. A chariot constructed of boiled lobsters and shrimps raced toward the punch bowl, behind which loomed a scaled reproduction of the Eiffel Tower in nougat.

In the middle of the table sat a low oblong box into which great quantities of sand had been poured. Footmen handed out tiny silver shovels and pails, and guests were invited to dig out the favors: silver cuff links, stickpins, rings. "It costed him plenty," she heard someone say.

Arms encircled her waist from behind. She smelled Haw's sweat, and leaned her head back against his soft shoulder. "Why the Eiffel Tower?"

"Because Denver's to Colorado what Paris used to be to France."

She spun around and kissed his naked chin. She didn't care who was watching, who wasn't. "Used to be?"

"Have you talked to Moffat yet?"

"I couldn't find him in this mob."

"This mob is the cream of Capitol Hill."

Well, almost. Baby looked around. Haw'd tried so hard she didn't really have the heart to explain it to him. She couldn't just walk up to Mrs. Senator Teller and start a conversation, Horace. The room would fall silent. She'd die, she'd explode. Haw didn't know. What a perfect child he was! Me kowtow to Mrs. Teller? Who she? Her dress wasn't bad but her hair was plain vulgar. Tufts of white or tinted feathers in coiffures were so outré it's a wonder she hadn't been laughed from the room. I could teach her, though. I could loan her my hairdresser. I could take her on a tour of my closets at home, with the Paris gowns still tissued in their coffins. . . .

Baby turned in her direction, shocked to find her so close. She felt herself shrink. Haw touched her cheek. Stay with me, Horace, my nerves are shot tonight. Don't walk away. Stand right beside me.

His large warm hands swallowed her little cold ones.

She felt every eye in that room upon her.

"Gunnison's a tough place. Moffat carries his pistol in hand after dark. Did I mention, *in hand?*"

"Perhaps you shouldn't go there."

"Business is business."

"Is Moffat on the board?"

"Him and me *is* the board." Haw tells me everything. I'm practically his partner. *I* could be on the board of every bank he ever started. Haw likes people and people like him. People come to him, he gives and he takes, he multiplies assets like loaves and fishes. He's a mountain of satisfaction with springs, a spring for every mouth. He sacrificed a political career to marry me, so I *have* to help him, there's really no choice. He could have been governor, maybe even president. Instead, he makes money and lets me keep track of it. Everything he touches hardens to silver! "Come meet Amy Abbot." He'd hooked her bare arm. He dragged her through the crowd.

Where was her champagne? Denver nights and Denver mornings, you could drink champagne as though lapping up the Milky Way. Champagne didn't halt the aging process, just put it in perspective.

The best part of Denver was always that time when the servants carried in the velvet cagecovers and put the canaries and parrots to sleep and induced the monkeys to come down from the chandeliers and hop back into their boxes: then the singing and comical squawking stopped and the drapes were all closed and she and Haw sipped champagne alone by the fire with its splendid mantelpiece of Indian marble, those were the best, those Colorado evenings.

"Miss Abbot, Mrs. Tabor."

"We thank you for the lily, Mrs. Tabor."

She'd looked younger on stage. Like Baby she fawned, but her shyness was fake, the innocent bow to her head disposed carefully to improve upon her looks. It hid the flaps of skin beneath her chin. Stage makeup still caked the lines beside her mouth, the crannies on her brow.

"Mr. Wilde loved lilies, when he was here. We named our daughter Lily. Lily's my flower."

"I'm sure I'll cherish this one." Her grainy voice wasn't what you'd expect after hearing her sing. It was younger in timbre, older in wear. She laced it with sarcasm. When she spoke, it seemed, a hidden eye winked at their hidden interlocutor, Baby's worse half.

"I admire your singing greatly." Miss Abbot smiled. Haw drifted off. "I once sang myself. I danced, I sang. Did you ever dance too, in your younger days?"

She dropped her smile. "We're a pair, you and me."

What did that mean? Baby noticed that Billy Bush's majordomo, Mr. Chambers, had slipped past the footmen. No doubt scouting out singers and actresses. He always chose two, paid them a fee, and shipped them off in a landau to Billy. "I played a Clementi. I danced, I sang. I skated exquisitely. Picturesquely. I haven't skated in years, but I used to win medals. Dear me, excuse me, I'm talking about myself. Where do you go from here, Miss Abbot?"

"Someplace called Pueblo."

"You're on the Silver Circuit. My husband devised it because, he

All for Love

said, it cost $656 in fares and baggage fees alone to bring Lawrence Barrett here from Kansas City. To overcome this disadvantage he organized a circuit of opera houses, in Colorado, Wyoming, and Utah, in other words. It spreads out the charges."

Miss Abbot had composed a rubbery smile. Her height made her gloat, gazing down upon Baby. She looked away.

"Did you ever play at the Harding Opera House in Oshkosh, Wisconsin? My most fervent dream, when I was a child, was to go on stage. Now look at me!"

Miss Abbot didn't. "You're lovely, Mrs. Tabor, I'm sure." She'd begun to incline toward the buffet table.

"I organized theatricals among our young people, the gay dogs and smart set of Oshkosh, Miss Abbot. We had such a swell time. I was Julie de Mortemar in *Richelieu,* honorably loved by the Chevalier, dishonorably pursued by the king. I was Cleopatra in *All for Love.* I never could get enough applause, can you? Clapping wasn't enough, I wanted hoots, whistles, foot stomping, bravos. How about you? Once on stage you never leave it. All the world's a stage, ha ha. I feel like I'm always reciting lines. I'm playing a role. I keep on looking for the *X*'s on the floor. Walk this way, pivot, kick my train, stagger . . . clutch my heaving bosom. Do I shoot myself now?"

Miss Abbot's bare shoulder, floating off, offered no cue. Baby found herself standing alone in the geographical center of the room. Every man here had a wife who entertained, every woman an invitation list that she weeded perpetually, dropping undesirables, adding more and more desirables. She spotted Haw near a ceiling-high window. Behind him, outside, light snow had begun. He'd collared Judge Stone and was waving his arms. Baby knew what he was saying. Increase the quantity of money and prices will rise and businessmen make a decent profit. There ain't enough gold in circulation to make a decent profit, that's why we need silver, cock a doodle doo. The more animated he became, the more the long sag of his face lit up. She pictured him tossing Cupid in the air. He'd recited "The Face on the Barroom Floor" before tucking her in once. Now she commanded it each night, sometimes mornings too. Cupid thought it was a real face, torn off someone's head. She thought she might step on it.

Haw spotted his wife standing alone. He clutched Judge Stone's arm, backing off. He began to lumber toward her, a big grin on his face. There was only one Horace, but how many Baby Does? Whenever she became blissfully happy she recognized the fragile nature of the happiness, and that plunged her into misery again. Not Haw, though. Shamelessly absorbed in one thing at a time, he was always in view, on deck, at hand. Nothing hidden, no fickle moods. She felt sorry for him, Mr. big clumsy oaf, Mr. cigar-sucking backslapping chairman of everything, with his finger in everyone's pie, for their own good. The closer he came, the larger he grew, the more she wanted to protect his swaying bulk. She'd shoot all his enemies and shield his body with her own. She drank him, he filled her. His schemes and plans were her spiritual nourishment. What did he really feel? Did he wonder what people said behind his back? Don't worry about them birds, she told him, they had each other. And they did! She thought of him stretched out helpless in bed, hairy chest heaving. With the spittle on her lips she tied knots in the hair.

He swaggered closer. Well-being spread through her.

She turned her head and spotted the haunted face of Augusta Tabor outside the door. Spare cheeks, tight lips. She nodded at Baby. Was she seeking admittance? She looked so forlorn.

No calling cards on the silver salver, but plenty of mail. Baby lay back on the sofa in the music room. The black and gold bamboo furniture, the parquet floors, mahogany paneling, ferns, flowers, tree-ferns in pots—the silk palace rug and small orientals and temple jars of the Yung Chang period—the disappearing back of the butler—all made her feel cozy and sad. It may have been excessive, like grace, but somehow it felt rationed. With many rooms to choose from, whichever one you chose became reflexively enjoyed, as in, Here I am enjoying it. You could sit in such rooms and the things you thought about magically appeared. She'd just thought about mail, now here it was.

She thought about Haw. The room remained empty.

The nurse had removed Cupid for her nap. She'd been petulant, fussy. Baby possessed a large capacity for embracing bad humor, and smothered it with dreamy distracted attention. Eventually, Cupid fell asleep on the rug, curled around the leg of a table. Nurse carried her off.

Mrs. Wurtzebach requests the honor of your company this afternoon for a drive—will wait here for an answer and trust it to be favorable.

Well, let her wait. If Baby didn't go, what else to do but wait? Mrs. W. knew better than to call, since the servants, per instructions, always said she was out. And if the servants had the afternoon off, Baby did it herself; she crouched behind the door and grunted with maleness, *Go away, she's not home.*

Permit me to inform you that your name was balloted for, and accepted in, the Veteran Relief Corps, at their last meeting, and the Corps will be glad to see you at an early day, for initiation, and welcome you as one of its members. We meet on Thursday, the 7th, at 2:30 PM, also every Tuesday.

We await your pleasure.

I am Respectfully,
Mrs. M. J. Handyside
Cor. Sec. Vet. R. C.

John Vernon

Mrs. M. J. Handyside? What a laugh! The Veteran Relief Corps was just a notch above such dregs as the Astra Club, the I.D.K.C. Club, and the South Broadway Social Club. Their tableau entitled "The Dream of a Bereaved Mother" had been presented to barely throttled snickers at last year's charity ball. Baby'd read between the lines in the newspaper's account, not having attended the ball herself.

Another request from Father Guida for money, this one for roofing the new College of the Sacred Heart in North Denver. A letter to Haw from E. H. Beck requested an Annual Pass to the Tabor Grand. He gave away passes to the opera house freely.

In his absence she had license to open his mail.

What's this? A letter from Harvey Doe, return address the Iron Horse Inn on Market Street. Sounded like a flophouse. Poor Harvey!

> Friend Lizzie—Deserous of having a meating with you through my friend Mr. Day. if you will allow me the privilege to see you at your most earliest convenience, I want to propose something beneficial to you. The same greeting as by gone days. Harvey.

She tossed it on the floor. One luxury of wealth was doing nothing, was letting the undone pile up disregarded. After their divorce, Harvey'd gone back to Wisconsin, but here he was in Denver. The shrinking world pressed. But not if you ignored it.

Last in the pile was a cable to Haw from Mr. Reed in Boston. As she read it, her heart drained.

> Have secured mortgage on Tabor Block and Grand Opera Block for $350,000 with the two blocks as security. Five years at 6%, 10% at maturity if principal unpaid. Reply requested.

She balled it up and threw it to the floor. She retrieved it and carefully flattened it out and placed it on the table and kicked the table over. Where was Haw when she needed him? In Gunnison, with his pistol.

All for Love

He'd discussed this with her, mortgaging the Tabor block, but she never thought he'd really do it. Better to sell the copper fields in Texas!

All at once she felt herself moving very cautiously. She stood up with prudence, settled back on the sofa so as not to crush the cushions. Dear God in heaven, don't let Haw get hurt. She pictured him swaggering down a wooden sidewalk. Don't let him go inspect any new mines or ride on a horse or get into a poker game. And if we're not married in your eyes, God—let Harvey and Augusta die. Let them expire of natural causes, or have an accident. I'll make six novenas, I'll send Father Guida enough money to take the whole parish to Jerusalem. I won't go myself, though, because I'm not worthy. I may be a sinner, but I've never hurt a soul. I'll let a dog bite me and offer it up....

She lay back on the sofa thinking bad thoughts; for example, strewing broken glass in Mrs. Senator Teller's cake batter. She closed her eyes and with her fingers plugged her ears. She breathed through the hollow flutes of her nose. Children stamped. Somewhere in the distance a muffled chorus chanted Latin. When she squeezed her eyes, clouds rubbed her eardrums. Was someone in the house? Someone walking down the hallway, pushing doors open, searching for her? Her eyes flew open.

The room looked perfectly still and empty. But the softened afternoon light was a cheat. It claim-jumped dreams. Well, let him mortgage the blocks. Haw did business the way he made love, he never said what it was he really wanted. She had to guess. He was due home today, this afternoon. She wouldn't mention the cable. Let him find it himself, let him bring it up. Nobody these days ever owned things anyway. Banks did, and boards. Slowly and deeply, like uncoiling snakes, her bowels opened up, her milk ducts loosened, her blood sank inside her. Let the house of cards collapse.

She'd read rumors in the paper that he was courting insolvency. Haw always laughed them off. Together, they'd planned the expansion of his empire. If it never stopped expanding it never could collapse. They sank a million dollars into the Overland Broadgauge Railroad Company, which hadn't, nonetheless, yet laid a tie. They bought patent rights to the cyanide process of extracting gold; purchased new mines in New Mexico, Arizona, Nevada, and Texas; and bought grazing rights to a half-million acres in southern Colorado. The bank in Gunnison, stockyards in Chicago, hotels, glassworks, steam companies, telephone systems—futures, options, patents, stocks. Haw'd recently scouted the Chihuahua region in Mexico and they'd bought three mines there. It was his notion that the nouveau riche of America required vast reservoirs of mahogany to panel their new mansions, so for a million dollars they'd purchased two hundred square miles of forest in Honduras, plus a grant of mineral rights for an additional hundred and fifty square miles. They planned steamship and rail lines, logging operations, sawmills, lumber towns. For weeks, they pored over maps of their property. Baby saw herself visiting this kingdom in her Queen of the Night dress, with the fringe of silver crescents and stars, and the jeweled waist-girdle in the shape of a serpent. Natives would carry her canopied chair past fruits and birds of fantastic shapes and colors, beneath towering trees with umbrella leaves flapping, past slimy bark thin and green as frogskin which, if you cut it, oozed jeweled yellow resin. Spiders large as kittens clung to bananas, blossoms splashed foreheads, six-fingered hands waved. Vegetable life arranged in profusion staged anatomy lessons around her. Nothing stank. Buckets of slime and moss manured sweet dreams. Perfumed galls burst. . . .

She squirmed on the couch, touching her throat. She dug her fuzzy buttocks into the cushions. The first time Haw ever fumbled to enter her, his sperm snaked reluctantly out against her thigh. It hesitated, pumping as though weakly attempting to suck itself back, then he detumesced and slumped, sound asleep on the bed.

After that, things improved. Her tender, forgiving nature helped, also her complicated lust. She could tell he liked innocence, so she conjured its devices, and learned to play the novice, but with accidental pinches and squeals. She increased his gratitude. She made him conquer her. Each night began with every hair in place, Baby laced up and rouged and eyeblacked, but ended with her beneath him—or on top—whipping her hair back and forth and snarling; it seemed to excite him. Lust had to be imagined first, apparently. You pictured yourself in every conceivable posture of degradation and victory: against the wall, battering the headboard, splayed across pillows. Then, to actually do what you imagined doubled the pleasure, by giving it body. What delicious stratagems. . . .

Haw also learned to play the beast, with coaxing. He became a bull thrashing above her. With drooling muzzle and popping eyes, his enormous head bellowed and roared. He covered her face with his hot smelly breath, his spawl rained upon her, his bristles, raw and stiff, scraped her tender skin. The noise he made shook the bed and rattled the windows and broke her open, then his bull head and horns lashed back and forth with consummate fury and he blanketed her face with his great heavy tongue. His skin smelled of urine. Not from having leaked; he bathed regularly now, often four times a day. She could smell it *through* the skin, as though it ran in his veins.

He liked to lie in bed upstairs and call for her to come. *Baby, I'm ready!* She pictured him, hairy and large, like a hippo. No, hippos were hairless. Maybe a bear struck by lightning, say, temporarily disabled, thrown on his back—tongue hanging out—*Baaaby!* His smell, his dirt, his growl, what else? Even four baths a day weren't enough to deodorize his skin, tarnished and pungent like the leather on a saddle —like copper and salt. Billy Bush had smelled of cheap Macassar oil and some sort of immigrant minty lamb sauce. Haw's breath smelled of American grease. He smelled like good dirt. His coarse hair tickled. His growl, his big round pillowy flesh. . . . He never trimmed the long claws on his fingers, which sliced her poor shoulders. His wide mouth cracked his big face in two.

She'd gone moist below. She longed for his body. She thought of it all day and they did it every night, when he was home. He was always twice as large when he was with her. She was small and he was big. Was her chin too fat? Inside herself, she still felt like a little girl. With his length and girth and years—fifty-six now—sometimes it became a triumph for Haw just to climb on top of his wife. In her hands, he felt powerful and adept—and he was! Even token passion worked, she knew. It was true what Nealie said; men acknowledged the inferiority of their sex by the pride they took in beholding gratified women beneath them.

But he couldn't touch her secrets. He was short and thick, not long and deep. His balls, like baskets of fruit, hung below. The crack of his ass was the Great Divide, the Grand Canyon. His donkey gasp and honk when he finished. . . . Often she was left still gazing down the maw of unthinkable things, the bloody toothless mouth. Pack my fudge, Haw, don't churn my butter. Sometimes he just went on and on forever, leaving her behind, and she cried out, he'd abandoned her. Wait for me, Daddy! He'd crossed a hill up ahead, but when she breeched the top what did she see, she saw a mean wolf. Crouched, fangs exposed, he sprang for her throat. . . .

They were copies, she and Haw, reproductions of the real Baby Doe and Horace Tabor, floating in a heaven shaped like the Tabor Grand.

"Baaaby!" He was home! Haw had come home. "Baby, I'm ready!" She stood. She rushed upstairs. When had he arrived?

Two weeks later, Baby and Horace sat up in bed drinking champagne while the servants laid out their clothes for the day and the nurse led in the world's most beautiful child. Two-year-old Cupid clung to her doll while Mrs. Page clutched the child by her waist and swung her up on the bed between her parents. "Cupid!"

"I changed my bed!"

"Good for you, sweetheart."

"I put the pillow down the bottom." She stressed the last three words with nods of her head, pronouncing "bottom" as "bomb," then mugged for Mommy as though rehearsing astonishment. A maid commenced to pull the curtains back and unwrap another Colorado morning, with sunlight breaking through the bare trees and frost silvering the lawn. Cupid called it frosting. To the west, they knew, looming over the horizon, were galloping mountains, one could see them from the attic. "Stop makin that noise!" Cupid shouted at the maid. "You're drybin me crazy! You're makin me nervous!"

Everyone laughed.

They knew she was the world's most beautiful child because *Harper's Bazaar* had put her on their cover, drawn by Thomas Nast, and now they'd been flooded with letters and cables from people all over offering praise, requesting photos, asking for money, and cautioning the Tabors to be on guard against kidnapers. The *Harper's* cover hung framed on the wall. Below it was mounted a silver tomahawk presented to Haw by the Gunnison Chamber of Commerce, and beside that a real human scalp, rumored to be the work of Kit Carson. The dignitaries in Gunnison had given these tokens to Haw in recognition for his contributions to humanity. He and Baby had marveled at the scalp, at the fine black hair, the wooden hoop inside stretching the skin, the feathers and beads on the knotted thong. It seemed quite old. Cupid thought it was left from the face that got nailed on the barroom floor, but now it hung below her picture like darkness visible conquered by light.

In Thomas Nast's depiction she was wide-eyed, curly-haired, dimple-chinned, bare-shouldered, and so innocent and ripe you wished to devour her. He'd arranged holly and branches about her head and shoulders, with a glowing star beneath them at the level of her navel, since this was the holiday season, and Cupid was the Tabors' gift to the world. The magazine—A Repository of Fashion, Pleasure, and Instruction—had appeared last week, and every last issue was sold out now, no one ever saw the like. Baby sipped her champagne and waited for her salver to fill with calling cards. In truth, more than a few married ladies had left their cards that week, though not yet la crème. But they'll come now. God will make them come. Everyone wanted to see the real Cupid.

Beneath the picture Nast had written, "Christ-Kindchen," suggesting that Cupid represented all of Christianity. Father Guida'd nearly fainted with joy. On page 2, of course, she was identified as the daughter of Governor and Mrs. Tabor of Denver. Journalists still referred to Haw as Governor.

"Here, Daddy." Cupid held out Horace's glass. "Drink it." Haw took the champagne and toasted Cupid's picture. "Is it good?"

"Yes."

"Is it good, Mommy?"

"Yes."

"Daddy, 'Face on Ballroom Floor'! 'Face on Ballroom Floor'!"

What a big nose Daddy had, and what a big round brow, climbing all the way to the top of his head! Cupid pinched his nose. She inserted a knuckle into one nostril. He laughed and laughed and sipped more champagne. She hung on his mustache and he swung left and right, like a roped steer.

Astir the Pine in sombre lay.
'Twas a bawmy autumn night,
And the godly-lot was there,
That over-saw Joe's bar-room
As court on the square;
And as song in wit as story ekes
Of oaken door, a vagabond stept lowly
In askan upon the floor.
What does it want! Whiskey! Rum! or Gin!
See! Tobe, Sic! Joe's can do the work,
I wouldn't touch with a fork it'd fetid as a turk.
As barinage the myscreant stood in static grace

As one intact as one of place, and bending
Low as embers fall nods inturn as secret call. . . .

Haw puffed his cheeks and sucked in his Adam's apple, growling and snorting the half-baked words and lifting his eyebrows and rolling his tongue. He sat up in bed in nightshirt and glasses with half his face still flat from sleeping. Only someone whose voice was heavy clay could bite and chew each line as he did, and still bellow. The poem filled the room. Haw bugged his eyes. He sprayed, but Cupid didn't mind, she faced the storm bravely. She stood on his lap holding onto his mustache and watched his big lips and flapping cheeks. Baby leaned on his shoulder, feeling his lungs boom. How could he muster so much zeal for something he'd done at least a hundred times now? Cupid's little butterfly mouth shaped the words with him.

Baby smiled and closed her eyes. She thought of the servants downstairs uncovering the cages, of the chattering and singing slowly enlarging and filling the house, the largest mansion in Denver! Her love of animals made people admire her, in spite of themselves. When the frost got burned off, the groundskeepers would release their hundred peacocks, to wander around the bronze Psyches, Nimrods, and Dianas on the lawn. She'd be the only Denver Brahmin forced to cage up her monkeys when she had her "day." To celebrate the *Harper's* cover, they'd purchased a litter of wolfhound puppies, and Baby heard them yipping now. She opened her eyes and looked to the door, where Mrs. Page held them boiling in a basket.

Haw concluded with a flourish. He emphasized certain words queerly—stressed on the upbeat, pinched on the outbreath—and ran his pop-started eyes up his brow:

Say, Joe a brace and
I'll feel better, glad! and draw right here in
Mem'ry the one that drove me mad.
Fetch the char you mark the whiskey score and

See her face in fancy on the bar-room floor.
O image divine at pillow pane as wont and
Rougishly shy she came in her girlish caress
And solace goodbye—

Haw scratched his head. " 'Nother as will-'o-clock tram!" screamed Cupid.

Another as will-'o-clock dram and knelt with
Char askan at sketch of one might stir the soul
Of any man; then a truant mem'ry lock in account
Low 'Madjeline' thous mistook one! struggles to
Rise and in cry as phantom of droad leaped as in
Her arms forgiven and fell on the picture dead.

Cupid squealed. Mrs. Page dumped the puppies on the bed. Haw roared, Baby laughed. Cupid crawled under the covers and thrashed about. The puppies snapped and rolled on the bed and one squatted to pee before Baby could stop it. Oh well, the little darling, she couldn't help herself. Baby picked up the squirming creature and buried her face in its downy fur. Haw climbed out of bed to dress for the office. Cupid popped up as naked as a flower. She leaned back against the headboard and spread her arms.

"What happened to your clothes, you little muffin?"

"Inside the bed!"

Haw stood there to admire her, and Baby's face beamed, with the puppy at her ear. Even the other pups seemed to pause. What a glad day!

No one else left cards. No invitations came. The trickle died out as fast as it'd started. It's the snow, Baby thought. They'd had a big storm, but people had so adjusted to bare streets their cutters weren't ready.

It's the cold, it's la grippe, it's Haw's beery smell, it's the Irish servants. . . .

She sat in the sunroom on a rare cloudy day. In Denver, either it snowed or it shone. The blue paving tiles from Sienna still radiated warmth from yesterday's sun, it felt cozy. She lay back in a love seat beneath a lamb's-wool lap robe remembering the day she'd fallen asleep in this very spot and woken upstairs in bed. The unused rooms in this overlarge house clung to the edge of one's mind like linty dreams. No less than five life-sized oil paintings of Baby hung in the house, to oversee its blank hush.

"Who's in there?" Haw shouted from the hallway.

"No one. It's me."

"All right, I'm going."

The worst thing about her utter lack of social conquests was its effect upon Horace. If he ever regretted his marriage to her she'd shoot herself, she'd go home to Mamma, she'd enter a convent. . . .

The sun filled the room for all of five seconds, then God pinched it out.

What was it, years later, that made her think it was a dream? Fifty years or so after the fact who could distinguish dreams from memories, or memories of dreams from dreams of memories? Everything happens eventually, even dreams. Nothing stays the same, nothing changes, everything flows in the granite of history.

Through the plasm of the house with its liquid walls and doors and gassy air clotted in sluggish currents, she heard the electric annunciator buzzing. She'd been running her fingers across her lips in wonder at their shape and feel. Her heart leapt. At last, they're beginning to call! Soon a voice droned from the door, "Mrs. Tabor."

"Yes?"

"No. That is, Mrs. Tabor is *here,* madame."

"But I'm Mrs. Tabor!"

Baby sat up. Augusta walked in. She's up to some dirty trick, Baby thought. She's found a way to lure him back. But Augusta looked desperate, long-faced, wide-eyed. Baby's heart went out to her. I'll shower you with money! What do you need?

"I've come here with great reluctance," she began.

"Please sit down."

"I musn't stay long, Mrs.—"

"Doe," Baby blurted. She stood up and gestured toward the love seat. Augusta, erect, shook her spare head. She bowed with politeness. Her very face looked thrifty. Her nondescript clothes were black, but dignified. Her tall thin head and prominent chin, her bifocals resting high on her nose, where it buttressed her brow, her tightly pursed lips. . . . Baby realized she was smiling. The columnists were right, she looked like a schoolmarm.

Baby knew what she was thinking: *shameless hussy!* The second Mrs. Tabor sat down again and lounged with becoming ease on the loveseat.

"Quite frankly, I wasn't certain whether to come. It seemed to me that if I called, others might follow."

"That's very kind of you."

"I wouldn't want you to think I bore a grudge. I used to think I loved him more, that it wasn't just his money. Now I don't know. I'm getting old, I suppose. We all are, of course. No one I ever heard about in this world ever got young, did they, Mrs.—"

Baby yawned.

"I used to think he'd do the same thing to you he done to me, then I could gloat. He'd find another mistress and you'd be out on your ear. The minute you got a little fat or old he'd toss you in the trash just like he done to me. I'm over it now, I've no wish for revenge."

"I know how you feel, I'm the same way too. Come here and sit beside me." Baby patted the love seat. "My first husband, Harvey, I caught him once with my own eyes coming out of a brothel. Imagine how I felt! I found it in my heart to forgive him, Mrs. Tabor, I've always been forgiving . . . it's part of my nature. May I call you Augusta? There are no words on earth to describe a person's torment when tongues start wagging, I'll vouch for that. What can I do, I could kneel in the street and beg them to stop, I could throw myself bodily in front of their carriages, I could jump off a cliff, but life goes on anyway. Haw's love keeps me going. I never thought he'd marry me. I was ready to go back to Mamma and Daddy and help them scrape by. It wasn't his fault, he couldn't help himself. Wasn't your fault neither, no one's to blame. I've suffered too. I still go four or five nights in a row without a lick of sleep, while Haw honks and snores. Sometimes I see things. I saw angels singing. I gave him a beautiful daughter, an angel. I love him more than you did!"

"You've had more practice."

"You knew him longer, you had your turn. We're not rivals, we're— we're sisters, Augusta. Come sit here beside me." At last she sat down. Baby gently touched her forearm. "You spent how many years with him, twenty-five? What were they like?"

"I did laundry in the mining camps for fifty cents a shirt, so we'd have a nest egg. I sold milk to settlers and made butter to sell, I opened a bakery and sold pies and bread, I nursed men in the camps when they had mining fever. I panned gold with Tabor!"

Augusta's lap looked so warm and soft, Baby couldn't help herself, she collapsed slowly toward it. "True devotion like that will never be forgotten." What was she saying? Already, she'd forgotten.

"Unfortunately, he thought of me in terms of scraping by and mean scrimping and petty habits of thrift." She stroked Baby's head. "We slowly saved enough to start a store. Those were the days, but Tabor didn't think so. Things began to change after we got rich. Usage dulls the affection. Does he ever mention me?"

"He often does, with real fondness . . ."

It wasn't clear now who was comforting whom. They lay on the love seat in each other's arms, stroking brows, patting heads, tasting salty tears. "There, there," they said. They fell asleep lying there, Mrs. Tabor and Mrs. Tabor. . . .

After that, things improved. Everyone called. The world came to

Baby's doorstep! Her "day" each week was Tuesday, but she had to add another, the house wasn't large enough. Then Haw decided to throw a ball, the largest and grandest Denver'd ever seen, too large for their house. Let's use the Tabor Grand!

It cost twenty-five thousand and some-odd dollars but was worth every penny. Carpenters laid the dance floor immediately after the last performance of *Pearl of Pekin,* on a Thursday night. They worked all night, stretching the floor level with the stage right across the top of the orchestra seats. Rich floral trains hid the boxes, trees and holly decked the back of the stage. Upon a terrace extending around the stage, lilies, azaleas, and roses bloomed, in hothouse soil imported from California. All day Friday, all Friday night, and most of Saturday the decorators worked. They suspended a false ceiling of wire from the dome over the whole auditorium, on the level of the lower gallery, and covered this with smilax and holly, creating a canopy of cool shadowy green. The lower gallery was transformed into a mountain of green with yellow flowers and garlands of roses. Around the ballroom, on raised platforms richly carpeted, were divans and sofas amid trees of tropic growth and shrubs of rare culture and blooming flowers and ferns. Incandescent lamplight. Perfumed fountains. Candles in cut glass hanging from the ceiling!

The lobby too was a dense mass of green. Against thick walls of clinging southern vines stood palm trees and orange trees in pots, and great columns of trailing clematis, its waxy leaves reflecting the light. The broad stairways flanking the entrance were transformed into terraces of moss and ivy with palm and orange trees rising in tiers, each row a little loftier. Cypress trees screened the corridors. Ivy curtained all the doors.

It was feared that the program would be interfered with and that, though the ball was a private one, the service of champagne after 1:00 A.M. would be prevented by police. But thanks to the influence of Governor Tabor, no such interference was attempted.

The approach to the Tabor Grand wasn't promising. The main en-

All for Love

trance was shut up by a huge shed of pine boards, as raw and bare as could be. And the flunkies provided to open carriage doors and assist the ladies were very clumsy in the main. It was only by the grace of God that serious accidents didn't occur. After her attendant stumbled and caught her train, one lady—Mrs. Senator Teller—lost her footing and fell full length upon the dirty snow.

Mrs. Tabor assisted her.

At eleven o'clock, one of the most admired ladies in Denver society, Mrs. Baby Doe Tabor, received the guests. As one's name was announced, Mrs. Tabor stepped forward, extending her hand, in a Worth gown of extraordinary beauty, of a light brocade with a very long train of the same material, and a décolleté bodice and a stomacher of diamonds, a diamond tiara, and of course her famous necklace with the Isabella Pearls.

She stood no more than ten feet from the dance floor. When the guests passed her they were met by the gay strains of Strauss's "Vienna Women," played by a hidden orchestra. The music seemed to rise from the floor.

In the supper rooms upstairs covers were laid for twelve hundred persons on two hundred tables, with continuous service from the first dance to the last, of consommé à la princesse, huîtres à la poulette, homard à la Newberg, croquettes de volaille, térapène à la Pinard, dinde farcie à la Toulouse, filet de boeuf aux champignons, saumon mayonnaise à la Richelieu, galantine de chapon aux truffes, aspic de pâté de foie gras à la Newport, salade de volaille, perdreau piqué à la gelée, chau-froid de cailles à la Lucullus, gâteaux assortis, fruits glacés, pièces montées, café, and of course, Louis Roederer Brut and Moet & Chandon Brut Imperial, and Apollinaris, to mention only the main dishes.

The great quadrille d'honneur, and the stately measures of Sir Roger de Coverley, began promptly at one o'clock. The four sets, each with twelve ladies and twelve gentlemen, stretched in parallel lines across the width of the room. Here was a veritable garland of buds, with

John Vernon

young beauties assigned to the outer sets, and social prominence to the inner. Both came together in the person of the hostess, Mrs. Haw Tabor, who led one inner set with her husband, while Senator and Mrs. Teller led the other. The cotillion at two o'clock was the largest ever danced in Denver—or the world!—with two hundred couples, led by Henry Stewart with Mrs. Tabor, known as Baby, followed by Mr. and Mrs. Charles Denisin, Mr. and Mrs. J. C. Shattuck, Mr. and Mrs. H. B. Chamberlin, Mr. and Mrs. Charles Ballin, Honorable and Mrs. J. B. Grant, Mr. and Mrs. Eugene Knight, Miss Bomberger and Mr. Ashley, Mr. Keenan and Mrs. Wickersham, Mr. Bush and Mrs. Augusta Tabor—

Oh dear, something happened. Mrs. Senator Teller's tulle cape had brushed a candle and was merrily burning. Quickly. Quickly. Extinguish it. Please.

It spread. What a shame, thought Baby, once your hair caught fire you were probably doomed. Your scalp melted off. Mrs. Teller's gown of maize-colored moiré reached flashpoint and she became a human torch. The violets trimming the mousseline de soie on the front and sides of her dress vaporized just like that. At the end, her burning flesh disrobed her bones and curled in sizzling scraps to the floor. Others around her had caught fire by now, as the crowd was tightly packed. Baby watched from a portico flanking the stage. Haw took her hand. The guests began to panic and run for the entrances, but there the fire was worse and drove them back. Fire climbed the trellised and draped theater walls and peeled back and floated down on the big wigs. A red banner of flame shot across the ballroom, something exploded, a tremendous roar began. The place became a furnace. Specks of flame and spark, odds and ends of dying light, condensed to form a pillar or a balcony here and there. Currents of flame eddied back and forth, searching. The false ceiling of smilax had burned completely off, leaving a framework of hot glowing wire. Bits of burning silk rose in spirals toward the dome. Burning hair smelled bad. The floor began to burn. Not a single groan or cry of any sort, nay, not a ripple, rose from the ballroom. Screams, Baby realized, were nipped in the bud, because people burned from the inside out, having breathed in the flames. Their lungs burned first, and fire sucked the oxygen right from their blood. They merely threw their arms up into the air and fell through the floor with never a peep.

I'm not happy, she grinned. Not at all, she told Haw. And only she and Haw escaped to crow about it.

6. Denver 1893

Compania Santa Eduwiges
Estado de Chihuahua

Jesus Maria, Mexico   September 24, 1893

My Darling Darling Wife

Oh how I do want to see you and have a lot of your love It
seems like an age since I left you at Depot. I do hope you are not
worried to death with business complications. I have no idea
about our affairs there except by your telegrams which say all
OK. Matters here are wonderfully grand—this mine will give
money enough to enable us to dispense charity again with a
liberal hand as long as we may and leave our children with lots
of money. I read Peters letter he wrote you last night his estimate
is all right It is now a little after 6 AM and such a beautiful
Sunday morning the sun does not reach the boarding house until
about 9 AM and it leaves us about 4-30 on account of such high
mountains both side of the gulch we had one of the storms that
troubles us so much here three days ago and stopped the mill for
36 hours by breaking the flume and filling up some of the ditch
You ought to see a tropical rain the clouds open up and the water
dashes out in terrific quantities this trouble lasts for only a
period of three months and we will probably have no more for
nine months the water raised in the gulch ten feet in 20 minutes
and the gulch will average steeper than 13th street from Sherman to Broadway and the bottom is filled with large boulders

some as large as a small house. It was a sight to see this muddy water tearing along and we could hear big boulders roll and bang about. but enough of this It is wonderful about the safeness of the trail and road we are safer a thousand times than in the city of Denver never any trouble about looting bullion on its way out.

Pete told you in his letter about the change we are compelled to make in the management. We did not like to do it but were compelled. but we will have a man who is as competent as Hart and strictly honest I know him. again referring to mine I was awfully well pleased to see all of the surface and we have about 14 hundred feet of new ground in which is many a bonanza. there is as I believe ore enough in sight of good paying value to last out present mill any way 20 years, and immense probability it will give us from $5000 to $20,000 per month and never less than the first figure. It will not be long for with so much new machinery we have had hot bearings and many little stoppages which always happens with a large plant.

I dream of you almost every night and I love you so hard all the time your letters are so lovely but I know or rather fear you are terribly annoyed and worried. My dear girl do take care of yourself for you are my all. do not fear we have time and again overcome all obstacles I forgot I had to make a draft on you at ten days sight for $1709.00 I had to do it for if I had shown the least weakness Creel would not have advanced the money. It will be there for your acceptance in about six days and that gives you 13 days before payment due. I also send you a bill of 831$ which be sure to send to W. Souza & Co. 378 California Street San Francisco Cal be sure and send this within three days after you get this letter. I love you to death and am trying so hard to get things so we can always be together Kiss Babies for me and be my love until death does us part

Horace

Haw'd been in Mexico three months now. He'd shouted at the station what he whispered in his letters, "Kiss babies for me!" then lumbered on the train, not yet too old, at sixty-three, to travel a thousand miles for the privilege of grubbing in mines, patching up steam hoists, hauling ore to the mill, calculating yields, excavating hope. All for her! All for love. For their family, their future, their girls, their house—for the bottomless debts, the slow dreamy crash, the money left running like an open faucet—for their discounted name, the bankruptcy courts, the smug business rivals offering condolences.

Don't give up, Horace. Never surrender. Work until you drop.

He never signed his letters EGYPT anymore, not even NORWICH: Knickers Off Ready When I Come Home. Nary a bush, flower or leaf appeared in the forest of his scrawl, no snakes nor monkeys neither. The country down there must have been barren. As for him, he claimed to be in splendid health. Roughing it did wonders for his aging body. He'd lost weight, down to two hundred pounds. One letter said he and Pete hadn't shaved in six or seven weeks, and she wondered how they smelled. Were there women in the mountains? Peter was learning Spanish, but Haw didn't care to, also he didn't like the food, it'd kill a decent American hog. Wouldn't kill Haw, though. . . .

She missed the big oaf, missed his sweet cigar breath. A sense of weight was absent from the house. Sure, his shoulders slumped forward more and more now—due to rheumatism, he claimed—his hairline had receded more and more, the vestige of hair too thin to dye, but the silver tone gave him a stately air. He was decent and large, so his decency was large, but he'd lost a certain edge, younger men were outfatiguing him. He worried about her "admirers" in Denver. Her brother Pete kept an eye on *him*, he assured her. But Peter's letters were business front to back. He never mentioned anything personal at all, she had no idea whether he felt he'd been dragged down to Mexico by Horace, pushed there by Baby, was it hell on earth, did he fear the bloodthirsty Apaches? If you were male they smashed your skull, bit off your fingers, boiled your brains, and if you were female . . .

"Letter from Poppa?" Cupid sat at the piano sprinkling notes, now and then banging them as though smashing vermin.

"Quiet," hissed Baby, "Honeymaid's sleeping." She folded the letter and slipped it in her bosom. The piano noise was Cupid's way of protesting the cancellation of her music lesson, though still she hadn't made the call. "My mother's sick. She has a headache." She used to enjoy saying such things, she'd coo the words pertly. Now she just whined about not taking lessons she used to whine about taking. If she didn't call soon, Professor Kempton would show up, and Baby would have to hide behind the door and disguise her voice: *She's not home. Go away....*

They were in the music room, with its bamboo furniture. Workmen had rolled up the silk palace rug and smaller orientals and carried them off with the temple jars of the Yung Chang period weeks ago now, she hadn't asked where. Was the life of issuing invitations in the third person to which the invited declined, also in the third, over at last? Horrors!

She laughed.

Horace, your four percent of the wonderful Calumet and Chicago Canal and Dock Company fetched only $6,000 today. I used it to pay the interest on our notes at the Union National. Mr. Fletcher from Denver offered us his house with $30,000 against it for our Larimer Street Block with $100,000 against it, but we might do better. My plan is this: Mr. Creel might agree to extend one of his notes. Maybe you can take an option on the Bavicanora, say 60,000 Mexican money, half payable in two years and half in three years, that's $36,571 American, if the dollar doesn't fall. If President Cleveland, lickspittle to Wall Street, doesn't lower the price of silver still more.... The newspapers are saying he's bound to repeal the Silver Purchase Act, that's why Geer and Company denied our loan for a million dollars at five and a half percent, they don't care for the notion of debts being paid in silver dollars whose real worth, they say, is just fifty-three cents. But we might try obtaining the loan in Europe, Mr. Geer suggests that. Send me to Washington, darling, I'll tickle Grover Cleveland's fat ribs with a pitchfork!

"What, Mommy?"

I'll pawn all my jewels, I'll sell all the paintings. . . . Since you left, Haw, the railroads in Denver have begun offering free transportation back East to the unemployed. Twelve banks closed last week. Most of the mines in Leadville are closing, and Mr. Kelly at the Matchless wrote to ask how I thought he could live on twenty-five dollars a month, especially when we don't pay him anyway, and this must stop right here or he shall leave the premises.

"Cupid."

"What, Mommy?"

"It's all the fault of that fatso, Mr. Cleveland."

"What is, Mommy?"

"Come here, darling."

Cupid climbed down from the piano bench and ran across the room to join Baby at the love seat. "Can I have my lesson?"

"We can't afford it." Go play with the peacocks, you beauty, break my heart. "Cuddle up, Lily. I threw out my corset. I'm planning to be . . . an old lady soon. Can I shoot myself now? Remind me when it's time. Don't push."

"She pinched me!"

"Honeymaid! Sweetheart!" Silver Dollar Rose Marie Echo Honeymaid had flown into the room on powerful moth wings and squeezed between Cupid and Baby, the runt, pressed by flesh on all sides. She was five, Cupid nine. They all crushed together, a grain of life trying to unhatch themselves in one small spot lost in that big house. "Honeymaid, that's my velvet polonaise!"

"I like it, Mamma. You gave it to me."

"I never. You pinchbug."

"She scratched my neck!" Elizabeth slammed a fist hard as rock behind Silver Dollar's biceps, waking buried bruises. Honeymaid kicked her older sister's pretty white ankle. "Little bitch."

"Haybag! Slut!"

Baby caressed them. She couldn't stop her hands and fingers from stroking. Her lips brushed their hair, she bit the ribbons and pulled out the bows, first one then the other. . . .

"Mommy, don't!"

Mrs. Page in her apron stood at the door. "Thank you. Thanks." Baby couldn't be short, she tried to smile sweetly, who knows what she wanted . . . her wages, maybe. At last the mouse-faced woman walked off.

"Is President Cleveland really a fatso?"

"How long were you listening?"

"Is he bigger than Poppa? Could he squeeze Poppa's guts out?"

"That's exactly what he's doing."

"Why?! Why?!"

"The papers say part of his brain was removed. They performed an operation on a billiards table, on a ferryboat somewhere, I don't know. Inside the saloon on the boat. His brains were leaking down through a crack in his mouth-top. They took out a plug of hot tar or something. That's why they call him a Dimmycrack, darlings."

"Is he crazy, Mommy?"

"Of course he's crazy."

"Tell us about the moon's a silver apple and the goldbugs want to eat it."

"The moon's a silver apple. Stop squirming, Honeymaid! This silver apple, imagine, it belongs to everybody, to the rich and poor, to the work-worn and dust-grimed. So. You and me, darlings, we're the creatures of the moon, and he's our friend, he's made out of silver. He belongs to the miners and the mine owners too, but that's not the main thing. The main thing is the goldbugs want to eat him, so. We come out at night, he does too, but the goldbugs want to eat the poor moon, just the tiniest, littlest nibbles at first. . . . They eat him like you eat cookies, darlings, they nibble around the edges at first. . . ."

Silver Dollar slipped out and ran across the room, screaming, "Chester! Chester!" Two stately wolfhounds had just walked in. The dogs had the run of the house these days, they were the masters, the humans obeyed them. Silver reached up to embrace her friend Chester with little bruised arms. She never liked cuddling her mother regardless, partial instead to dogs and peacocks. Over the yellow velvet polonaise with the silver buttons, she also wore Baby's toreador jacket, the black one with white stitching and silver studs. She'll get hairs all over my clothes, Baby thought, but no one can blame me, it's not my fault.

Baby felt her older daughter relax and worm closer, uncurling her spine. Her mother's love put meat on her bones, made her open up tall, like a flower in the sun. "Now the sun, the goldbugs worship the sun. . . ."

"Mommy, do you have a headache?" Cupid whispered.

"Just a little bit."

"Can I rub your temple?"

"Of course, my little Cupid."

Elizabeth . . . Cupid . . . Lily . . . reached up and massaged Baby's forehead with her finger pads, all of them. "You look old, Mommy. You have wrinkles on your face."

"Look, Mommy!" Silver clung to the dog's mane and let him drag her toward the love seat.

Lily whispered as she rubbed, "Mommy, who's worse, Billy Bush or the President?"

"Anyone who hates us, they're all just as bad."

"What about Mrs. Ballin?"

"She's the worst of the lot. She and all her Lady Mucks and their dinner parties."

"Did Billy Bush lower the price of silver?"

"He's to blame, ask your father. He cheated us out of so much money, and we were too nice to ask for it back."

Lily continued to rub her mother's brow. "Would he kidnap Honeymaid? Would he kill her, Mommy?"

"He Bushed us, Cupid. We can't go anywhere, we have no money. We might as well be in jail, I don't know. We're being punished. I'll die if this continues. Tell me when it's over. . . ."

She realized she'd fallen asleep when the annunciator buzzed. "Cupid, get the door." Her voice echoed strangely. Where were her daughters? The maids had all left in the last month or two, only Mrs. Page and her husband'd stayed on, having no choice. They were even older than Haw. "Cupid, sweetheart, it's Professor Kempton, I know it. You never called him!" She stood and crossed the room, stopping at the mirror to adjust her shirtwaist and plain brown skirt. Simple clothes for meager times, but not too simple, she still wore the blue traveling cloak, the one edged with swansdown. Her hands brushed off hairs. Light from the chintz curtains in the windows seemed thick with pollen, the goldbugs were coming. . . .

Were their late afternoon lessons over forever? A little Schubert blows away cares. The insides of her elbows felt damp. Light ran straight into the room as though . . . as though naked sun people stood at each window calmly effusing, she thought. Piss-colored light. She brushed at her cloak. Even if she was a night and moon person, this light right now looked best on her skin, the dying gold made her glow. How warm it felt. . . . She didn't look bad, not for her age. . . .

Hairs everywhere! Even in the entry, hairballs and dustballs swirled at her skirts, fine-boned skeletons left by air creatures. Lacking servants to clean them, the floors of her house had become an ossuary. It reminded her of the ankle fogs used for Wagner recitals at the Tabor Grand.

Leaded glass in the door showed a human form. She could tell him to leave, no one home, go away. . . . Her inner thighs trembled, having walked downtown and back that morning. They were down to one landau and no grooms to harness it. She felt vaguely afraid, the air seemed to furrow, and why was her throat bare? "Professor Kempton!"

He stood on the step below the open door less than a foot from her

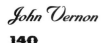

bosom. "I saw Lily in the field of grass behind the house. Does she know the time?"

She studied him, she painted his body. Professor Kempton didn't have . . . degrees, of course. Thin and short, long curly hair, dark eyes, intense. His frock coat had just been cleaned, she could tell. She noted that his teeth were very white and his lips quite thick. A whitish scar creased his upper lip. His features looked Jewish, but she'd never asked; a shrunken, condensed Jake Sandelowsky. And just about Jake's age, when she knew him. "She didn't call you?"

"No."

"I'm afraid we must cancel the lesson today. I'm very sorry."

This news seemed to bring him to a point; the lift and push of his eyes, she could tell, were concern fanning out. He colored. Looked contagious! "She's not . . . indisposed?"

"No, but"—she caressed her throat. "I am."

He looked down at his feet. "Well. She should have called."

"I asked her to call."

He shifted his leather case to both hands, held in front of his hips. "You don't feel well?" He looked up.

Her eyes wandered over his body. "No."

"I do wish Lily or someone had called, this walk to your house . . . Her lessons should not . . . Both girls, Mrs. Tabor, I've never had more talented pupils. Every lesson counts, regularity in lessons is very important. When two young ladies have such eminent, such natural ability . . ."

"I'm very sorry."

"You don't feel well?"

A carriage on the road dragged a plume of dust behind it. Professor Kempton shifted his weight. She didn't even know his first name.

"And then," he continued, "you know, of course, I'm in pressing need. . . . It's been two months—I can't continue without . . ."

"I'm very sorry. Has it been that long? I'll be in town tomorrow. I shall drop by the bank."

All for Love

141

"Oh, there's no urgency. . . ."

She had to shade her eyes to see him now, he'd shifted too far, on the portico, to the west. And raising her hand to her brow meant adjustments, meant lifting her breast inside her shirtwaist, which rubbed against the nipple. . . .

He backed up. "Well. Good day, Mrs. Tabor."

"Goodbye. I'm sorry."

"I do hope you feel better soon."

"Thank you. I may."

She closed the door and let out her breath. Dead hairs of wolfhounds snapped at her ankles. And there was Silver Dollar on the staircase, two fingers in her mouth! "Honeymaid, darling. . . ." She rushed up the stairs and smothered her youngest daughter with kisses. "Honey, let's try on my diamond necklaces. You can wear my waist girdle. With the African diamonds?" Her heart rose in her throat like a sparrow in a flue, rose and fell back. And inside that heart another heart fluttered, small as a seed.

Compania Santa Eduwiges
Estado de Chihuahua

Jesus Maria, Mexico   April 18, 1894

My Darling Wife,

When we got up this morning there was one inch of snow which is the first here all year it is now 10 AM and it is going fast by noon it will be all gone except in the shady places. Last week Pete came in and told me that the tramway cable had broke we are putting in a splice and will soon be going again but with the accident one Mexican was killed and since then we've been running some pretty poor ore we have lost about four or five days and every hour seems to me a year I am so anxious for good results this ore being worth $20 a ton American money as I wrote you before shows only $11 American in new assays. If I had known this would not have got my ideas up where I had them I now hope and expect this month about 35,000 Mex money if lucky. You know how hard I have struggled here for it seems to me that I have been away from you for years but I well know it is not quite nine months

It seems so quiet here today for not a wheel is turning in the mill for want of ore for the tramway must run or mill cannot we will start up again prob tomorrow AM. I do hope you are not worried too badly and that you will not be whiteheaded when we meet again I hope you can do all you expect to but fear you have not mentioned Bennett & Myers. They are no doubt eager to get our buildings. How can a man pay his debts if they keep lowering the price of silver tell me that the bankers want to wipe silver off the face of the earth so the value of their gold gets doubled which doubles their debt securities and how can we pay if our debts is doubled I know you will do all in your power for us none can do more and let the result be what it may if bad 99/100 of my feeling bad over it will be on your account for myself I care but little, enough.

I fear the power of attorney I sent you will do you no good because the properties are incorporated and it will take a resolution of the corporation by a quorum of the directors before you can sell anything and give title and you cannot have a quorum there without either Peter or myself and I do not think in fact am sure I cannot give you a power of attorney for the president of the co. so if you can sell anything I will have to come to make title but that is nothing it is nothing for me to travel and you make sale to take affect July 1st and I will probably be ready to come to Denver then Oh I do so hope I can come before that time

Now my loving wife do not worry. We will do all in our power

All for Love

and we will surely pull out I dream of you almost every night for the last ten nights often twice in a night. The children are often associated with you the dreams are in the main satisfactory as dreams can be sometimes quite unsatisfactory. They are caused by my knowing that you are badly worried about some of our affairs and by thinking of you when I go to sleep but enough you may call this nonsense perhaps it is just love me hard all the time and know each night as you lay your head on the pillow that I am thinking of you and our babies   love love love

Horace

She'd managed, just, to scrape up the $2,500 interest for the note held by Bennett & Myers, and convinced them to extend it for another six months. Wore the black chantilly over yellow satin for that one, and a bonnet of violets, since after all it was nearly spring. Unhappily, two buttons on her jacket were missing, and a loose nail in her left shoe worried her heel walking back from downtown, past the Tabor Block, still called that, with its grilled iron front, fine cut stone, and modified Ionic cornice topped by balustrades, a railing, and fourteen little towers. It still commanded downtown Denver, its size and weight made her drift as she walked, list to the side.

Not one person on the sidewalk didn't know who she was. A man smelling of drink gave her a note which said he was a good yankee-doodle, no Fritz or bogtrotter, but'd lost his tongue in a fight and couldn't find work and did she have any. She handed it back.

At home, the small hole in her heel looked unfriendly. She pictured it oozing rust-thickened water.

The shares in the Republic of Honduras–Campbell Reduction Company had proved worthless, no one would buy them. There wasn't anything of value Haw hadn't mortgaged, including the Opera Block, the Tabor Block, the opera house in Leadville, the Clarendon Hotel, every mill and mine. The Denver properties had a second mortgage

he'd secured from the Northwestern Mutual Loan Company to pay off a $300,000 loan to the New England Mutual Life Company, and now there was talk that Laura Smith, doyenne and financier, who'd never once shared canapés with Baby, would purchase the Bennett and Myers first mortgage of $350,000. She planned to file first on the scenery and furnishings of the Tabor Grand, being a lover of opera. Everywhere Baby turned she discovered new loans Haw hadn't bothered to mention, and notes renewed, sold, forgiven, remembered, called in . . . back taxes due, insurance premiums. . . . Her considerable account at Hughes and Keith was long past due, they were in pressing need. We millionaires must stick together, she told Thomas Hughes in his office.

"We?"

And she'd worn, that day, the purple satin dress with yellow side panels, somewhat faded, plus a small purple bonnet and red ostrich plumes! Eyeblack, bloom of roses.

Maybe she could lease the Eclipse Mine in Boulder, Haw hadn't mentioned that. And if she sold whatever jewelry still lay around. . . .

She thought of silver leaking through cracks in the earth, squeezed up and pooling like slapjacks in sand.

They'd given a dinner party one time years ago for Haw's business associates, and served soup made from the turtles in their ponds. She'd once sent a check to Father Guida for the church, and he came in person to thank her. How many zeroes could we, if we were bad, have added to the end of the amount, he joked? Until you fell off the paper, you goose.

She'd ordered a fireplace mantel from India carved in white marble, and when it arrived sent it straight back with precise instructions as to how to recarve it. The champagne always helped on days when they were merely customarily disgruntled. The tiles from Sienna, the Persian rugs, the Parisian gowns. . . .

I'm so bored I think I'll shoot myself.

We're being punished for our sins, that's clear. But listen, God, could you please redeem the mortgage on the Tabor Grand? It would pull us out.

I'm a businessman, Mrs. Tabor, not a magician. I appreciate your sentimental feelings about the opera house, but in that case you shouldn't have mortgaged it.

Fine. I understand. You could take a third mortgage, though, God, that might help. . . .

The day the nail worked up through her shoe and she limped back home and got caught in a thunderstorm, she decided there was no God. No rhyme or reason, no order to things. But at home, in sheer terror, she knelt on the bare floor next to her bed and prayed for forgiveness, with her rosary beads, holy cards, St. Blaise candles, palms, vials of water and packets of sand from the Holy Land spread out before her.

She found herself chasing Cupid and Honeymaid around the dining room table, but for what transgression she couldn't remember. She punished them by locking her door and shouting "Leave me alone!" when they knocked. "I'm sick," she screamed, "you're getting on my nerves." Reduced to weeping lumps in the hallway, deprived of Mommy's kisses and caresses, they managed to make their presence felt even when they tried to be quiet. She opened the door and threw things at them, sachet packets, brushes, corsets, pillows, bolsters, anything at hand. Anyway, here was something to enjoy, the animal panic skinning their faces. . . .

The wolfhounds got hungry, and one day one of them, chasing another outside in doggy play, veered off into the peacocks instead and commenced chasing *them*. He nudged one with his nose, then nipped at its back. The ferocious bird dropped its sails, wheeled around, and snapped at the dog, who pinned it with his forepaws and broke its fragile neck with one bite. "Mommy, come here." Silver watched from the porch. "Mamma," she whispered, but no one heard. Soon the other dogs smelled blood, and peacocks screamed, feathers flew, viscera smeared the dogs' long noses. In seconds, twenty or so peacocks lay

John Vernon

146

dead on the lawn, some with their bellies torn open. Whining dogs nosed and pawed at the corpses, wagging their tails. They seemed disappointed now in the birds' lack of substance, as though digging with their teeth through those colorful feathers and wings had only exposed more feathers and wings. Blood maculated their grinning faces.

Moving drays hauled off most of the furniture, leaving Baby's clothes, a few chairs, and their beds. "Not my pony cart!" Cupid screamed. Workmen came to shut off the gas, lights, and water, forcing them, that evening, to spread a picnic cloth on the floor of the pantry and eat sausages from tins and bonbons out of boxes. They drank water from a barrel that had to be filled by pails at the courthouse pump, two blocks off. They'd gone there after dark so no one would see them, but Cupid stayed home. She refused to help. It wasn't *fair*. Somebody should do something. She'd heard her mother tell the workmen that morning that Poppa had founded the very companies shutting them off now!

Maybe she could go live with Doris Kirby's family, maybe they'd adopt her. The thought of anyone spotting poor Lily hauling a pail of water down Sherman Street so consumed her with shame she feared bursting into flames.

Baby filled the house with candles. Candlelight was good for not seeing the trash and colonies of dog hair everywhere you walked. Honeymaid speared a little sausage with a toothpick and held it to a candle, but Baby said it was already cooked. Still, she turned it carefully in the flame, and not until every bit of its surface had been well scorched did she pop it in her mouth.

Baby read them a letter from Professor Kempton. " 'I presume you do not wish me to resume Misses Lily's and Honeymaid's lessons, at least not until your business troubles are settled. I have been several times to the house and also to the Opera House to see you, but failed. My interest in your lovely two children is so great—and not wishing to intrude on you—that I beg leave to inquire about their present state of health. I must say, it has never been my good fortune before, to meet so amiable and talented children. Will you therefore kindly excuse my impatience to resume their lessons as soon as convenient?' "

"Will we, Mommy?"

"No, darlings. How can you possibly play the piano without a piano to play?"

This logic seemed airtight until Cupid said, "I could play Doris Kirby's."

"Can I shoot myself now, Mommy?" said her sister. "Is it time?"

"Hush," said Baby.

"Shut up, Silver," said Lily.

"Shut up, Silver," said Silver.

"Mom, she's doing it again."

"Mom, she's doing it again."

Lily pinched her sister's arm, but Silver Dollar refused to scream. She was waiting for Lily to say something else so she could echo it. Echo, after all, was one of her names.

"Tell her to stop, Mommy."

"Tell her to stop, Mommy."

"I'm such a nit I wish someone would pinch me."

"I'm such a nit I wish someone would pinch me."

Lily lunged at her sister with both hands, infesting her with pinches. "Shitface!"

"Shitface!"

Baby softly hummed to herself and finished the sausages. Let them eat bonbons. Seeking protection, Honeymaid poured into her mother's arms, crushing herself against her ribs. Baby felt her daughter's body about to quiver. Her bruises drained into her mother's bosom. Pumped full of secret needs, she made a squashy noise. Unconsciously, Baby squeezed and caressed her, running her fingers across her soft hair and its thicket of curls. Memories surfaced: snakes at the springhouse back in Oshkosh; her sister Nealie in bed with scarlet fever and everyone praying; Daddy in a rage trying to read Holy Scripture. "You darlings don't know how easy you've got it. I had to walk to the outhouse barefoot in winter."

"Mommy, where do we peepee now?"

"Outside. I had to walk barefoot to school and the other children bullyragged me and I had to take it even if I didn't want to. I asked myself, should I spit in their faces? And I couldn't decide. It was agonizing! My coat was never warm enough and I wore out my hands with slappaty-pouch. Nobody liked me. They did everything to tease me. And you're worried about carrying pails around, Lily!"

"No I'm not."

"Why should you care? Just laugh in their faces. Nobody likes us anyway, what difference does it make? They've done everything to Bush us. I won't leave a will, I've decided that. I'm not leaving them a penny, I don't care. Imagine their faces! They can kill each other to get the scraps I leave behind. No one can blame me, I've done all I could. Lay down, Honeymaid. Cupid, lay down. Get some pillows from the closet, Cupid, did they leave us any pillows? So. When Poppa comes back, they'll get what they deserve. He'll become rich again, and they'll fall at his feet, they'll kiss his hands, you wait and see. He's a powerful man, no one knows how powerful! They'll come begging at our door and I won't even open it. I don't trust them the teeniest tiniest bit. You'll see what happens. I'll open a bank and they'll come to me for loans and I'll turn them all down."

"Who, Mommy?"

"All of them, every single one. I won't give them a penny. They don't trust me, I won't trust them. Mr. Arnold at the store always raises his prices when he sees me coming, so. I pretend not to notice. It's beneath my attention. Sure, it drives me loony, but I don't let them see that. I've been poor before, I can be poor again, what difference does it make? I don't care. Let them laugh, let them say what they want about me. It doesn't make the slightest difference. I don't care about them, you shouldn't either. What do you care about Doris Kirby?"

"Nothing," said Lily, looking down at her lap.

"Mommy, is there any more sausages?"

"No, Honeymaid."

"Tell us about the Great Unknown. What happened after General Coxey expelled him?" Silver Dollar's voice rose like the warmth from a bowl of heated milk. Pooled in her mother's lap, her face had unpeeled from Baby's ribs, where the stories began, and gazed up so lovely, so pure and full of light! Maybe she'll go on stage, Baby thought. She'll become a concert pianist, a soprano. She'll sing the Habanera from *Carmen*. But what about her lisp . . . ?

Candlelight in ovals wavered on the ceiling. Empty counters and pantries softly rocked. "He went off with the Veiled Lady, Honeymaid. Christopher Columbus Jones followed them, and watched them join the goldbugs of Wall Street, who tore out their eyes. The bugs of the sun fly into your eyes and lay their eggs there. Then the babies get born and eat their way out. It's like looking at the sun, it claws at your eyesight. Don't let me catch either one of you ever looking at the sun, you darlings and dears . . . you loons and goons."

"We won't, Mommy."

"Don't even try it, you mink and you stink. . . . "

Compania Santa Eduwiges
Estado de Chihuahua

Jesus Maria, Mexico   May 9, 1894

My Darling Wife,

I have been looking for a long loving letter from you I want one which is personal the letters for Peter and myself are to common. You know what I mean. It is lovely here nice and warm days and cool nights but not cold no ice in creek. You say if the property is a failure sell it, well it is not a failure but its not as good as we thought but it has had very rich ore and I am confident it will repeat itself many times, but it is far from civilization and I want rest and love with you and this is no place for you and children So this and the Vulture both of them sell at whatever worth you can get if you can get an offer which will make us comfortable.

Mrs. Smith wrote me I'll tell you what she said. She told me a party told her he had the money in hand to loan her to pay off the Northwestern note but that he would not talk to her about it until she was in possession I wrote her to get a thirty days option and she flatly replied she would not take a penny less than three hundred and fifty thousand dollars but of course if we can establish it as a mortgage in the courts she will have to accept three hundred thousand the amount at which she bid it in If she gets possession of our buildings it will cost me many thousands of dollars on account of her management therefore we must leave nothing undone to defeat the same. You know my angel it is the same exactly as in a time of war and the judges have power to issue any order that will protect the country My funds were always freely used for the good of the people and all I want is to keep what rightly belongs to me and lead a good quiet life at home I feel if you will go to court and ask them to issue a order restraining her from taking possession until my time expires for redemption with the Northwestern note which would leave her 3 months to secure a loan if I failed she being a judgment creditor I feel that the court will not refuse you but they will recognize this is an actual war. It will not only save me but will help our silver cause and such an act will be admired by the toiling masses who are clamoring as we are for free coinage. An order that the assignees stay in possession for both parties the full time of my redemption with the Northwestern God help us giving Mrs. Smith all the money over and above running expenses because the assignees are economical and trustworthy tell them that they will do it for you my darling wife if we trust in God.

All for Love

Whatever you do no matter what happens to me my angel
don't let go of the Matchless Mine hang on to that. There is still
ore in the mine, when silver comes back it will make millions.
That's our best hope

The long red flowers I sent you and the children were orchids
pronounced orkid they grow on the back of trees

I love you to death love me too my darling Hug & kiss our
babies for me.

Horace

Windy Oliver, hurry up your stumps! One-of-the-dogs, stop biting
fleas. Pay attention, you're getting on my nerves. Forward
...... march!

Coxey's army trooped down Wall Street as far as the White House,
then turned through the gate and clamored up the stairs. Legal Tender
Coxey, youngest of the lot, fell over the balustrade, whoosh, flop. President Cleveland, come out and give us money! The Kickapoo Indian
banged on the door. . . .

"Honeymaid, hush." Baby rolled over and faced away, but it didn't
stop her fartleberries. Gently, Silver Dollar lay her own pillow across
Mamma's profile, muting the snores. The bolster could just as well do
for the White House, except Silver's thimbles tended to roll off. Cleveland and his tippybobs rushed out and boxed Windy Oliver's ears, but
up jumps the Great Unknown, back on Coxey's side. And here comes
the Veiled Lady! The Goddess of Peace. . . .

General Coxey, I surrender, said Mr. Cleveland.

Kneel, you old fatso! Give us money!

Thimbles clicked headrails, rolled to the mattress, fell to the floor.
Trouble was, Honeymaid couldn't stop squirming, sprawled on her
stomach. The sheets got tugged, the mattress shook, Baby Doe

groaned, then flailed with her arm. "Hush up, Honeymaid, lie down, be still. . . ."

Silver slipped out of the bed trailing thimbles. More boxes of thimbles sat on the taboret, armies in waiting. She gazed down at her mother, whose face had surfaced between the two pillows, whose nose once again honked raucous dilberries. Her cheeks looked smudged. Wrinkles had softened. In the thin gauzy light she looked, somehow . . . windy. Wind pushing water. . . . Pudding swelled out just before it boils. Leave me alone, I'm sick, I have a headache. I don't feel well, I'll die if this continues. . . .

I could eat you up, Mommy, I love you so much. Professor Kempton kissed me on the ear. He touched my naughty bits. He said How come you wear those farting crackers, they look like a boy's dirty old breeches. I told him you were mending my dresses.

She turned and walked out. The bins of shoes in Baby's dressing room reminded her daughter of coal bins in the basement. Two hundred pairs of shoes glowed in moonlight! Silver chose some low slippers whose dragging heels on her feet caused the toes to slap the floor with each gawky step. From one trunk she selected a short woolen skirt, then found in a big chest-sized drawer a feather boa and chantilly shawl. In one of the long dark closets, she located by feel a sealskin cape on a lower shelf. The bonnets and headdresses loomed out of reach, but not the gloves, they were in the next closet. Honeymaid had to wade through fallen clothes devolving to rags. She picked up something to knot around her waist. Gee, the gloves all felt like pillow slips on her arms, so she sat on the floor and pulled them on her . . . legs! How nice, now the slippers didn't flop!

Back in the dressing room, next to the window, she saw in the moonlight how the gloves she'd chosen were spangled in patterns with tiny mirrors and baby pearls and raised ridges flexing up and down their length. How precious, how moony, how Windy Oliver. Poppa always said Honeymaid was precious. . . .

The skirt stopped at her ankles, being Mommy's shortest. The bright moonlight bleached it of color, but Silver Dollar knew it was green. The shawl, the fur cape, let's see.... In a trunk she found a complicated corset, birdcage of cloth, and strapped it on backwards to hold everything in place. The full moon filling fly-spotted windows eddied through floating panels of dust. The dressing room floor was littered with pages of Mommy's big dress catalogue, on each of which had been glued a photograph of one Parisian dress plus a swatch of material. Stray stockings and gloves had gathered in corners, an overturned lamp ... baskets of buttons.

She selected a button and put it under her tongue.

Thus armatured, she walked out the back way, through the maid's hall, careful not to spill. Is it time to shoot myself? Don't even try it. I'll die if this continues, I have a splitting headache, you're driving me crazy....

Put that vase back, Lily, you're such a dumb bunny!

Silver Dollar's head felt bare. She thought of brushing out Mommy's tresses, a task she and Cupid fought over nightly. One got the brush and one got the comb and it didn't amount to a hill of beans which one you got, you wanted the other. Stop tormenting me, her mother always said. Someday you'll have children, you'll see what it's like. Enjoy it while you can, goons and loons....

Her head felt bare, but she couldn't reach the hats. So.... In a room they called the junk room, she poked her finger in one of the holes of a screen depicting, top to bottom, clouds, irises, lily pads, and fish. She could only reach the fish. Once, she'd seen Mommy with a silver dagger rip open the back of a chair in this room and magically pull out a fistful of jewels. She took them to the store and sold them to the man. After that, Silver told her sister Lily how she'd learned that stores were in fact where you sold things. Nitwit! Blubberbrain! Lily died laughing.

Everything here was soft and hard. Light from the moon through tall dormer windows collected and pooled in the alleys between things. On the wall hung a row of leather saddles whose diamond borders had been sliced and ripped out. Strewn on the floor were open cigar boxes, some with loose jewels. A stack of chromos, broken pieces of marble, scrapbooks, watch chains, ink bottles, baled rugs. Gosh, a silver tomahawk presented to Poppa by the Gunnison, Colorado Chamber of Commerce. Glory be, a squeeze box, skates, what's this . . . a stereo viewer, an Indian drum. . . . A strange-looking wig with long black hair. Silver put it on. The wooden hoop inside just fit her head. Its leathery lining clung to her scalp, so now her tresses were longer than Mommy's . . . blacker, too. It had feathers and beads!

The silver tomahawk didn't weigh much, she could tell it was a toy. About the size of a spoon. So, if she couldn't be the Veiled Lady she settled for the Kickapoo Indian Blood Remedy. Worship the moon, President Cleveland! Oh Mr. Moon, when you coming down? Give us our money! The glorious moon stuffed her with silver. She waded through peelings and parings of moon, a fog dry as dead hair. Our day will come, darlings and dears. We'll get back on our feet again, monkeys and moons.

She angled downstairs, bulk teeter-tottering. Long black hair smelling like feet. The empty rooms echoed. Well, not exactly empty. Newspapers, letters, envelopes, and calendars cluttered the floor. Wires curled from walls. Heavy curtains, half ripped, hung in arches and doorways. The chandeliers that Lily once said were Mommy's earrings still hovered overhead, and leaping between them were ghosts of monkeys, chattering monkeys, fresh from the forest. . . . Little hard logs from the dogs lay around. Rags, once clothes, stuffed a hole in one wall, smelling of ashes. A door smelled of pee. Ghost choirs of canaries rose from empty cages mashed on the floor, criminy me, enjoy it while you can! You're special, Mommy said. *Precious,* said Poppa. You mink and you stink. . . .

How thrilling to see your house shut off and stripped of pretty furniture, paintings, and rugs, leaving only the trash! It made Mommy sad, sure, but her two cute babies relished watching walls whose only real purpose was to stiffen the familiar step forward and become

All for Love

155

undressed by grown-ups without a shred of importance . . . at least this baby did. I'll race you to the dray. . . . It was *so* magnificent! Silver couldn't sleep!

When she entered the parlor, two large shapes slowly passed beneath the dining room arch with a stiff-legged, halting, droopy roll. Silver froze. One turned in her direction and growled long and low. He stood there facing her. One-of-the-dogs.

She turned and headed back for the stairs.

Quiet as an Indian, she mounted the staircase, walked down the hallway, and crept into Cupid's room. Her sister lay on her brass bed, strings cut. Cupid had managed to keep her dollhouse when the furniture was auctioned, darling spoiled Cupid. It was almost as tall as Silver! She lifted the roof and chopped up some tables and chairs with the hatchet. Injun raid, Cupid, hold onto your scalp. The redskins ravished the pretty young girls and raised them to eat puddings of bear guts. They didn't have pianos or big fancy houses.

In a bowl of moonlight, in Cupid's room, Silver Dollar Tabor, impossibly happy, stood wearing Mommy's corset over Mommy's lovely clothes, black shiny hair with feathers and beads hanging down to her calves.

Part Two

So Said Honeymaid

7. Chicago 1925

"Welcome to Paradise."

"I never saw such a lousy bunch of cheapskates."

"Try some fuck-me dances, Silver. The big come-on squeeze."

"Ruthie, you don't get it. The gentleman falls quicker for a lady that keeps the talk on a high plane than for some bird who comes across with a crude proposition by a thrust of her hips."

"Is that so? Get a load of *you*. How many tickets you collect so far?"

"Three."

"You might have to compromise your principles. What do you do, talk about books? Seen any good pictures lately? No, I haven't. Me neither, let's fuck."

"This traveling salesman meets a girl? Listen, he says, I can't piddle around, I'm only here a few hours, do you or don't you? She rolls a big soft-boiled eye in his direction and demurely sighs, Well, I don't usually . . . but you talked me into it."

"Hey, that's cute."

"Move it, girls, this ain't a social club!"

Squeals, groans, muttered insults, wild oaths. "Feast your eyes, bozo, it's a *bahth*room full of monkeys." The man at the door mock-squinted at the toilets. Stoop-shouldered and round-faced, he distastefully pinched a bit of lint off his tongue and wiped it on his suit. Taxi dancers pulled down their dresses, stuffed powder puffs into their stocking tops, and slowly rose from benches lining the walls. Others backed away from the mirrors pursing their lips, painting, lipsticking . . . lighting cigarettes.

"All you girls are going straight to hell."

"What can we do?"

"Quit smoking like chimneys."

A toilet flushed. "Sammy, did your Mommy let you lick the bowl, or did you hafta pull the chain like everyone else?"

"Very funny. Remind me to laugh next Sunday. New girl, what's the matter?"

Silver Dollar was washing her knee. "I spilled chocolate on my white stocking, Teacher, then Mamma tried to paint it over with some white paint, but that made it worse."

"Get your cannister out there."

She uncoiled and rose, taking her sweet time. Her friend Ruthie stood waiting. "Ace of a guy," Silver whispered. "Who is he?"

They slouched past beneath his gaze. At the door, Silver felt him pivot and follow. "He's the butcher," Ruthie hissed. "You don't keep in line, next week someone finds your earring in their sausage."

"What a sap."

Bony fingers squeezed her elbow. "New girl. What's your name?"

"Silver Dollar Tabor."

"I mean your real name."

She felt like spitting in his face. Fleshy cheeks, small nose. That *is* my real name, Mr. Moon. "Rose Marie. . . ."

"How old are you?"

"Twenty-four."

"That's a damn lie. If you're under thirty I'll eat my hat."

"Go ahead. I'll get sad."

"You're wasting our time." He squeezed her arm; she could feel it bruising, congealing between his finger and thumb to a yellow-grey knob. "Don't lemme see you dancing for free."

He pushed her away, she stumbled, someone caught her. A dark Filipino man dressed to the nines held her in his arms, but she shrugged him off. "I don't dance with Flips." Sammy the butcher walked back toward the bathroom with a squeamish, disgusting rotation of his hips.

John Vernon

160

"Here's a nickel," Silver muttered to his back. "Go call all your friends."

From the low pressed-tin ceiling, streamers of red and yellow crepe paper ran the length of the room. Wall panels of painted mountain scenery made Silver think of home. Colored spotlights roamed back and forth across the dancers so that some flared up in a blaze of red, others greyly shrunk. Silver'd rouged so heavily no one could have guessed how old she was, could they? Then again, maybe that's how he knew. . . . The taxi girls mostly wore silk dresses with short skirts that swished about, and they'd rolled down their socks to expose their pretty legs. Men lining the walls ranged from flash Filipinos in high white collars and tailored suits to factory workers fresh from the farm in ill-fitting store-boughts, to college students, store clerks, Chinese in coats and vests, Mexicans, Slavs, Greeks . . . not to mention the pockmarked, maimed, dwarfed, and crippled misfits she'd promised herself to refuse all dances no matter how many tickets they thrust in her face.

Not to worry, Honeymaid. Not a brute had approached her.

Clenching couples galloped and stomped, weaving in and out of others doing one-steps or barely moving, locked in loving embraces drained by swaying hips. "I like your size, I like your eyes, who wouldn't?" sang a thin man holding a cornet. On the stage behind him, the clarinet, trombone, bull fiddle, drums, piano, and violin scratched, blew, and thumped. Men holding strings of unused tickets like limp empty leashes looped the dance floor aimlessly. Gotta make 'em last, a day's paycheck of squeeze. . . . If not the turkey trot, then the rabbit hop, if not that then the stomp, the blue slump, the grizzly hug, best of all the shimmy. . . .

Silver popped a chickle in her mouth. I don't dance with big talkers, scrappers, writers, braggarts, monkey chasers, dupes, boozers, lady's men, flashy dudes, or fellows with little noses, she'd told Ruthie.

Little noses?

Generally they're little inside.

All for Love

Loop hounds and Flips, that's all there is here. "Back to the line, boys, back to the line." A cop patrolled the painted line on the floor, loosely swinging his club. On the wall, a sign forbade improper dancing at the Paradise Dance Club. What the hell, thought Silver. She yanked a few kinky locks down her forehead. It's all a game anyway. . . . Chewing, she snatched a ticket from a fish and said, "You look aces to me. Come on."

"*Qué?*"

She locked the bones of her hips against his and felt him relax. The little Filipino man looked around the dance floor, eye whites widening. Dapperly dressed and somewhat clumsy, he only came up as high as her nose. She could smell his rancid Macassar oil. For crying out loud, now I'm dealing in coal. . . .

When that dance was over, she gave him a free one. The dances only lasted ninety seconds. Then he was out of tickets, so she sent him scooting back to the glass booth for more, my goodness, he'd barely gotten hard. So what if all the other nickel hoppers were younger, Silver Dollar knew how to please. She didn't have to blondine her hair either. The sheer control of her involuntary muscles, the major and minor pectorals, the abdominals, enabled oscillations and undulations to cross in waves back and forth across her body and make any man come just as clean as a peeled egg.

Standing in the middle of the floor, she swayed to the music, waiting for her little Flip. The slow dreamy waltz had words like these: "I wish I had my old girl back again, I miss her more than ever now." Ah, there he was, bright teeth and white eyes, a yard-long row of tickets in his hand. But just as he arrived, a boy cut him off, a tall drink of milk.

"My love for you is incurable," he said.

"Oh yeah? How many tickets you got?"

"Enough to make it last."

Her fingers fluttered down below his buttocks. What fun! What a swell time! She pulled him against her. . . .

John Vernon

162

Five tickets later they still scraped and rubbed. He was a dozen years younger than her, at least. Strange how he never thrust back with his hips, even though he'd grown large. She made slow festoons with her underbelly, feeling it pressing her. Some boys wielded their manhood like clubs, others pretended it didn't exist, it was home on a shelf with their rock collection. What a mysterious implement cursed the male groin! Wasn't where to put it always a problem? How many men had she seen on the street cars adjusting themselves, in obvious discomfort? Some stared at her face, bold and ashamed, and she always stared back.

It was the motion of the streetcar, she'd learned; steel rubbing steel, felt through the buttocks.

Others, like this fish she'd hooked, had somehow managed to disconnect themselves from it. Well, if it had a life of its own, you might just as well go about your business. "Quite a harem you got here," he said.

"Yes, it's weird and dim and redolent with mystery." She felt conscious of her lisp, but plowed on. To compensate for it, her voice dropped an octave and grew more silky. "We lure men behind screens depicting bestial deeds, and ply them with coffee—unadulturated with tingling concoctions, of course—and we flirt with them through veils. What time did your Mamma say to be home?"

Hips still pasted to her belly, he leaned back and regarded her. "Mamma's home in Riverside, I'm at the University. I'm older than I look." When he smiled, his eyes narrowed. With the white down of hair on his forehead and cheeks, he looked like a Brian or Duncan, she thought, but turned out to be an Ernest, Ernie for short. Whitish complexion, sandy thin hair, tall bony features, small tidy ears. Everything softened his smile's irritation. He had to be at least six three. Because of his height, his chin, like a boot heel, sat on her head as they danced and danced. Her nose warmed his boiled shirt. Was he wearing linen? She probed with her tongue.... "And you," he said. "No question of you going home to Mamma, is there?"

"Mamma's back in Colorado, in the mountains I love. Give me my pony and wild dash down the mountain trail any old day, give me the freedom to do and dare as nature bids."

"You talk with real swing, Miss. . . ."

"Rose Marie. Call me Silver."

"Silver?"

"It's how my Mamma and Poppa got rich. They pet-named me after their wealth."

"How original. Wealth, mountains, ponies. . . . It fairly staggers the fancy. What are you doing here, may I ask?"

"Dancing with you."

"Yes, of course. In Chicago. You must like Chicago."

"I despise it absolutely! I don't like the big city. Money's the God of Chicago, for one thing. Bright lights, music, revelry, this and that, it's all a mask for your misery. Manhood and womanhood and character are all that count in the mountains."

"I see. You hate Chicago, it disgusts you. Yet here you are dancing with me for, how much? I pay ten cents per ticket, minimum twelve. What fraction of that are you allowed to keep?"

"A nickel. Say, I could ask you the same thing. What are you doing here?"

"I was lonesome."

"You could go to the Lonesome Club or the big halls."

"The girls aren't as pretty. They don't dance as close."

"They don't charge you, neither."

"The God of Chicago."

"I don't do it for the money, smarty-pants. You may have noticed the last two dances you ran out of tickets and no one's collecting."

"What do you do it for?"

"Sweet love, who knows? I could dance till I drop. I like clutching warm flesh. I'm collecting material."

"For what?"

"I'm a writer!"

"A writer?" Suddenly he spasmed. She clutched his bottom, his breath whooshed out, then he carried on dancing. Pumping bodies surrounded them, hircine smells, smashed laughter, nauseating cigar and cigarette smoke, all throbbing to the music. Had anyone noticed? Spotlights swept the room. The man on the stage sang to someone named Honey Bunch how much he loved her, how much he thought of her. Ernie's voice, for such a young man, had roots in his feet. He hadn't deflated yet. Really, he hadn't missed a step. "What do you write?"

"Sob and special stuff. The usual. Wild escapades, daring adventures, dandy and slapdash, hot love, bloody deeds."

"How exciting."

"I write about the Wild West, where I grew up. You should of seen me, my glorious bronze hair racing in the wind looked too beautiful to be real. I was a Turkish pipe dream. Still am, but now you want more pipe. I had scads of admirers in knee britches, Ernie. In Colorado, you could find me riding into town with a colored kerchief tied around my throat, a cowboy hat, pistol strapped to my side, whooping my pony downhill to the store just to buy a can of tomatoes for supper. Mamma was always afraid some bad person would kidnap her daughters. Hence, the pistol. Golly, those were the days—"

"New girl, where's your tickets?"

"In my apron, here."

Sammy the butcher stood beside them in all his wienerwurst majesty. His triumphant face billowed with cracked veins. "I count eleven tickets, sister, I been watching you. You like to do your friends kind, ain't that so? By my count you danced fifteen dances since your last powder."

"Who taught you to count?"

"See that sign? No improper dancing, it says. You been dancing too lewd and giving free rides. This ain't no shimmy joint."

"Hey, let her arm go." Ernie, my hero! My Star of Blood!

"Get your keister outa here."

"Meet me downstairs," Silver implored. Her eyes widened, but Ernie just quizzically smiled, watching her. "I have to get my coat," she added. She held both his hands. Were his yellow eyes amused or in love, and what difference did it make? I've got him, he's mine, what a catch, what fun. . . .

"We should get a cut!" Sammy yelled behind her.

In the wardrobe, she pulled the silver flask from her coat and swallowed half the contents, to protect against cold.

Outside, North Clark Street blew sleet in their faces. They walked toward the Loop, searching for a place where the chop suey looked like it came on clean plates. Silver knew one called the Canton Tea Garden, but couldn't remember exactly which street. She pulled out a cigarette, he lit it for her, she gave it to him then pulled out another. When they passed beneath the iron sky of the El, a train overhead showered sparks. The squeal and rumble of sliding iron and clacking boards did something to your spirits, it made you want to howl. Motorcars with their lamps lit chugged down the street. One or two horse wagons, several yellow cabs. . . . The sleet kept on turning to snow fine as black sand, then back to sleet. Like an acid, it smeared across rising dark buildings, blotting them out. If you listened carefully, you might hear in the distance explosions and gunshots on this winter night. The *Unione Siciliana.* . . .

Actually, this was the very evening Johnny Torrio's jaw got blown off but he survived and fled to New York, leaving his assistant Al Capone to take over.

Silver knew how to pick 'em. In the Canton Tea Garden, the chop suey didn't taste the least bit of floor. Across the table, flushed by the wind, Ernie looked happy. Why did God create woman if not for moments like these in which, filled with fiery impulses and longing, she could learn to play her part and snag a husband?

He studied anthropology at the University of Chicago, he told her. What's that?

You know, old bones, old customs, old gods.

Oh sure, she knew all about it, heavens to Betsy, she'd once found an arrowhead outside a mine in Leadville.

Leadville?

"Sure. Where Poppa made his millions, in the mountains. We grew up in Denver with cast-iron deer on the lawn and bronze statues of Venus and real flesh-and-blood wolfhounds and peacocks all about. It was A–Number One heavenly, Ernie, but after Poppa died Mamma took us back to Leadville. That's where I learned how to be a cowgirl and to race around the mountains bareback on ponies."

"Brothers or sisters?"

"Just me and Mamma. Lily ran off and met a man, now she lives in Wisconsin, she was my sister. Actually, she married her cousin. We see each other seldom. Me, I worked for the Pike's Peak Film Company. I had my own newspaper for a while, the *Silver Dollar Weekly*. I met Teddy Roosevelt and wrote a song about him, published in Denver, 'Our President Roosevelt's Colorado Hunt.' I modeled, I what." Swimming in suey, Silver still had the presence of mind to edit out infected glands, one ovary excised, and various other skirtings of death and reminders of age. She didn't mention the Big Review of 1919, nor did she say anything about Florence Wheeler in Denver, who'd accused Silver Dollar of stealing her ring—for which Silver was jailed—only to reveal the next day that she'd pinned it under her dress and forgotten it.

He'd drunk four cups of tea before she produced the flask and offered to spike it for him. Chagrined grin. Ernie held up his own flask. Evidently, it had been wedged between his legs and continually in use throughout the meal!

Red dragons and palaces writhed on the walls. Paper lanterns slowly twisted.

"Tell me about your writing."

"*Star of Blood?* It's a novel. 'The final chapter is not finished. Perhaps it has not yet begun in the life of the daringest, most heartless yet resoluble desperado that ever struck the hidden vein of terror in the bold heart of the heroic West,' I'm quoting now. Get a load of *you*, you should see your face."

"I feel struck dumb."

"Those are the opening lines of the thing. I just fool around. Will it make me famous? 'Brigandage and wholesale slaughter were the cards he nonchalantly played in his game of life.' Righto. Tom Mix could play the hero if they made it a movie."

"Any women?"

"Just Artie. Artie Dallas. She dies. 'She had fiducially answered the call of death when quick consumption laid its fatal hold upon her dissipated body and she faded, rapidly and silently as a flower. There, in a notorious resort in the underworld she closed her eyes, her wild, startled black eyes that hopelessly flashed from out her flying dark hair.' " Silver flung her hands open, shrugged, and smiled. Her head felt too large. Her curly brown hair, her own startled black eyes, heavily painted.... She was dark, Ernie was light, she was older, he was young. She felt like a mine full of hidden riches. Peering over the edge with wonder, he tossed in a pebble. Bony long fingers, soft as a woman's. Cut your nails, Ernie. Some men pour out of the womb fully groomed and puffing a cigar, do they not? He'd walked beside her through sleet and snow clutching his fedora, yet look at him now, not a hair out of place. Placid as a just-fed cat. His quizzical smile looked so fresh, so boyish, so full of teeth....

"More, tell me more. Was your childhood happy?"

"Oh, happy as a clam. Have you ever been West? It's super. It's the cheese."

"The cat's—what? How do you say it?"

"The cat's meow, the duck's quack, the pig's wings, the elephant's wrist, the sardine's whiskers. I know every satisfying, modern, and clever expression for classy. My favorite is, it's not half bad. My childhood was divine. I went through a nifty Indian craze, and wore a beaded headband, a fringed shirt, and moccasins. Utah Charlie was a friend of mine. I slept out at night under the stars and cooked my own bacon and eggs on a fire. I kid you not. When I got too big for my pony, I'd go to the Opera House Barns in Leadville, and Mr. Younger gave me the best horse he had, a swell palomino with a yellow bridle. Dolly. He never charged. I was fifteen years old and thought to be wild. Mamma used to follow me around, to make sure I behaved. I loved horses. I loved animals. We had monkeys and cats and birds when I was little. I had a baby wildcat later on. I'll never forget the time it got stolen or carried off by an eagle or something. The smell was something ghastly. It stank out loud. What else? I managed our mining properties, with Mamma, but I was restless. I had to be on my own. I worked for the Lambert Shows in Colorado farm towns and learned an Egyptian dance, which helped somewhat when I needed money. I used to think when a woman reaches twenty-three she should gaze back upon a gaily trodden road. Pleasure should have walked with her on that road, riding should have filled the empty days, dances and theaters the lonesome nights, young company should have thronged it. Who wants to gaze back on empty roads in which the pleasure-feasting people of the world never ventured, Ernie? The ones who have gay times? And then, and then . . ." Silver pursed her lips and looked at the ceiling. "After I became a grown-up woman, the main improvement in my life was better clothes. But I wanted to be a writer most of all. I once wrote a letter to Buffalo Bill and asked him about his buffalo hunts and his fights with the Indians. I was thinking of writing a book about it. You know what he said? He wrote back from the Hoffman House in New York. He said he never killed buffalo nor fought with the Injuns without haunting feelings of remorse and regret. But someone had to do it, he said. Someone had to stand between civilization and savagery. Someone had to make it possible for civilization to advance."

"Did he really say that?"

"Yes, he did. I wrote back and told him, don't look at me." She thumped her sternum with her knuckles. "What else? My father? He was a great man. Truly. He died when I was ten. He owned half the world, I do believe. He bounced me on his knees and so forth. His face was enormous. I think my mother kept him solvent. Is that anything like sober, ha ha? She manages the properties by herself now. She's a very remarkable woman, Ernie. What else, what else?"

"No painful experiences? No traumatisms to impair a happy childhood?"

"Well, the fact is, I *believe* in pain. It's all I've got. Can material things last forever, I wonder? If so, I'm out of luck. Some things, let's face it, you hope for an end to."

"Some things like what?"

"Like too many questions. Like nosy children. Enjoy the chop suey, what difference does it make? Time is pain, money is pain, stuff is pain, I mean rubbish and effects. That's why I believe in the spirit. The spirit survives. The spirit of Silver!"

destroy this letter

General Delivery, Chicago   Jan. 14, 1925

My Dear Mamma:

I can't understand why I don't hear from you. Why don't you ever write me any of the news back home? Do you go to Denver anymore. Do you ever hear from Phil or Blanche? I surely would love to know what is going on back there, but I never hear. I have been ill and could not write before. I lost my job because of my clothes, well I'll try to hold out with 47 cents in my purse and my comb and brush and toothbrush. I'll try to brave it out, I am in rags now. At church I met a man, Ernie Frick (I call him *Earnest*) whose people here are of high standing and wealthy. I told him that I was from Colorado and my people were wealthy. I told him that you were wealthy. That was when I first knew him

John Vernon

and just expected to have him as a passing acquaintance and as time went on and we became better friends I never contradicted what I had said but still said you were wealthy. Mamma, God alone knows how I have longed for a little home all my own so I could put the ups and downs of life behind me and have someone who cared for me to take care of me. And as he grew attached to me I dreamed of that. He often made the wish to meet you but I discouraged him going to Colorado for fear he would hear that you were poor and about me having been in jail and all that. One week ago he came over to see me and told me he was introduced to a man from Denver and heard terrible reports about me, that I was married before and my husband was a crook. He said he was not going to take anyone's word for it but was going to Colorado to look up my people and find out the truth. There is one thing I know, I must get away before Ernie returns as I could not stand the shame of seeing him after he had heard all those lies about me.

Mamma, you are my only friend and I ask a favor of you in Jesus name. I told Ernie that you were very religious and was so modest in your living that no one would know you were wealthy. If you see him or hear from him, for my sake please let him think you are wealthy and try to keep from him the fact that I was in jail there. Maybe you could write to him and tell him that it was all a foul lie about my being married, but please don't tell him that I said I expected a home from him or any of that. I told him that I was going to write you about some of those lies, so if you write and say that I wrote you and gave you his name and said he was coming to Colorado to see you and you thought you would drop him a line about it and not go into any details about anything else except the lie and leave a wealthy impression it might keep him away from Colorado as I cannot stand the idea of him finding out how unfortunate I really have been. You are my only friend and take my advice about what to say as I am on the

All for Love

ground and I know what is best in this case. If you write him use fair stationary and do not give any address as if you apparently forgot it. You are not supposed to know about me going to Nebraska. Please don't mention the Minstrel Maid Company, or the Slide for Life by my teeth at Lakeside Park. I'm awfully disgusted with all the men here, I've seen too many of them but Ernest is different, a student with a bright future. I discouraged him about going to see you and said that was because I had not thought that you would approve of me seeing a man, you wanted me to join a convent. Mamma, could you send me some money at least until he returns? Don't mention my age at least knock it down some, I rely upon you and our God and God knows I need the help of both.

Your loving
Silver

Matchless Mine
Leadville, Colo   Jan. 21, 1925

My own darling Silver,

I am in bed prostrate with grief from your letter. Shall I write to any wicked man who comes along and you probably in the family-way and if you go on it will be a repetition of my martyred Sister Nealie, one child in her womb, one nursing at her breast, one on her lap, one on her dress at her feet, four scarcely able to walk, consequently her blood was impoverished and she went to a premature grave. You are not strong enough to protect yourself neither was Nealie, one of the most beautiful characters ever sent into this world. What do you mean by wealthy, do you mean that you are denying our Lord Jesus Christ and his sufferings? I think that you are making a mistake if you don't tell your friends that I send you money, not on my account but on your own,

John Vernon

because the public always wonders where a person without a visible income gets his or her money. By letting people know that I help you when I can people will think all the more of you, especially as you are a girl. 5$ encl.

Tell your friend not to write not to come, I won't see him.

Now that I am also steeped in grief I may as well tell you that I will be very much surprised if you will ever see me in the world again for last month I was struck down suddenly and only saved by a miracle. I wrote our beloved Father Guida whose prayers must have saved me from death. Twenty-eighth day of December I was working down the mine with the windlass. A man by the name of Atkins was on the other side of it. We were hoisting rock from a shaft sixty-five feet deep, that was two hundred and forty-four feet underground where we were. We would lower the buckets sixty-five feet to a man by name of Wilbur Simmons who would fill them and we would pull them up. Mr. Atkins took the bucket of rock and dragged it some thirty feet through the drift as I am too old and I would let out the rope for him. I was silently praying to Saint Anthony when Mr. Atkins suddenly calls to me, this is the kind of stuff you are looking for, come see this bucket! I walked over and as I came near the open shaft I received such a terrible blow in the forehead that it knocked me backwards right on top of the open shaft. I felt my old body going down heavy and screamed for I knew that I would be killed and the man underneath me too and Mr. Atkins was so horror struck that he could not move. I was lifted right out of that hole and placed on the boards beside it and no one knows who did it or how it was done but we know that it was our blessed Saviour. I was unharmed and not a sign of pain or soreness was on my forehead where I was struck that mighty blow and no sign of it or bad effects in any way except that for many nights I woke up thinking I was going down that hole. It was Satan that struck me, he wants to kill me, he knows I am going to save the Matchless

Mine, but God in His mercy has attended with mighty Angels all through this battle.

Please excuse lead pencil, no ink where I am as I am in Leadville. Come home to me and all will be good, I would never have consented to your going away except for your writing and music but you don't mention that. Oh my precious darling Honeymaid come home at once and telegraph me that you will come and never leave me again, we both will be happy and comfortable forever don't fail me my darling you know you were half my poor heart and Lily the other half come home, I love you.

Forever your devoted and loving
Mamma

General Delivery, Chicago   Feb. 2, 1925

Mrs. Tabor:

You have given me more sorrow than I ever expected to have, I had to move out so he would not follow me. Under no condition show my letters or repeat one thing in them—that favor you *must* grant in the name of Jesus. I will not come back never again. The Mine will never do me any good in the years to come, I will be somewhere else in another part of the world, and good riddance apparently lost and you nor no one shall ever know where. No you do not love me, if you did you would help me like I ask and not ruin my life. A life without happiness or home life or love. So believe me, you will pay. When you ruin my life and break my heart and rob me of love—you shall pay. How dare you refuse to help me, what would Poppa say if he knew what you did to his Honeymaid! I will never see you again by my efforts. A woman, human and in love and having anticipated marriage and home and happiness will do all things for the one she loves, even if he has been torn from her. May God pity you I don't. I will have to join a convent.

And if God does pity you and you ever see Poppa after you die, tell him that you sent his Honeymaid adrift in the world by having no pity for her and you drug the love from her very hands. Tell him that her frail figure is swaying in the storm, battered by the fires of life, that she is alone with a broken heart thinking of the happiness she almost had. And tell him that I loved my Poppa and longed for his help and his protection. And in the future when you wonder where and how I am just think of me as "The leaf in the storm," suffering, battling for existence, alone and nursing the wounds of love.

The picture you sent I can make hide nor hair of. Who is the woman in the bed, why are the two men staring out the window, whose baby is that in the basket so tiny? Is the mother your sister?

May God Pity you.

The leaf in the storm.

Do not show this letter to anyone in the world. No one must know about my broken heart.

Alone and helpless
The leaf in the storm

I paid Mrs. Krebbs the 5$ you sent, am now free of debt. To whom it may concern, I Silver Tabor, this February 2, 1925, at 2:40 AM state that I am going insane or something else, dying of grief. What terrible suffering.

• • •

Beauty contests, radios, autos at the Indianapolis Speedway exceeding a hundred miles an hour—dance marathons, road houses, championship prizefights, football stadiums sporting Doric columns and costing six million dollars to construct, so fans could feel classy as well as rich—speakeasies, hot jazz, cabarets, violent and scabrous dances performed in furs. . . . Because nightclubs in America grossed twenty-two million dollars in 1923, Dion O'Bannion, the former altar boy who loved flowers and his mother, shot the doorknobs off toilets in Chicago nightspots as encouragement for their greedy owners to share and share alike with him and his friends. O'Bannion himself, while preparing floral displays for Mike Merlo's funeral, was still shaking hands with Frankie Yale when six bullets fired by Albert Anselmi and John Scalise ripped through his head, chest, cheek, and larynx, blowing him into the chrysanthemums and roses. Anselmi and Scalise will forever be remembered as the bloody pulps left behind after a splendid dinner party given by Al Capone, who personally clubbed each of them to death with a sawed-off baseball bat in front of his friends.

In the Apache Club on Cottage Grove Avenue, Capone liked to hand out twenty-dollar bills to the waitresses and busboys after a day's hard work of serving mungy at his soup kitchen. People kissed his hand! Like everyone else in America, he spent the mid-twenties reciting after Emil Coué: "Every day in every way I am getting better and better." Emil Coué was a craze, so was jazz. A craze craze had swept the country. Goldfish swallowing, platform squatting, quintuplets, kidnapping. . . . But nothing held a candle to the Apache dance, an adult Punch and Judy show employing real bodies. The Apache Club was a black-and-tan cabaret; the races mingled freely. Roulette, dice tables, Twenty-six games, house poker in one room; in the other, through a wide pillared archway, the carefully devised Parisian squalor of smallish round tables, wire chairs, flaking yellow plaster, dim lights, cigarette smoke, an overhead fan. Only the Moulin Rouge silhouettes pasted on the walls looked at all American. Ernie Frick appreciated the irony, having been to Paris, having seen the real thing, that is, not real Apaches, but real Parisian dancers portraying thugs whose savagery naturally got labeled . . . Apache.

He'd lost all his money at the Twenty-six tables, the girls with the dice cups being so pretty. Scrutinizing each one, looking for Silver Dollar, he kept on forgetting to add up his points or keep track of his throws, but what the hell, it was only money, forty-seven dollars to be exact. So what if his daddy had cut him off and his grades at the U. had taken a nosedive? He'd developed a taste for bad fun, for hasty compensation for imminent loss. Debt was part of the fun . . . so was flirting. It wasn't his fault that the girls were children, unripe versions of Silver. What haunted him was her elastic quality, the way she yielded and sprang back, soul and mind of eager clay. Whatever it was, she had tried it. She was damaged goods, sure, but so was he now. They were the classic opposition, he light and she dark, *claritas* and *profundus,* upon which the world turned, said all his professors. You could deeply probe the sun and find darkness, the blind opaque source, or, screw that, pirouette through hazard while keeping your composure, thus shedding light on the darkest practices. That sounded good, yes, give that a try.

Silver's posture was snaky. Her lisp was a hiss from the shallows of her soul. The long river of her flesh seemed boneless when she pressed up against him with such complete surrender he didn't know what to do, he'd never felt such a blessing. Loaves and fishes! She'd made herself increase, then just disappeared, moved, without warning, out of her rooming house, no forwarding address. That's when he'd still had money enough to bribe obtuse German landladies, but Silver had covered her tracks too well. She'd drawn him in, he'd flooded the darkness, then woken in a cold swamp of wet sheets. . . .

Ernie was nothing if not . . . resoluble. Resolutely dissolvable. One thin spine like a needle held him up. The idea of Twenty-Six, with its piddling bets, was to get you drinking to excess, so the girls withheld the dice cup if your glass was empty. He couldn't leave, he still owed. A short man with shrunken feet in spats kept looking in his direction.

All for Love

As though not to hide, he leaned on a pillar between the two rooms, breathing deeply of smoke. On the cabaret side, a tall black man in a cabbage-leaf suit buttoned up tightly, and a bandanna tied around his neck . . . Apache cap on his head . . . *slunk* down the aisle between tables perfectly erect, if that was even possible. The spine branched across his back like reinforced armor, but his legs and arms flexed. He paused with each deliberately lingering step, body swinging from his crucified shoulders; stood with one foot extended out front, arms hanging down. The piano, fiddle, and drums were now playing jazzed-up tango rhythms, fractured and unsqueezed.

Suddenly, he dropped into a crouch. Looked around. Saw a woman at a table. Fixed her with his stare. Well, she couldn't resist, she sullenly stood, swayed like a snake, and Ernie saw at once who it was. As though being dragged, reluctant and defiant, Silver Dollar approached her black Apache. He grabbed her by the wrist, pulled her against him, spun her around, flung her away. She crouched, afraid and fascinated, waiting.

Ernie couldn't help it, he was getting hard, as though a bony finger probing his gut had found a puckered flap of skin hung from his belly, all but forgotten. Silver smoldered. Darkled. She hadn't seen Ernie, she couldn't see anyone else in the room—that was the fiction— except her partner. They approached, fell back, approached again, her swaying steps with exaggerated stealth mocking his. What a wormy cat she was! The tight striped jersey compressed her breasts so you couldn't detect how much they sagged, though Ernie knew, he'd ski jumped off them. . . . Was she supposed to look used up, or young? In the flickering light, she lurched back and forth from ripened and desperate, exploded at the eyes, to wiry and firm but helpless as a girl. That's why she was so good at this, he realized, she ran the whole gamut. She too had loosely knotted a bandanna around her neck. Her short green skirt flared when she spun, exposing the tops of her long silk stockings.

She smiled in wistful pleasure. Clearly a trap. The man's furrowed brow expressed chilly hauteur, Ernie felt a pinprick of jealousy. This black man was very tall and handsome, with bulging muscles even on his cheeks. He pulled her to him and twirled her around, now they were waltzing, dipping and gliding, though he never bent his back. She threw her head back, mouth slackly open, looking up into his eyes as they austerely danced.

He seized her throat in his strong grip, pushed it back, and held it a moment, watching it at arm's length, as though it were a slimy snake —then threw it away and walked off. Throats seemed to be very prominent here, but Ernie knew why, he'd seen this dance before . . . in Paris. The man's throat was sprung out, a skein of cords, while hers, even in dim smoky light, looked red and bruised where he'd grabbed it. Why not stop this right here, walk up and grab her wrist? Come to Riverside and meet my mother, the deaconess. Safety pins popped open inside Ernie's heart. . . .

Silver crouched, submissive, watching her partner. She looked properly debauched. Panting, she rose, slid toward him, looked down. He'd turned by now, raised her by the chin, jailed her in his arms and waltzed around some more with intricate complicated sectioned-off steps. Every movement was constrained and formally prescribed, every turn and gesture stiff and angular and jerky, but somehow they managed to step up the pace, to make it exciting, though there were sluggish interludes, thought Ernie—trying to be bored—followed by bursts of frenetic action, the climax was coming. Suddenly, he threw her off but held her wrist, and on the rebound they crashed into each other, he cold and hard, she trembling and distraught. What a sackful of jittering moth-nerves she'd become! He pulled her back, they waltzed furiously around, angry at the world, he threw her away and dragged her back again, threw and dragged back, more violently each time.

He flung her to the floor and pulled her to her feet. Now they waltzed around nicely and she, chastened, hung more and more limply from his arms. They waltzed faster and faster, a dancing bomb. When they stopped, it seemed as though something kept spinning, the blurred atoms of their souls. The musicians still blithely banged away, but he shouted, *"Taisez-vous!"* So . . . he was French. Capone had imported him, like bootleg. The music reached a confused little climax, tidied by the drum. That Negro was *angry*. Silver was slung back across his thigh, he'd lowered to a crouch. With one hand on her forehead he pushed her head back, and with the other drew a knife, slashed her throat, and let her drop. Ernie, of course, having seen this before, knew it wasn't real, but that made it worse. Silver just lay there. No one applauded. He wanted to rush out and nurse her back to life, but instead he continued standing by the pillar, erect, in a sweat. He was flushed all over, he realized now. One pocketed hand rattled some change. The lights brightened. Silver jumped up and raised the black Apache's hand and the audience applauded while the drum made little rolls.

"I've been looking for you all over town."

"Here I am."

Ernie sat at Silver's table. Well, she was smiling, she seemed glad to see him. She looked worried, haughty, exhausted, peppy. Decide what it is you want to be! "Where did you go?"

"I had to move. I owed Mrs. Krebbs. You don't know how it is in this town for a woman with talent, an artiste. It's not easy." She lit up a cigarette, looking around. The man with the spats watched them from a pillar.

"Since when have you been on the ebony?"

"He's my dancing partner. We are artistes."

"I suppose it's better than taxi dancing. You must make a decent wage."

"More than a nickel a dance, for crying out loud. This place is where rich folks go anymore. How have you been?"

"Sad and lonely."

"How was Colorado? Did you like my mountains?"

"I never went. Could not afford a ticket."

"With all your jack?"

"Easy come, easy go." She seemed to be melting. She oozed to the side, tipping her head. "What's wrong?"

"I lost an earring."

"It's in your hand."

"Jeez." She laughed. "I feel like a bozo." What plastic features! A face seen through blown glass. . . . Eruptions in her soul, quakes and calms, caprices, shifts of mood, nothing was masked. Everything about her cried out loud. It made him feel positively protective. She leaned across the table, crushing her bosom against the hard marble. "Buy me a drink."

"I'm afraid I can't."

"Mamma wouldn't approve?"

"Not that. It's my . . . banker." He nodded at the man in the spats.

Silver waved him over. He heavily approached. For all his surveillance of Ernie that evening, he wouldn't even glance at him now. "This bird with you?" He spoke to Silver Dollar.

"To the end of time, Ralph. Till hell freezes over."

"He owes the house fifty-nine bucks."

"Forty-seven!" cried Ernie.

"Interest," said Ralph, watching Silver. His jaw pushed up, blistering the lips. Words came out bruised. Wide-apart eyes made him look froggy. His meaty face glistened.

Silver touched Ralph's arm. "Put it on my tab," she said. "Tell Pete to bring us two Johnny Walkers."

He bent down and lipped her earlobe. "You'll carry this guy?"

"Till the cows come home. Till death do us part."

"He likes to lose money."

"So do I."

• • •

Bed creak. Soft breath in Ernie's ear. The heel of his hand lay discreetly on the small of her back. His fingertip made her brown button pucker. Peck the sticky star. He lay on his back, she lay wrapped around him, thus crushing her lower lips against his thigh. One breast upon his arm.

He didn't have to look, he was growing stiff again, in contemplation of what he had to say. "The infliction of pain is an act of love."

Her head, on his shoulder, raised itself up. Her arm across his belly felt quite rough, since Ernie was relatively hairless, smooth as a baby in fact. Beside them, on a table, her cigarette burned in a saucer. Smoke tried to eddy but merely hung.

Lying there with a sheet loosely draped across their hips. . . . Ernie later believed that was the first time he'd noticed the scabs running up and down her forearm. But in just a few weeks he'd be the one seeking out her good veins, her hands shook so much. He learned to prepare the needle himself, gradually diminishing the doses, the only cure for morphinism. "Ernie, put it down."

His left arm, gliding over their heads, held a human scalp. He shook it; the hair waved. "Where did you get this?"

"It used to be Mamma's."

He trailed the hairs of the thing along her side, pulling her closer with his right hand. His finger went in. "In our culture, pleasure deriving from the suffering of another is not socially acceptable."

"It ain't? I should hope not."

"Herodotus gives an account of scalping amongst the Scythians."

"What does he say?" She was biting his chest, gently tugging with her teeth.

"He says they chiefly desired to bring back the bodies of enemies killed in battle, to be maltreated to satiation . . . but if the distance was too great, only parts were brought back, in most cases the head. If the distance was even greater, however, the scalp would have to do. The Scythian warrior decapitated his enemy, sawed the top off his head, and saved the skull for a cup. He peeled off the scalp and scraped it clean with an ox rib, then worked it in his fingers until it grew supple. It must have looked like this. Maybe not such long hair." He lowered it to their faces. The thing smelled of trunks and rooming house closets, musty and unchaste. "They used them for handkerchiefs. Great warriors hung them on the bridles of their horses. Some sewed a bunch together to make a sort of cloak."

"Jeez, what barbarity. Men are such lousy animals, Ernie." She writhed against him, suctioning his hip. "The sins of the father and mother shall be visited upon the children," she hissed, "even unto the fourth and fifth generations."

"You know your Bible well."

"That's in *Star of Blood*. It has been so historically, I wrote, and will be so eternally. The gapless chain of ancestral barbarity which takes the modern back to the primitive . . . had . . ." She gasped. "Perhaps, what, oh shit . . ." Asquirm, she raised up, locking their glances. "Had perhaps filled his throbbing heart with cruelty."

He looked away, at the cigarette beside them. "What about eye for eye, tooth for tooth, hand for hand, foot for foot? The Tupi Indians took eyes, not scalps."

"Jesus."

"The northern tribes of the Athapascans, especially the Eskimos, never scalped. Nor the southern tribes, till they came into contact with those that did, such as Mexicans and whites. The governor of Chihuahua in Mexico paid one hundred and fifty dollars a scalp for unfriendly male Indians . . . one hundred for females."

"Just like a man."

"If you scalp someone, you gain control of his soul. His spirit has no rest in the afterlife, and, refused admission to the Mansions of Bliss, now it sees everything through a glass, darkly. Meanwhile, the power of the scalp's owner is thereby increased a hundredfold."

"Oh, Ernie, oh . . ." He lay straight as a board, hard and cold as rock, as though crystals grew from his dripping brain. She'd climbed on top and straddled his hips. He let the scalp drop. She fit herself on and started working up and down, very careful and very slow. He'd never felt so large before. From the table beside them he picked up the cigarette, burned down to half. The paper, brown and dry, had cupped the glowing tip like the untrimmed nail of a snifter's pinky. He took a deep drag to burn it off. He flicked the long ash in the saucer, then held it between his first two fingers above her plunging back.

With his middle finger he tapped the base of her spine. Just his finger, but it gave her a jolt and thrust her down, pushing him deeper. She raised her head and locked his eyes bravely, game as a trooper . . . grotesquely childish. Her face had gone rubbery. It seemed to say, I can take it, Ernie, I've got it coming, I've been a naughty girl.

He tried being brave too, like a big boy. He smiled to himself, what a bounder I've been. I'm doing this now. It's *transpiring,* he thought. The cigarette's tip burned closer to his fingers. He held it above the small of her back. He lay there motionless, mind blank and numb. He was proud of himself. He didn't feel a thing.

There was a young girl
Who retired for the night,
She was both young and handsome.
She took off her shoes and the rest of her clothes
And the rain blew through the transom. Chorus!
The old jaw bone.
It was three o'clock, near the hour of one
A figure appears and it strikes you dumb. Chorus!
The old jaw bone.
I tried it on the pedestal
I tried it on the chair
I tried it nearly every place
But couldn't get it there. Chorus!
The old jaw bone.

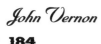

"Van Osten, you son of a bitch, tell a joke!"

Crowds at the Spit Box were like that, impatient.

"Two Swedes apply for a marriage license. 'Name?' 'Ollie Olson.' 'And yours?' 'Lena Olson.' 'Any connection?' The bride turns red. 'Only vunce. He yumped me.'" Drumroll.

"Tell a good one, for Christ's sake."

"Say boys, that's enough hooting. What's the difference between a sharpshooter and a constipated owl? The sharpshooter shoots and shoots and never hits. The owl hoots and hoots . . ."

"Tell 'James, fuck the duck'!"

"French maid: 'What means fuck?' English butler: 'It means, To serve.' Next night at supper, maid haughtily announces to the butler, 'James, fuck the duck.' 'How jolly,' says the visiting Brit. 'May I stick my prick in the mahshed potahtoes?'"

"Tough audience," Van Osten told Pocahontas backstage. It didn't bother Silver Dollar though, she always found relief in advance, twenty-five grains' worth, her daily allowance. But sometimes it took thirty to make her happy.

She'd lost weight, her nails had turned brittle, her skin dried up, so Ernie rubbed sweet oil all over her body before each performance. The glistening result muddled sags and wasted skin, and reinforced the image of an Indian princess who'd smeared herself with bear grease to welcome her lovers. . . .

Tom-tom effects. "Ten Little Indians," the only fitting tune the pianist knew. Catcalls and hoots from the stags at the Spit Box, some of whom whooped like spunky young braves when Pocahontas emerged dancing toe-heel and dispatching her imaginary enemies left and right with a little silver hatchet. She was carving up air, so much yellow oleo. Her bright eyes sucked light and with perfect clarity registered each red streak made by the slashing arms whirling like windmills at the edge of her mind. Moments like this, mind and body were one, and joy filled her limbs and freed her from shapes. She acted out the story Mamma'd once told her, of how Kit Carson had scalped a vile savage to thwart a poor white woman's impending outrage. It wasn't ten little Indians but ten little white girls, each rescued from defilement. Darlings and dears, here's your redemption just in the nick of time, your ticket back to innocence. You're on your way home, mink and stink, here's your bliss back. . . .

Before throwing off her Navajo blanket she stood there and shouted, "How!"

"*Hooow!*"

Even Ernie and Ralph looked up from their table. Through eddies of smoke she saw Ernie's sad eyes. In the dumps again? She knew why. The *Unione* would garnishee her wages every night this week to pay off his debts. As the shaking began, she tried meeting his eyes. This is for you, kiss kiss. Pectorals, deltoids, abdominals, dorsals. . . . At cruising speed, her frantic shimmying positively blew off the blanket, and she stood there in such a state of vibration the smoke roiled around her. Planting her feet apart, raising her arms, she squatted a bit to imply smutty things, with feathers for pasties, a scalp for a G-string.

"You mean you've been *de*creasing the doses? No wonder it don't work. You run up your debts and run down my dope."

"It's out of my hands. We can't afford it."

"Who's we? It's my money, Ernie. *I* can afford it. I got enough."

"Where?"

"Oh sure. Like to get your hands on it, nest pah? You make me sick. I got you pegged. It's money you want, go home to mamma. Go bury your face to the neck in her titties, I know your kind." She was running down South Clark, full of the Old Nick.

"Silver!"

"Get lost . . ." Morphinists could summon up tanks of high octane and burn through it pronto, then run empty on the fumes for hours and hours, she'd done it before. Just like the Slide for Life by her teeth. . . . Sooner or later she'd crash, of course, vomit her guts, get the shakes and dry chills. Soul wrapped in wet sheets. Lips dry as frayed ropes. She hailed a taxi before he could catch up, glancing back quickly. He stood there forlorn under a street lamp outside a dry cleaners. . . .

"Twenty-second and Wentworth."

This wasn't a good idea, not really. She had to sit still, and couldn't help sinking, like punched dough deflating. Many Silver Dollars rained from her shoulders, dropped to the seat. "Let me out here."

"It's only Eighteenth."

From the bank between her breasts she whipped out a dollar. On Eighteenth, she found the Chicago, Rock Island & Pacific tracks, and walked south through cinders. Dear Mamma, don't worry, things are just swell. How come you don't write. Send fifty dollars. My own darling fairies, I love you so much, send me a box of beautiful hankies, some little eating dishes, a dozen tiny spoons, some candy, a book that tells all about the heavens, a little pair of sharp-pointed scissors . . . some candy . . . fairy silk thread . . . a beautiful pair of glass ball-slippers. . . .

She stopped to light a smoke. Some sort of high-pitched squeal filled the air. Warehouses, weeds, a night pall over everything. It seemed that she managed to stumble in the dark despite having stopped walking. The match echoed inside her mind before she struck it. For a change it wasn't windy, but her back humped anyway, of its own accord. A small flat explosion, a convex circle of crown-shaped sparks, already debris, then one tongue of flame whipping out, sucked back. Then slowly uncurling, testing its tumescence. Morbid and slow and teasing and bright. A gurgling noise came out of her throat. Something bothered her tongue, a speck of debris she couldn't scrape off, not with her teeth nor with her nails. . . .

She lit the cigarette and deeply inhaled. Every speck of Chicago passed through her lungs.

This was not good. The sinking sensation had found her again, like a wandering pit. At a break in a board fence, she crossed a weedy lot tripping over shapes—corpses—of dogs, of horses, goats, cats, people. . . . This was where the mammals came to die and pile up their bones, like they said about elephants. Someone had started a fire in an icebox. The squeal filled the air, getting louder.

Twenty-first Street. She felt faint, but followed the noise down an alley, then up another street. More like a very high whistle or buzz. The closer she got the stronger she felt, but the strength was defective, strength of a puppet with nerves made of horse hairs. Brick buildings gave way to colored flags and pagoda balconies, spicy smells, shops selling fireworks. She found a narrow street and turned up an alley, every cell in her flesh too parched to scream. This is not exactly bliss, Honeymaid. I'd like to scrape that whistling sound from my eardrums with a sharp ice pick, I don't like it a nickel.

Go ahead. Be my guest.

With shaking hands, she fumbled in her soft bank, trying to locate a five she'd been saving for this moment, five lovely dollars. At the alley's dead end, a weak shaded light painted a door. The top third of the door was a glass window exposing a Chinese man's lumpish face and chest. Such a large face, so yellow and thick, so alert, so . . . asleep. Anyway, his eyes were closed. He sat there in a closet.

She thrust the fist grasping the five into a hole below the window. Gently, he tugged. The money released. With a sigh of relief she watched him load the syringe from a vial with a stoppered top. That's the ticket, good, all the way to the bottom. She closed her eyes, hunched, felt the sting on her arm, then for a cavernous moment waited. The world held its breath.

Well-being spread through her, dressing all her wounds. It plugged every one of her tormenting leaks. By the time she'd straightened up and withdrawn her arm, the noise had stopped, the night air cooled, the world thrown itself back together again.

• • •

John Vernon

"Jesus! Fucking's the best thing in the world, ain't it, Ralph?"

"It sure is."

"Do you like it?"

"It's swell."

"Make me come!"

"I'm working on it."

"What the queen said to the king, you know that one? 'So peasants call this fucking? It's too good for them.' "

"Ha ha."

"Do you like it?"

"I like it fine. Shut up."

She woke up when he smacked her. "What'd you do that for?"

"You fell asleep." He grabbed her wrist and dragged her out of bed. "Have a drink with me." He was dressed in his underwear, she in her pink brassiere and skirt slip. The room was quite warm for late March. Her stockings hung from wires nailed on the wall. On one wall was a framed chromo of a cowboy, on another the Sacred Heart of Jesus. Beside the bed stood an upended crate with a pretty lace doily on top, and on top of that a plate boiling over with cigarette butts.

The kitchen was the other end of the room. Really, the place was too hot for a fire, but he'd started one in the stove. On top, a large kettle of water steamed. "What's that for?" she asked.

"In case you wanna take a bath. You stink."

"Go to hell."

She sat at the table strewn with last week's newspapers, matches, playing cards, cheap silverware. A pan held greasy water and a sausage, left there from yesterday. Silver wasn't hungry. Ralph poured them each two fingers of whiskey, then stood with his hand over her glass. "Here, you drink this one." Somehow his skivvies made his ears stick out, or so thought Silver. His shoulders sprouted black hairs. His sluggish lips pursed and he sipped his own whiskey, pushing hers across the table.

"Put some water in it."

"You don't need water."

"It's bullfrog booze. You take a sip, hop a little, then you croak."

"Ha ha, that's a good one."

She hummed a tune, happy not to feel anything, not even happiness. Her face stung a little. Through the bare window nailed shut beside her bed, Ellis Avenue shouted and honked.

"What's that you're humming?" he asked.

" 'In a Dream I Loved You.' " Watching him standing there, she tipped her glass, extended her tongue with her mouth wide open, and worming the tip around, tested the whiskey. She shrugged and swallowed. "I wrote it."

"You look terrible."

"Thanks."

"Where's your boyfriend?"

"Home with mamma."

"I thought you told me he was rich."

"He is."

"Then how come you live in a dump like this?"

Silver shrugged. "Good question."

He poured her more whiskey. "You told me you'd carry him."

"I did. I will."

"What you make won't even cover his vigorish. You encouraged him to borrow, encourage him to pay."

"Me? You encouraged him."

"Are you listening to me? Did you tell me you'd carry him?"

"You just want to tap into his daddy's bank account."

"Encourage him to pay. I urge you to do so."

"Encourage him yourself." Silver stood up, holding onto the table. She felt him watching her. A towel hung from a nail on the wall, but the effort to wipe her hands on the filthy thing seemed enormous. Her hands had fisted, God knows why. They felt like stones. She felt herself aging, hung on her bones. She stared at the wallpaper, unable to decide what it represented. Yellow jellyfish rising through water stains and spattered coffee. . . .

Rumble and snap on the cast-iron stove. "Your water's boiling," she said. "I'm gonna open the window."

"It's nailed shut, dumbo." The room was so hot! She staggered to the bed. What a harum-scarum Ralph Capone was. He'd violated her soul, they all had. She was pregnant with sin, with its sticky effluvium, and soon, through the festering rip where body and soul intersected, where sin repeatedly thrust itself in, she'd give birth to a . . . dead frog resembling Ralph. She laughed out loud and sank onto the bed. A wave of fear passed over her body. . . .

From the wainscotted stairs Ernie heard the first scream, and ran up shouting her name, *Silver!* Her weak second scream broke into shivers of moaning disgust, utter loathing and dread and abomination, a raw animal sound spewing fitfully from her innards. Seventy years later he still heard that sound. He heard it in his dreams. In old age he still asked himself the same thing he asked then: Ernie, are you ready for this? Something real, something true, something perfectly horrible. . . .

The flat was full of steam. Beside the stove in his underwear, Ralph looked ridiculous. Steam rose from the bed and from puddles on the floor. At the foot of the bed, Silver's trunk was open and clothes crazily pulled out. A pair of red shoes steamed on the wet sheets. She knelt beside the bed trying futilely to climb back up. In her brassiere and slip she looked red as a lobster. As she tried to climb onto the bed she slid down, but the parboiled skin of her arms was still wet and stuck to the wet sheets and pulled, turning white. Sliding down, she pivoted, having heard someone come in. She looked in his direction with eyes pink and limp, smeared in their sockets. She couldn't see anything, Ernie could tell. Her upper lip was pulled back against her teeth, and she made that ghastly sound. He started toward the bed.

Ralph stepped in front of him, hand up. "Let's talk."

Her funeral was held in a room called a chapel, not long before a junk shop. The priest led a hymn:

Though your sins be as scarlet,
  They shall be white as snow,
Though they be crimson,
  They shall be as wool.

Newspaper reporters found Lily in Wisconsin. "I haven't seen my sister in years. I never approved of her. She's no more to me than a dead woman in Chicago. Why should I, who have pride and position, and like only quiet and nice things, have to embrace her in this kind of death?"

The police shipped Silver's trunk to Leadville, where Baby Doe claimed it. She insisted her daughter was still alive, she was just getting rid of her earthly possessions in preparation for taking her vows. "That woman in the papers isn't my Silver Dollar," she told the reporters. "Silver's in a convent. I had a letter from her just last week."

8. Leadville 1935

Empty road. Cold. Walls of dust fine as talc blown down from the mountains. Arkansas River just a large stream here. Dirt road, river, brown rangeland and forests rising to the west, crushed by massive white mountains, the Sawatch Range. To the east: foothills puddled with snow, blue sky turning black along the horizon. Ripped horizon blown in shreds across the sky, transparent and black. On a day like this, the radiant depthless enormous blue sky dragged shadows through squints of the human specks below. The sound of the wind wasn't misery hung with chains and howling, no, though this was the depth of the Great Depression. It was more like sound's absence, stranded power, great pipes of air filled with static pressure unable to explode. Only when you splayed your fingers over your head could you hear the wind moan.

She tried it, held up her hand. . . . Alone on the road, walking north toward Leadville, she wore a sort of tent buttoned up the front, too thin for the season; the cold needled through it. But she was big: six two, one ninety. She walked like a farmer, neither fast nor slow, as though all destinations were circumscribed already. Yet here she was on the top of the world! Black hair flared out beneath her watch cap. Hard to tell if the darkness of her skin was due to dirt or complexion. Small face, big mouth, large brown eyes. Large hips. Young. Everything she owned in the world was contained in a gunnysack hanging from one pudgy hand, seven-tenths of it blanket. She'd slept in an empty schoolhouse last night, wrapped in the blanket, cold as ice . . . but slept.

The high thin cold air, empty and wide, sucked an extra giddy bounce from her step. Late winter sun tongued the back of her neck. Not a single car had passed her that morning. She walked on the west side to minimize road dust whipped up by gusts. Both of her shoes had worn completely through, but she walked neither flinching nor breaking stride, the soles of her feet being thick as leather.

The town called Granite consisted of frozen mud, a filling station, some trailers. Gas pumps the shape of upside-down thermometers. She asked the man inside if he knew anyone going north into Leadville. As they were talking, a Packard pulled up. The attendant went out and spoke with the driver, then waved her outside.

It was colder to ride than to walk, but quicker. The driver wore a huge fur coat. "Whereabouts in Leadville?"

She shrugged.

He let her off on Harrison Ave., the town's only paved street. The place seemed empty. Two men stood in an alley on either side of a smoking oil drum. Nine or ten cars were parked at a slant to a WPA sidewalk of poured cement. She heard a click and glanced overhead to see a traffic light hung on a wire between two poles change from red to green, then the Packard drove off.

"Little boy!"

A boy on the sidewalk walked over.

"Tell me the way to Mrs. Tabor's."

"I can take you as far as the road to her place."

"I don't have any money."

"That don't matter." He took her free hand, and together they walked down Harrison Ave. toward East Seventh Street. Half of the stores and saloons were boarded up. The frame buildings needed paint, the brick ones were filthy. Every window was thick with grime. Through one, she spotted herself and her guide pass in a mirror behind two barber chairs, then a dog barked somewhere out on the street and a cigarette truck honked, and the driver waved.

She walked by herself up East Seventh. Frozen mud and brown weeds. One house was shingled with shakes of wood stenciled, "For

Fire Use Only." Beyond the railroad tracks, abandoned headframes stood amid hills of yellow waste. Rusted tracks crossed viaducts of slag and tailings leading nowhere. Below, rusted oil drums, rusted roofs and fences, looked dumped there haphazardly. Buildings were mouse brown, earth grey and yellow. The smokestacks still standing poured out nothing into nowhere. Old mine shafts everywhere. Timbered holes that once yielded silver had become dumps, with a spume of rags and shoes, busted-up furniture, tin cans, chopped crates, stumps of shovels and picks overflowing their mouths.

Ahead walked a man carrying two pails of water on a pole across his shoulders. He wore brown wool long johns over lumpy layers she guessed were newspaper. When he heard her coming up, he stopped and turned. "Which cabin is Mrs. Tabor's?" she asked.

"Mrs. Who?" He stood there watching her, hung from the pole, in the posture of crucifixion. "Do me a favor, Missy."

"What?"

"Scratch my nose."

"Whereabouts?"

"On the left side, there. No, lower down. You got nice long nails."

She scratched it gently. It resembled a big toe. Dirty and raw, his whole face squinted looking up at her. She thought he might sneeze on her bosom. His rheumy eyes smiled.

"Don't Mrs. Tabor live up here?"

"You any kin to her?"

"No."

"What's your business?"

"No business to speak of. I read about her and thought I'd come see her. She sounded like she might need a friend."

He looked her up and down. "Well, sometimes she's funny. She's a good shot too. She don't see many people, tell you the truth. I'm bringing her this water. Guess you can come."

Together, they walked up the hill to the Matchless. Before he could protest, she'd relieved him of the pole and placed it across her own shoulders. Not a drop of water spilled. She was taller than him by nearly a foot. Her gunnysack, pinned by the pole, resembled a goiter slung back across her shoulder. The pails were smaller now. She started to sing. Her pace didn't slow, it picked up, and he had to jog-trot to match it.

"What's your name?"

"Sue Bonnie."

"Where you from?"

"Everywhere. I'm a hobo."

She sang "Sometimes I'm Happy." The road snaked up between heaves of earth. Leadville had sunk out of sight behind them, leaving just sky and mountains across the Arkansas Valley. They took a road left past a Keep Out sign. A shack with a tin roof and lean-to on one end came into view beyond a clearing. Drifts of unmelted snow banked ridges of waste. On the slope behind the shack stood a large barnlike building from which cables emerged leading to a headframe. More shacks and headframes in the distance. Nothing grew on the earth. A good half mile away young pines rimmed this wasteland, having appeared since the demand for timbering mines had ended years back. Beyond them, forests climbed the sloping mountains toward Arkansas Pass.

"Smoke in the stovepipe. She's home," said Sue.

"Most always is home." They dumped the water in a barrel inside the lean-to. Sue heard scuffles from the shack. This lean-to protected the entrance from the weather; the water-man knocked. "Mrs. Tabor, it's me, Albin. Here's your water."

An aeroplane slowly droned by overhead.

"Here's a girl with me tired and cold who come here to see you from God knows where. Won't you please let her in and give her something to eat?"

"Mrs. Tabor's downtown," said a voice.

"Aw, Mrs. Tabor, she's tired and she's cold."

"Mrs. Tabor is not home, go away."

John Vernon

"Then who am I talking to anymore?"

"The night watchman."

Albin's lips fizzled. Sue backed out and looked at the cabin. Two small windows just under the roofline were covered with newspapers from the inside. Unpainted, the weathered boards' grain had gullied and turned black in streaks running down the thin ridges. Albin emerged from the lean-to holding out the August page of a 1933 John Hancock calendar. "My payment." Sue took it. They walked toward the road. "She leaves it for me beneath an old flowerpot." Sue looked at the page. "Turn it over."

Share Warrants to Bearer, it said in pencil. *Two (2) Shares in Matchless Mine. Leadville, Colorado, 1935.*

She handed it back. He smashed it up and stuffed it in his pocket. Walking downhill, she watched massive mountains across the valley sinking like ships with each step she took. Within the next hour the sun would set, and already the air had begun turning colder. She pictured the cold air flowing from mine shafts, flooding the hillside, then realized she was crying. "There, there," said Albin. "I know someplace you can stay."

With the sound of the knock a light popped behind her eyes, filled her skull, contracted. Eye-flaps still shut, she followed it down. . . . A thief with candle descending a mine shaft, a fizzled-out bird flying back into its egg. . . .

"Mrs. Tabor, my name's Sue Bonnie. I come all the way from Kansas to see you."

That's not so far. . . . Baby's eyes flew open. Ripped paper on the ceiling, morning light, something scratching in the roof. It seemed she attracted crazy people and pack rats. I'm sleep. Gone out shopping.

"Won't you let me in?"

"I'm taking a bath."

"I just want to meet you. I thought we could talk."

"Come back some other time. I am taking a bath." Baby Doe sucked in her breath and waited. Must be a little bird, hardly made any noise. Go back to Kansas, little chick. Get some corn shucks for my mattress. "Come back tomorrow."

"What time?"

"Come for tea."

"What time is that?"

Teatime, you ninny. I'll hide in the shaft house, climb down the mine shaft.... But since George Schmidt froze to death last year in the shaft house, Baby Doe hadn't stepped inside it, except to throw out all his rubbish, including the cage with his dead canary. It still made a pile outside near the headframe. She could take the things one by one this summer and toss them down the Little Pittsburg or the Giddy Betsy, they'd begun to cave in. Those mines in which scoundrels hadn't built stills made pretty good trash dumps, but, God forbid, not the Matchless. The Matchless was like a dead man's pockets full of hidden riches. She'd dreamed of the sixth level just last night. "Where's my pencil?"

"Mrs. Tabor?"

"Go away, damn it!"

Heavy rocks glued to the bones of her back.... What a curse to grow old, to pool up with blood.... She rolled out of bed and ascended to her feet with both hands on her thighs, then her knees, then up, as though climbing a ladder. Shuffling steps to the oilcloth table. Tea bags, pie plates, old photos, newspapers, empty tin cans, last year's calendar, a blizzard of paper. Pencil!

On the back of July she wrote, *April 3*.

> *I saw in a dream myself down the no. 6 shaft in drift 244 level & saw the most wonderful strike of rich lead ore & another close by of rich zinc ore small piece of rich galena ore out of no. 6 shaft in my hands*

Someone could just drift a little farther north on the fifth level, or sink a winze through to that stope on the fourth, if the thieves and claim jumpers didn't get there first. Spies from the banks, Wall Street leeches. . . .

"All right, then. I'll come back tomorrow."

Baby Doe scowled. At the corner window, she lifted the newspaper. . . . Jumped back as though stung. A round moony face flecked with dirt trying to grin. . . . It looked startled too! Hardly a bird. She was tall, with large shoulders and muscular arms, the Beef Trust type. May Howard, but taller. Looking right at her, just two feet away! The impudent Amazonian waved her stubby fingers!

She lowered the newspaper.

Heavy tread outside, like something pacing a cage. At last the footsteps waned. Baby lifted the newspaper. She was larger than most men, and walked like a lumberjack. Generous strides. Strong and young.

Long after Sue had disappeared Baby Doe continued staring out the window, having torn down the paper. Spring in Leadville meant the worst storms, and dark clouds had climbed the hill to her shack, ripped themselves open, shaken out their snow. It blew sideways and up, everywhere but down. Where her unknown visitor had rounded a corner, an old tire clung to the side of a hill, sprinkled with new snow. Old snow inside it. She'd never noticed it before. Had she thrown it there, or one of her laborers, years ago perhaps? It was quite far away, yet each minor detail—worn treads, bald patches, shags of ice inside —looked every bit as clear as the palm of her hand. Shredded rubber boiling out. Against the backdrop of a further hill and a bush with lower branches chewed by some mammal, she could trace the skeletal threads of a membrane, the webby lines linking far and near . . . the secret stitches. Messages sewn in the hem of a garment, prayers tattooed inside her pupils. . . . Shadows raced up, the sun broke through clouds. She made out a wet shape, coils of black and grey. A black dragon tied down, writhing in agony. He was tied around the middle and groaning horribly, and the action of kneading the earth with his claws rippled his back and tail in undulations. Meanwhile, a little old man with bald head—the one who'd tied him—kicked at some leaves and bushes behind and found clusters of strawberries. He looked at her window, stuffing his mouth. . . .

She turned and fished beneath the bed for her rosaries.

"I've been everywhere hoboing, through every single jerkwater town you could name, Mrs. Moberg."

"Call me Mary."

"I traveled the freights in the boxcars, on the bumpers, the rods, in the engine, and out on the cowcatchers."

"Ain't that cold?"

"I cured my consumption by riding a cowcatcher mouth wide open. I rode the Pullmans by telling the conductor sob stories of how I'd lost my ticket, or by hiding in the toilets or riding the blinds or decking it on top. On top you got to lie flat on your stomach and brace yourself with one hand over the side with the ventilator shutters between your legs so's you don't get blowed off."

"Now I've heard everything."

"I've hitchhiked everywhere too. The only time I wear a skirt is hitchhiking."

"When I was a child we used to sing, 'Hobo, hobo, where have you been?' What I want to know is, where did you start from? You had to start from someplace."

Everything dripped. The kettle on the stove gave off steam, so did the tub on the long kitchen table, in which Mary scrubbed the clothes with a washboard. Even the wringer cranked by Sue squeezed out steam. One by one, wrung shirts plopped to the oilcloth. Sue checked the water on the stove. "This needs more lye."

Mary eyeballed her, then stood up and studied the boiling water. "It

could use a tad more." With a paring knife, she cut shavings from the cake and threw them in the kettle, then quick-wrapped the soap in a little hanky and dropped it in her apron as though guarding family jewels. It was her mother's recipe: waste fat, ammonia, water, lye, borax, and sassafras oil.

Soon the minerals broke and the water grew soft. She dipped off the mineral scum with a ladle, then Sue dumped wrung shirts in the boiling water. "What's this for?" She held up a shirt with a knotted string tied on to its tail.

Mary beamed. "That's how I tell who belongs to what. See, in my book, everyone has a number. Let's say, Mr. Ackerson? He's number seven, so I tie a string to the tail of his shirt with seven knots."

"Nifty."

One piece of linoleum lay on the pine floor, buckled and cracked. Strangers had to be careful not to trip on its edges. Rags had been poked into cracks around the windows, whose panels were so steamed you couldn't see the ore dumps and tipples outside . . . the abandoned boxcars. An advantage of the steam was it kept down the soot from the woodstove. Soot vexed Mary. Pots and pans inside a warmer on the back of the stove were always coated with soot, nothing she could do. Behind, the stove pipe ran up and angled out the back wall, held in place by black wires. Streaks of rust ran down sections.

"I grew up in an orphanage."

"You poor thing."

"It don't matter, Mrs——. I don't think of myself as any way misfortunate. Nothing's bad or good but what you make of it. Things just happen and you got to accept them. I was taken by a doctor to a rooming house in Chicago, which was a combination of hobo college and hobohemia? Poets and spittoon philosophers and anarchists, plus dozens of children, no one knew whose. Grace before meals was a poem by Walt Whitman. We had noted professors and sociologists give talks, and poets said their poems and singers sang. Mary McCormic sang for us once and gave the super fifty dollars and sent him out to buy food and whiskey for the bunch. The King of the Hobos came and talked about the open road. I found out later there were lots of Kings of the Hobos, point of fact, also one or two Queens. I've met ten separate men who claimed to be King, including Jeff Davis. I've met them all."

"Aren't they all thieves and drunkards?"

"Not your true 'bo. Your hobo is somebody looking for work, but since there ain't any where they are, why they got to travel to find it. Your tramps, on the other hand, they're out for excitement. They're the unattached penniless adventurers, Mary. Bums are vagrants on booze and dope who don't care to work. Me, I like to work."

"Thank God for that."

"I worked on a farm in North Dakota. I been a nurse, a waitress, a typist, a beet picker. I washed clothes for timber gangs in Washington state and that's why I'm telling you, leave this to me. I know how to do it."

Mary blinked a lot, and felt small next to Sue. Well, she *was* small. Her big nose was square, and for washing she always put her hair up, but the steam collapsed it, so she put it up again. She was proud of her blond hair.

Her husband worked at the Climax Mine ten miles from Leadville, smelting molysulfide to be shipped to the Midwest. Automakers had learned about moly steel by observing the reluctance of tanks to be blown up during the Great War, and now the Climax was the only mine giving steady employment. No one wanted silver. Silver was down to 23.5 cents an ounce, the lowest price ever.

The night Albin brought Sue to the door and Mary reluctantly agreed to let her stay, Deke Moberg came home and slapped Sue's back and said she could board there as long as she wanted. She'd have to help his wife, of course. At first, that fueled Mary's aggravation; boarding folks wasn't too bad, but having them in your hair all day could crab things up pretty quickly. As it turned out, Sue did wear well, she felt that now. She was easy to talk to. For such a big woman, her voice was gentle and quiet, like a child's.

"Trouble is, I ain't happy till I'm on the road. I get hungry to see things. That's why I come here."

"Why?" Mary stirred the boiling clothes with a paddle. All it took was a nod, and Sue was holding the first rinsing tub up high by its handles. "Put it on the stove."

"I can hold it up."

"Oh, you . . ." With the paddle, she fished out the shirts and dumped them in the tub. It took a few minutes, but Sue never flagged. When all had been transferred, she set it on the table.

"Why is I read about Mrs. Tabor in the *Sunday Gazette*. They told how she was poor that once was so rich that her girls wore cambric diapers pinned up by gold pins garnished with diamonds. They said how she lived in a shack outside Leadville near the Matchless Mine which her late husband told her on his deathbed to cling to thirty-five years ago."

"Well, that's what she done."

"I thought I'd like to see her. She sounded like an awfully interesting woman. She used to wear ermine furs and the Isabella Pearls."

"She wears burlap now."

"I thought I could help her. Maybe she had some work I could do. We might like each other, I thought. I never knew my mother. People used to tell me stories. The article about Mrs. Tabor suggested she once was a fallen woman?"

"She never talks about the past."

"Why not?"

Mary shrugged. "She don't like to, I guess. A few years ago they made a motion picture about her life, but she never went to see it."

"A motion picture!"

"Everyone else but her went to see it."

"Was she bad? Did they make her sound bad?"

"Not very much. But Bebe Daniels don't look anything like her, that's what everyone said."

"The article I read made her sound good. She stayed faithful to her husband, even after they went broke. Anyway, I never held with that truck about certain things is more shameful than others. Like I said, nothing's bad except you make it so. I was sewing clothes in Kansas City for a dollar a week and rent and food relief."

"Well, I can do you better than that."

"And getting here was easy as flipping a freight. No schedules, no regular meals or sleep. . . ."

Someone halloed from the back porch and knocked. It sounded like a stick whacking the wall. Mary wiped her hands on her apron and pushed through the door. She was gone a few minutes. When Sue at last squeegeed some steam off a window with the side of her hand and looked out back, a little old woman dressed in black with a cap tied on by a scarf was walking off. She walked with the effort not to betray uncertain footing, but couldn't help careening now and then. Her feet were wrapped in burlap.

Mary came back with some droopy little snowdrops dying in her fist. "These are for you. She picked them herself. She wants you to go up and visit sometime."

"I've been up to see her three times already! She wouldn't let me in."

"Well, she said she would next time."

A bird come & clung to my screen calling me Oh God save the soul of one who is dying   I pray it is not one of my children

A spirit rubbing gently & soothingly my feet
At about the same time felt a large lump rising up inside of me from under my heart to the top of my neck on my left side   the dear hands rubbing my feet felt so soft & comforting & soothing

All at once I grew older & wondered at my own gravity—
tried to throw it off

Blessed Jesus saved me from the most horrible death by burn-
ing & electricity.   On the table close to its edge stood the electric
plate heavy made of iron & small on top of it stood my can of
boiling hot coffee   I stood on a rocking chair & reached to fix
electric cords & the devil only he toppled the chair so that it
threw me bending close over the boiling coffee & the red hot plate
had I fallen on it I would have been burnt & scalded to death
for had that red hot stove fallen on my heart I would have
fainted instantly & been burnt to death at once   then my body
falling would have pulled the live wires of electricity on me but
Jesus the only Power held me suspended above this red hot &
boiling mass & the chair shaking & instantly God had me
thrown over the back of the chair & away from the table

Baby Doe fished the bag from Sue's tea, then handed her the cup.
She dropped the bag in her own. "My brother sends me enough to get
by on. He's a well-to-do businessman. My sisters are all dead."

"At Home Colony some woman give me a picture there she claimed
was her and me, and she was my sister, named Enid." Sue sipped her
tea. "I'm sure I got blood kin still in this world, but God knows where.
She was no sister, she was a hustler. A bum."

"We're all bums, Sue. We've wasted our lives."

"Well, *I* ain't a bum. I might have chewed a cigar butt or two, but I
never lost control on my destiny. The difference between a bum and a
hobo is hobos are not a bunch of dumb ignoramuses. That's the truth.
You certainly are not a bum, Mrs. Tabor. You may be poor, but that's
no cause for shame. I've seen plenty of elegant women, but you take
the cake."

"Thank you."

"It's your smile. And the way you talk."

"It's my teeth. I still have my teeth."

"You've been blessed by God to live to an old age and have lovely memories."

Baby Doe smiled. Her sunken eyes looked perpetually worried, but the flesh around her mouth still clung to the muscles she'd had as a girl, still struck the same pose. Her teeth had parted to augment the smile, and Sue noticed her tongue silently clucking. "You don't know what tragedy I've seen."

"We all have our crosses."

"Most of the people I ever loved are dead. I should be too."

"You'll live to be a hundred."

"Time doesn't pass. It just piles up."

"What I can't figure is where it flies off to."

"It's no fun growing old."

"But look at the alternative."

"Sometimes I think my mind is going."

"Your mind's like a pail of water, I've found. Tip your head and it still stays level. Maybe I'm cursed with a level mind."

"Tip it *too* much and it spills," Baby said. She cocked her head and bit her tongue. Sue laughed. "You should count your blessings, Sue. Sound mind, sound body. How old are you?"

"Twenty-eight."

"You look healthy as a horse."

"One time I had the galloping consumption."

"You sure don't look it."

"It galloped right through me."

"I do get awfully cold, I'll say that. I haven't been warm for a long, long time."

"Who chops your firewood?"

"I chop it myself."

"You ought to let me do it. I have power in my arms. You have beauty in yours."

"Go on." Baby waved a limp hand and turned away smiling. The chair seemed to bend and turn with her. Its rockers had been tied up with twine. The ceiling was covered with butcher paper and the walls with pages of the *Rocky Mountain News.* On one wall hung a picture of the Virgin Mary outlined in tin from Ray-O-Vac batteries, with ferns and palms splayed out behind it. Across the room stood Baby Doe's iron cot, piled high with clothes—for blankets, Sue assumed. A woodstove poured out heat, too much for this spring day. In a corner sat a two-burner oil stove covered with grease, and close beside it uneasily leaned a stack of old newspapers and other rubbish . . . too close, Sue thought.

From the table beside them the striped cord of the hot plate ran up to a socket into which a plug was screwed. Piles of books, papers, tin plates, and other trash surrounded the hot plate. The papers held pencil scrawls, some looping around newspaper columns or calendar dates, for these were scraps of anything at hand, old envelopes, invoices, labels from cans. Sue turned one over and read *El Monte Peaches* above yellow quarter moons in a dish. She turned it back. *She fell on the floor and screamed in rage and acted terrible & scalded my foot through the mercy of God.* . . . "What's these?"

"My dreams. Things I see. How Jesus saved me."

"He saved you all these times?"

"Ramblings of a lonely woman. Jesus does not always prominently figure. But he is the ghost in every engine, the wheel within wheels. He protects old women like me from the fire and he rescues us from floods."

"Jeez." One of Baby Doe's eyes seemed to be vibrating. Their shade of blue was lovely, Sue thought, and the vibrating one looked puzzled and searching, but the other looked dead. The leather flight cap on her head was vintage Charles Lindbergh. A moth-eaten sweater with half the buttons missing forked at her hips, over layers and folds of black shirts and dresses, a palimpsest of stains. Sue knew from dirty clothes, having slept in hers all her life. "I could wash out some of those clothes for you," she said, nodding at the bed. "I'm helping Mary Moberg."

Baby Doe turned away. She picked something off her skirt and pulled her sweater tight across her bosom. "Thank you, that won't be necessary."

"It's no trouble at all."

She stood and dragged her chair closer to the stove, even though the room was hot. Rocking, she watched Sue. Between the stove and the sun beating on the tin roof, Sue guessed it was well over ninety inside.

"We could go outside and sit in the sun."

Baby looked at Sue as though a perfect stranger had materialized in her shack. This place was the size of a boxcar, Sue realized, having ridden plenty of boxcars with strangers. She'd crossed the West from Tucson to L.A. and back countless times not exchanging one word with 'boes crouched in corners expecting someone to pounce. In a shack like this you were inside someone's mind like a foreign word whispered through a door. Baby Doe seemed to be guarding the mess. She glowered from the stove. The room seemed to darken.

"Mrs. Tabor!" Someone knocked on the door.

Baby Doe stood, buttoning vanished buttons on her sweater. The walls shrunk with each knock. She looked around, puzzled. "Go away. She's not home."

"Mrs. Tabor, it's Tim Riley and Bill Durning."

"She's not home. She went downtown." Baby spotted Sue and waved her close, one finger on her lips. She whispered, "You go outside and tell them I'm not home, say I've gone away. Go ahead, quick."

"Who are they?"

"Just another nuisance. Go on."

She was squeezing Sue's elbow. Sue looked down. The old woman

smelled bad this close, but she was used to that. She couldn't help patting Baby Doe's head, then walked to the door. "You leave it to me." As she slipped outside, the door locked behind her.

The bright sun made her squint and sneeze. The two men had backed out of the lean-to and stood there watching Sue. It appeared that her size made them uneasy. They wore miner's clothes: canvas shirts, overalls, short-billed caps, laced-up boots. "Mrs. Tabor ain't home," she said.

"Sorry, ma'am. We'll come back some other time." They trudged off a few steps and one turned around. "We thought that was her voice."

"Think again."

"Tell her we just want to be paid."

"I'll give her the message."

Sue left Mary Moberg's house and took the road uphill with long hungry strokes of her powerful legs. The glorious light even recommended mud, with its miniature palaces and minarets. Wild irises had resurrected in the ditches. Delve! Mould! Pile the words of the earth!

She turned at the road to Baby's shack, propelled by the sun and its single muscle. This time when she knocked there was no answer. "Mrs. Tabor, open up, it's Sue." Silence.

"Sue, is that you?" Her shaky voice came from a distance. Sound of tools thrown into clattering piles behind the shack . . . shovels, or picks. Sue walked around the back and saw in the wasteland of dirt, rubbish, and stacks of boards, Baby in miner's clothes reaching for the crank on a windlass across an open shaft. Her arms folded up and her birdcage chest flung itself against the crank. It didn't budge.

In the past few weeks, the ground here had thawed, turned to mud, then dried in the sun as hard as concrete. Black rocks lay on the dead-white dirt. Sue marched up and stamped to a halt with pudgy fists balled on her hips. "What the hell are you doing?"

Baby straightened up and wiped her brow. The collar around this shaft looked fairly new, the windlass too. "Trying to haul up the bucket."

"You shouldn't ought to do such things at your age."

"Pshaw." She grinned broadly, the painful and mannish smile of a queen. She wore a man's khaki shirt, baggy trousers tied below the knees, brogans caked with dried mud, coarse stockings so loose they hung over the ankles. On her head sat a motoring cap tied beneath her chin with a ragged scarf.

Picks, jacks, a sledgehammer, hatchets, axes, and shovels lay beside the hole. It was late afternoon, the time Sue always came. She was no dumb bohunk. She knew that Baby Doe had set this stage carefully, then swung into action when she showed up. She even knew her own line: "Let me try that for you." Baby backed off and stood there swaying. Pushing at the crank, Sue felt steel seizing steel. "You got any grease?"

"In the shaft house."

They crossed the mine yard littered with shafts, six open mouths. Trash outside the sagging shaft house glittered in the sunlight. Sue slid a barn door on rollers aside, and they entered a mausoleum of rusted boilers, stovepipe sections, tables, dirt, rocks, old coats, tools, lockers, tin cans. Corpses of shovels hung from the walls. Crushed hats, rubber suits, a smashed coal bin, ropes and cables, an iron cot with its nightmarish mattress arthritically twisted on busted springs. Everything here was bleached of color. "Is this where that man froze to death?" Sue asked.

Baby was already out the door, a grease gun in her hand. Sue couldn't help thinking she walked like a boy with a load in his pants, hardly flexing her legs. At the windlass, she handed the grease gun to Sue with a bandaged smile. Her face was all dewlaps, neck to eyes. Flaccid smears of skin. But such eyes, so lovely and still so full of hope! That's why Sue had liked her right away. She was optimistical. Despite her ravaged face, she looked like a child. Her horizontal smile seemed lacking in the strength to curl up at the ends so instead it just pulled back, baring the teeth.

When Sue had at last raised the bucket, she saw why it felt so damn heavy: the thing was full of ore. Together, they dumped it. Sue dripped with sweat. "Did you fill this bucket yourself, Mrs. Tabor?"

"Dear me, no. Some men I hired."

"Those that come to the door?"

"Them and some others."

"They said they never been paid."

"I paid them. I gave them shares in the mine. And look how they treat me! I caught them high-grading."

"What's that?"

"Stealing ore."

"Is there really ore to steal? These mines are played out."

"Take a look yourself." Baby picked up a chunk.

"It's just rock to me."

"Carbonate of lead! The poor man's gold!" She dropped the mud-colored rock on the pile. "I knew it."

"Knew what?"

"When Mr. Johnson gave up my business, gave my Lake County Warrants and Bonds to Mr. Shibbs ... About the middle of February ... the Wells Fargo Express Company books will show that I took them out that very day. I gave them as security for express charges to Shibbs."

"Shibbs? Slow down. You ain't making any sense."

"Every judge, every banker, every scheming moneybags in Colorado knows the value of the Matchless Mine. You can't say they don't. I've redeemed it more times than I can count, I saved it from the fire and flood. You don't know all the mortgages, all the suits and countersuits, the leases and encumbrances I've rescued it from. Just imagine, Sue, I shored up the tunnels, pumped out the upper levels, greased the machinery."

All for Love

"You did that yourself?"

"I'm coming to that . . . no, not exactly. I haven't been down there in . . . quite some time. I thought maybe you could lower me in the bucket. I asked myself, who do I know with strength in her arms?"

"And who do I know with beauty in hers?" Of course, Sue thought. She felt her smile rising like cream in a bottle, and followed the script as though they'd rehearsed it. "You can't go down in that mine, Mrs. Tabor. You'd pretty near kill yourself. Let me do it. Once the bucket's run down with the tools, I'll descend on the rungs. You can tell me what to do. Is it hard?"

"Not to figure out, no it's not. But it's awfully hard work."

"That's me. I like to work."

"Somebody broken the boiler monkey." Baby's eyes opened. Once the words left her lips she forgot what they meant. They sounded like cornsilk whipping guitar strings. The meanings of things often did that, cracked open and expired, she realized. They whispered their secrets so low no one heard, the wind through dead grass . . . dust faintly stirring in lost declivities. . . .

Light remembered the room. Another morning. Watching it happen, she threw off the covers, remarkably weightless, full of air . . . deboned. Crawled out of bed, opened the stove, raked out banked coals, loaded it with slabwood she'd split herself. It was May already . . . August . . . another century. All at once she stood at the window peering in. Spotted an old lady feeding a woodstove. She was free! Outside, she could hike to Alaska, start a new life, invest in property . . . in smelters, mines. . . .

Instead, she opened the door and walked in. Baby Doe looked up. "How did you get in?" She inspected the room, examined the junk. The old shoes, she saw, were for burning in the stove. She fished through the trunk Silver'd shipped back before entering the convent, full of outlandish clothes, boas, wigs, and copies of her book, *Star of Blood.* "Make yourself at home, Mrs. Nosy."

She read some of the scribblings scattered on the table.

I heard the spirit of Lily Langtry   Had a strange visitor, a lonely cow with big white heart on its brow between the two eyes Saw a dragon in my coffee cup

Up in the air 6 feet high 3 round balls of blue green & bluish green   all sparkling with an edge around each one of bright yellow above Matchless mine & they fairly danced like dancing jewels

Dreamed of a large amount of raw beefsteak very red my bowels moved twice & each time as much as a bushel of snakes came out of my bowels all in a large wriggling heap it was remarkable the messes of snake or snake worms that passed from my bowels big piles on the floor

She surveyed the room, frightened. These writings were concatenations, formulas. All at once she felt exhausted, and lowered her sagging flesh to the bed, trying not to plummet. One arm across her eyes, she sank like a stone. So warm in the room. Who'd filled it with purple? Purple fog near the ceiling. . . .

Palms of angels caressed her, smiles of children made her weep. Her lungs filled with dust. A face at the window whispered unwholesome things. Ugly hairs in her nose, rotting eyes, horror. . . . She came to the door, leaked into the room. Don't let her touch my flesh, Jesus Lord. Don't let her steal anything, I'll pray six novenas. . . .

"Mrs. Tabor!" Loud knocks.

"Go away, she's not home."

Rush of blood through her veins. Blood-light in the room, tied in knots behind the eyes.

All for Love

"It's a summons, Mrs. Tabor. You better open up. Tim Riley and them others, they sued you for their wages."

But I promised them every other royalty check and settlement sheet from the George W. Casey lease on the Matchless Mine, Sheriff, until said sum with interest is paid. . . . "She's taking a bath. Get off my property."

"Mrs. Tabor, it's the law, you gotta let us in."

Haw, you were right, they'll resort to anything. It's getting so nobody's safe in their homes. I could offer them our shares in the Honduras-Campbell Reduction Company, they're somewhere in the lard box under the table. "She went downtown."

Muffled voices at the door, rattle of the latch. She climbed out of bed, heavy with sin and congealed fatigue. Every missed opportunity in her life swelled her heart. They're murdering my soul, Haw. You died before I got the dripping heart, lucky for you. Dr. Zander said there was only a few cases in the world, I should tell the priest to get himself ready. That was ten years ago. . . . I've had flattering offers to donate my organs, though I'm steeped in grief. I was struck down suddenly one night in Leadville. . . .

"Mrs. Tabor. . . ."

She found a box of shells on the table. With sudden clarity and control, she reached for the shotgun standing in the corner. Broke it over her knee, inserted the shells, walked to the door, *schlanged* the gun shut. "Get off my property if you know what's good for you. . . ."

Silence outside. The stove at her back was a roaring inferno.

Sue'd never suspected a mine would feel clammy. The warm air was close and sluggish. The hard work made dust, and dust coated her sweat. She wore just an undershirt and overalls at first, but after a while took them off and worked in the buff save for boots and hat, since no one could see her. Her flop hat once had been Baby's, from the time Baby Doe mucked in mines in Central City. Stiffened with resin, it was hard as a helmet, and deflected small annoyances, for example chunks of ore.

She sang while she worked. "Sweet Georgia Brown," "After You've Gone," "Sometimes I'm Happy." She'd never had time in her twenty-eight years to be confused by life. Work gave it meaning. But even Sue got fatigued mucking in the Matchless, endlessly swinging picks and sledges. She learned to single jack, to blast out a face, muck the ore, load it, and sort it. At first, there were hazards she hadn't suspected. On the fifth level, where she pushed her cart, several crosscuts were paved, just like sidewalks. This struck her as strange. She tried one and plunged through cymbals of ice, for it wasn't concrete but a winze filled with water whose surface had filmed with rock dust, stupid, and no one had warned her it looked like concrete! It might have been refreshing if it weren't so cold, so instantly numbing. For such a big oaf Sue bobbed up at once and shot from the water roaring naked and laughing and smacking her forehead. One by one, she untied her boots and poured out the water, shivering on a stone, whose sharp edges bit her buttocks.

She quickly learned to test every surface. One carbide lamp illuminated plenty, but was flatter even than light from a full moon; it didn't glow or reflect. She prodded weak timbers before entering adits, never picked up abandoned explosives, turned back at once at the least whiff of gas, and avoided drifts whose roofs had caved in. Below the fifth level, everything was flooded. The pumps had stopped running long ago in Leadville, the mines on Fryer Hill were filling with water, and neither the unfinished Malta nor the abandoned Canterbury Tunnels were much help to unwater them. It was the fourth level, though, that Baby'd told her to work, that's where she'd dreamed the ore was so rich that like ripened fruit it would drop of its own weight into your cart.

Hardly. It had to be encouraged. A lode stoped out here had been sheathed up and down with square-set timbers filling the cavities, rising like towers, stacked blocks of air—a skeletal cathedral inside the earth. Connecting the timbers were ladders and walkways, a maze which Sue had to gingerly learn the best routes through, avoiding rotten passages. She wandered back and forth on these Gothic monkey bars, selecting faces to blow out and rip down. The rock fell toward splintered chutes below, tearing out boards, filling every square inch of the air above with dust. She coughed, sweating, naked . . . singing in the uproar. "No gal made has got a shade on Sweet Georgia Brown. . . ."

Mornings, she helped Mary Moberg with the washing. Encouraged by Sue, Mary'd cut her prices, increased her volume, and in no time at all had doubled her profits. Really, Sue did most of the work. She'd even memorized the merchandise and dispensed with knotted strings, always careful to note new shirts and linen and file them in her brain.

In Mary's steaming kitchen, they threw sweet corn in the kettle once the laundry was finished, and ate corn on the cob, cold baked potatoes, and coffee soup: cowboy coffee poured over thick slices of bread Sue'd baked herself.

Afternoons, instead of teatime with Baby, she worked down the Matchless for two or three hours. Baby Doe set up a chair by the shaft head and, as Sue descended, shouted weakly down. We could sink a new winze right through that damn stope. . . . Sue, take a look at the 244 drift. . . . If the drift on the third level hadn't collapsed. . . .

Deep in the mine, Sue eviscerated the stope. When enough ore had clattered through the chutes, she descended the grillwork of timbers and rungs and shoveled the steaming ore through a winze to the fifth level below, having already positioned the cart underneath it. Not steaming, really. Powdery, dusty. But she'd worked in a stables in Oregon once, and this reminded her of it, this hauling off of waste from bowels never empty. She could tell by the sound when the cart was filled up. Back in the hoist shaft, she climbed down a level and followed the tracks to where the cart waited. Level five was the only one with tracks. She cleared away the spillage, stepped behind the cart, and pushed it toward the hoist shaft, sweating bullets. Here, she shoveled ore into the bucket; too much spilled if she tried to tip the

cart. She clothed herself and climbed up the shaft toward the molten eye of light where Baby waited, sometimes showing her face across the edge. "Get back, Mamma!" Sue had taken to calling Baby Mamma since Baby had said she was just like a daughter. At the shaft head, she hauled up the bucket and, together, she and Baby dumped it out.

All that summer and fall, the routine never varied. Standing in the bare mine yard in the sun, motoring cap tied on her head, Baby Doe helped with the final sorting, that is, she told Sue which was ore and which waste. Sometimes she fussily rescued a chunk from the waste pile herself, and lugged it to the ore pile. She couldn't throw the stuff, as Sue could.

Then Baby cooked them supper: corn griddle cakes, tomato soup, tea. Late summer was good for greens and wild tea, for watercress, wild onions, wild mustard, chamomile. After heavy rains, especially in August, Baby searched for puffballs, which she sliced thick as steaks and fried up in lard.

Once every few weeks, on Saturday mornings, Deke and Mary Moberg chugged up in his pickup, and together Sue and Deke filled it with ore. Baby waved them off to the smelter; leaving, they watched her in the mirror beaming ear to ear.

The roads were a bother with such a heavy load, and Deke couldn't take the ruts that slow downhill, since his brakes were bad. More often than not, once he'd floored the footbrake and ripped up the handbrake they still dragged forward. In town, they turned north toward Climax. Deke knew a place where someone had cut a rough logging road just before the first switchback up to Arkansas Pass. They bounced through the forest a hundred feet or so, enough not to be seen from the main road. Here they dumped their load, for of course the ore was worthless. Silver wouldn't fetch twenty-five cents an ounce, and every assay they'd run on this ore had come back at less than ten ounces to the ton. It would cost more to smelt than the silver was worth.

Then they drove home and Sue lay down and dropped off to sleep as though falling down a mine shaft.

All for Love

The next day, Sunday, Mary paid Sue for her laundry work: six dollars every two weeks. Sue brought it to Baby at teatime as payment for the ore they'd mined. Babe lamented the low price of silver and the lack of good help, excepting Sue of course. If the government started buying silver again, if a half-dozen miners as good as Sue could work alongside her.... They could run several shifts! Baby gave Sue two dollars, her share, and folded the rest and stuffed it in her bosom.

She sighed and wished out loud that she were strong enough to help. With such a horn of plenty in her own backyard.... Why, the Matchless was bottomless with wealth, Sue Bonnie!

Saw vision of a flying bug not solid all thin lips

The devil in the shape of a horrible ugly brownish weasel of little face tiny grey brown hand mouth opening & shutting as if he bit me

A medium sized man in kaki coat with long fishing pole stood in my door leaning against the side a long time

This morning I dreamed a little flower grew out of the palm of my hand left palm out of the brain & heart lines between the thumb and between the 1 & 2 fingers   it was a little pink flower with feathery green foliage about an inch in length it was strongly rooted in my hand & grew strong & fresh & healthy   I watched it growing in my palm & when I woke all day I felt that tingling sensation   Silver was dead in bed and the bed was covered with flowers

Saw many cattle cows all coming my way & passing me after that Silver was probably more than 150 feet in the air   then Silver was up in a steeple   after that men carried a pine coffin w. rope handles it was Papa Tabor laid out on a table Silver & I were looking at him & we knew he had been long dead when Tabor raised his head up to me & said Kiss me & held his mouth

wide O so wide open & showing his tongue which was so white &
begged me to kiss him in his mouth so I will get strong he said
I said I did not want to kiss the undertakers' embalming stuff &
Silver said we must wipe it off his head

I saw Silver in a rocking chair & her hands were up to her face
her face was very red & she was crying & telling me "Oh mamma
I am crazy I have gone mad & crazy" & her heart was broken

Winter came early, as it did every year. The wind blew hard, the earth seized up. Cold was the large bone everyone chewed. One night, Sue convinced Baby to walk downtown with her and the Mobergs, also Albin Erickson, and whoop it up at the Saddle Rock Café. Baby said she'd go and watch. On the way into Leadville, snow fine as sand blew in their faces and grained the frozen dirt, threading ruts on the road. The sun slid down like a frozen egg yolk behind the mountains, more clouds blew in, and pretty soon the white tatters whipping their ankles lay in scraps everywhere. "Maybe we should turn back," said Sue.

"When we come this far?" Baby trudged on.

They formed a moving shield around Baby. A general feeling of last chances set in. If they didn't have a good time tonight they might just have to wait till next June. "Is it always this cold in October?" Sue asked.

"Leadville's pure murder for winters," said Mary.

Sue kept on looking left and right. They'd come to the trestle across which trains had once hauled tons of precious ore to glowing smelters. She turned to Baby. "I don't see how you can stay by yourself in that shack all winter. You'd do yourself kind if you let me move in."

"You sing too much. I can't have a songbird all the time singing."

"Seriously, Mamma. What if something happened?"

"I can shift for myself."

"You can come stay with us," Mary offered.

Sue perked up. "Say, that's an idea."

"It's getting so this country can't feed a jackrabbit," said Deke. "Nothing but frozen dirt and snow."

"What's that suppose to mean? We can't help someone out?" Mary Moberg stared up at her husband like someone who wouldn't look away.

"It means any damn fool could understand if someone had to move in for a while. It's nobody's fault, it's the blistering freezing countryside here full of dirt and sage and squawking crows and rabbits so skinny they can't see their own shadows."

"You can move in with me, Mrs. Tabor," Albin offered. "You can sleep in my bed."

Sue pushed Albin, a little too hard. The tall skinny man felt like a loose bunch of pencils. "Why, Albin. You never asked *me* to sleep with you!"

Even in the dusk, they could see him blushing. "I didn't mean it that way. . . . I meant—on the floor."

"That's even worse!"

Inside the Saddle Rock, just the warm air and smoke and the yellow smell of beer was enough to intoxicate frozen pilgrims. Everyone there stared at Baby Doe. They'd all seen the motion picture about her, and knew she hadn't. She didn't care for the public attention, they assumed. Usually they steered strangers who inquired away from her house, and usually she only exposed herself in glimpses, at the backdoor of the convent, at Zaitz's grocery just before closing time. She took alleys, not streets, and went to early Mass on weekdays, when the church was mostly empty. Tonight was an occasion! In her long black skirts, black shirtwaist, black cape, in her work boots and fingerless gloves, she looked oddly . . . regal. She wouldn't remove the motoring cap tied on her head with a torn veil. Sue guessed she'd lost her hair. She'd never once seen Baby bareheaded. Around her neck a silver cross hung on a loop of twine.

Platters of fried chicken sat on the counter. Mrs. Cassidy brought some chicken and coleslaw to Baby Doe's table, compliments of the house. Eating, Baby cut her chicken with a fork and knife into dainty little pieces. Tim Riley and Bill Durning sat across the room glaring at Baby's table. After a while Tim walked over and stood above her. "Mrs. Tabor, when you gonna pay us?"

"Leave her alone," Deke said. "Can't you see she's busy?"

"A man's got a right to be paid for his work."

"You'll be paid," said Sue. "The mine's back in production."

"That worthless hole? She tricked us into working there a month. I saw the first day it was bunk. Played out."

"Then how come you worked there a month, you bohunk?" Sue raised her eyebrows.

"She said she'd pay us."

"On spec, you mean."

"It was strictly cash."

Sue stood up. "If it was cash, then you'd have no incentive to search out the good ore that's still in that mine to be found. What kind of a miner are you, Mr. Riley? Baby Doe Tabor would never agree to such a foolish agreement. She's a businesswoman." Tim Riley stood there rubbing his arm.

Baby Doe ate without looking up. "Did you send the sheriff to my house?" she asked.

"A man's got a right to sue for his wages."

Sue stepped toward Tim. She was large, but even larger was the zone of authority that outlined her body, like heat around a flame. "A mother's got a right to toss her baby in the river too, but that don't mean she should do it."

He seemed to see the logic. He backed up, nodding. He was still within earshot when Baby blotted her teeth with a napkin, turned, and said, "Tell your friends I got a new box of shells."

Deke and Mary Moberg broke into hoots. Five minutes later, Tim and Bill Durning were gone. People walked up to Baby Doe's table and thanked her for shooing those no-counts away. Others just came by to say hello. Some tried to give her money but she refused it. "We Tabors have always been proud," she said.

A piano, accordion, fiddle, and drums were playing on stage. The hardwood floor had been scattered with sand. Deke asked Baby to dance and she accepted, lifting her hand. Once on the dance floor, her stiff mannish staggers melted like snow. The band played "Nobody's Sweetheart," a two-step. The Red Sea of couples parted for Deke and Baby Doe, he of the tall spine straight as a flagpole, she of the flowing black skirts and broad smile. Sue and Mary danced and yoohooed Baby. Then the song was over and they changed partners: Deke danced with his wife and Sue with Baby Doe, to "The World Is Waiting for the Sunrise." It sounded just like the former song, though. "Play 'Gimme a Pigfoot,'" somebody shouted.

"Did you ever boogie-woogie, Mamma?"

"Dear me, no. Heavens to Betsy."

"I bet you were a swingster."

"Tabor and I never went out dancing. We preferred a quiet evening at home." This close, she smelled of mildew and horsehair mattresses and old trunks and urinous leaks. Their bosoms barely touched. Sue could tell that Baby'd stuffed newspapers under her clothes, front and back. Neither woman led, but Sue took the man's part. Her left hand held Baby's right, and her right hand cradled the small of her back. "You know what Deke asked me?" Baby leaned back and looked up at Sue's face, batting her lashes. She talked through a shy smile trying not to form.

"What?"

"For a kiss."

"What did you tell him?"

"First off, I told him this was the very place where I met Haw Tabor more than fifty years ago—the Saddle Rock Café. We were introduced here by a layabout pipsqueak named Billy Bush. I told him the last man I ever kissed was Haw. And the next man I kissed would be Haw too, in heaven. That wiseacre said, Are you sure he's there? I told him

I was sure as eggs is eggs. What do you think? You think there's a heaven?"

"You bet. We're in it."

Patton Hollow drove them home, Baby first. The snow had piled up and he'd put on his chains. Sue walked Baby into the shack and raked up her coals, filled her stove with wood, turned down the air vents. She covered Mamma with every blanket and coat she could find in the shack. "What'll we do about this snow?"

"We'll try and stay warm."

"I mean about the mine."

"It don't snow inside a mine."

"OK. I'll be here tomorrow."

I went to bed & had awful cramps in my legs & was in agony & got up & went to where Christ Jesus our Blessed Saviour appeared to me nailed on the cross the night of Nov 8 in front of stove pipe up high & I said Jesus take away these cramps & they instantly left.

I saw a small trap door open in the floor it was about 2 feet square & 4 men's heads were sticking up near the top & one said Mrs. Tabor unlock the door they were awful looking things & leered at me dirty I said all right I'll unlock the door and I closed the trap door on their heads it did not close down all the way

I was miles high in the air I was sailing all over the sky with nothing but a black dress

O great gorgeous curtain of green curling & thick curtain going & flowing from ceiling south to north on floor there is to be a war I saw visions of thousands of soldiers & men & horses men on them

Silver & I were in bed & in the bed was a fleshy man of medium age very clean & small smiling bald he was sitting up in bed

Saw someone as if their shadow was crossing very plain & big & strong pass close to my north window   quickly bolted the door without making a sound & looked out all windows   no one any where around   it was a dark big strong shadow a spirit sure

More snow. Sue no longer strode like Walt Whitman up to the Matchless with the earth expanding right hand and left hand—she had to plow and trudge through two feet of snow. Baby didn't sit outside by the shaft, she huddled in her shack next to the stove. Her chair beside the shaft head, pushed over on its side, lay buried in snow.

It was warmer down in the mine, of course, but hardly warm enough for Sue to work unclothed. Water dripped on her neck. In most places the rock face was harder to reach from her scaffolding of square-set timbers, she'd blasted so much of it out in recent months. She'd begun to expose some rotten quartz and wondered if this lode hadn't pinched out. She swung at some quartz with her pick and watched it drop. The work was good, the sheer strain of muscle, the pop of contact, sigh of release. Bone contends with rock and wins. What fun it was to sweat! When she swung at a prominent crack to the right a load of rock big as a truck engine dropped straight down and plunged out of sight. Her tower shook. Sounds of ripping and snapping wouldn't stop. A huge dull thump, then more roaring and sliding, and so much dust she began to choke. The timbers she stood on seemed to be swaying, then it seemed as though the whole mine was turning, then it paused and held. The timbers, she could tell, were under great strain. Carefully, she started climbing down through them. It felt like they'd been wedged askew and were threatening to burst. She could hear them groaning. Above, the roof of the mine hung uncertainly.

It loomed above her while she climbed down. Wait a minute, she'd left her pick up there on a timber. . . . Baby Doe always counted the tools. . . .

She lifted her lamp and peered beyond its vault of light overhead toward the darkness above. A groan came from somewhere; dirt sifted down. Shake out the fleas, Sue, get your ass down safe!

She realized when she'd reached the tunnel that the same square-set cribbing that cradled the lode and helped you reach its face in a stope as large as this one also held up the ceiling of rock, like a pillar. In a working mine you had to keep adding timbers. Baby'd never told her that! Her ceiling had dropped but the timbers held, like a bandy-legged hod carrier crushed by his load while climbing a ladder. . . .

She shuddered and let off a long and low whistle. She slapped her forehead and laughed out loud. She wanted to leap, but the roof on this tunnel was too low for leaping, why she'd smash her head. . . . The tunnel'd collapse! Climbing up the shaft, her limbs felt woozy. Her blood had thinned out. She pictured her hands letting go of the rungs and her carcass plunging down through the darkness like unsorted waste. . . .

When she told Baby Doe what had happened in the mine, Mamma just smiled and made Sue a cup of tea. She seemed slow and distracted. "Is the winze still free?"

"Which winze is that?"

"Between the fourth and fifth level."

"I didn't notice. I was scared out of my wits, for Pete's sake."

The shack felt warm enough, but Sue's feet were cold. Baby Doe wore two or three sweaters over long johns, and her feet were wrapped in burlap. A shelf on the wall near her table had collapsed at one end, and some cups and plates fallen, but Baby hadn't cleaned it up. Mice scratched in the ceiling. Burlap covered the windows. Sue's tea tasted like hot sugar water.

"Do you need any money?" Sue asked, then regretted it.

"Silver Dollar just sent me a check from Chicago."

"Who's that?"

"My daughter."

"I thought your daughter lived in Wisconsin."

"That's Lily. Silver's in a convent in Chicago."

"She's a nun?"

"The most holy nun they ever saw."

"Why'd she become a nun?"

"Because she wanted to. Why'd you become a hobo?"

She shrugged and sipped her tea. "Because I wanted to." Baby Doe stared at her. Sue tried to smile. "I figure in the spring we can hire a crew and shore up those timbers."

"Why wait until spring?"

"Well . . . I don't know. First let me recover." She shuddered and thought about almost dying, not for the first time. But it always seemed impossible to ponder your own death. It was never imminent save on special occasions, such as today, and that was now over. She realized she'd never climb down that mine again. "You can't hardly get no trucks up here now, and besides, how would you pay for the timbers?"

"They'll put it on my tab."

"The town's emptied out. Even the Climax is down to one shift."

"We can always find someone." Baby looked at Sue, a faint smile on her lips. The grey eruption of her face appeared spongy. It billowed with pores. "Sue, what's the matter? Don't I pay you enough?"

"I don't do it for the money! If I did it for the money I wouldn't be here."

"What do you do it for?"

"I *like* to work."

"Well, lots of us do. But you shouldn't ought to just think about yourself."

• • •

Baby's eyes popped open and flew to the ceiling. Dear Jesus, help me find someone good to check on the mine. Someone who won't try to take it away. . . .

She lay on her back beneath a huge pile of blankets, coats, and sweaters. Someone would have to crawl out of bed and stoke up the stove, someone, not me. . . . Small things were happening on her body. One blocked-up ear itched. Her lungs felt thready, windsocks full of holes. A shoulder spasmed. Sweaty feet cold as ice. Curved knuckling pains in the small of her back dug and probed. Eyelashes felt gritty. Joints inflamed. Her body, she knew, was becoming a thing, but had to go through this annoying stage, like a corpse thawing out. . . . No, that's not right. An old oven lit up rediscovering its smells. . . .

What strength and power she'd had when she was young! She was stronger than Sue. How she'd loved being in crowded rooms and pushing into people where they were thickest, and giving them her strength and receiving in turn their collective adoration, increased tenfold. She wrote songs and everyone sang them. . . .

Wait a minute, that was Silver. Still it was strange how many she'd herded ahead through the final exit, as though emptying a theater. At the end of a long, unfinished play she couldn't make heads or tails of anyway. . . . Haw's silhouette coffined by the doorway in a blaze of daylight beneath the Exit sign. . . . She could see his walking network of veins, muscles, bones, and thick language. Haw was dead, youth and strength were a joke. Weakness billowed inside her body like a stale wind, and bloated her flesh. . . . She threw off the covers and slowly crawled out of bed without standing. It was easier like this, but she still felt short of breath. She crept along the floor to the stove and touched it, to see if it was warm. It was! The warmth flowed into both hands up her arms to her heart, how cozy. Just what the doctor ordered.

She opened the stove, raked up the coals, stuffed it with wood. Another day, darlings. . . . "Mrs. Tabor!" Loud knock.

"She's not home."

"Mamma, open up. I brought you some hot food."

"Go away, she's not home. She went downtown."

"Nobody's downtown. There's six feet of snow. It took me most half the morning to get here."

Well then, the food couldn't be hot. Sue was lying again. "I'm taking a bath."

"Don't do this to me, Mamma. Please let me in."

Baby Doe sat on the floor before the stove. The open door smelled of stale creosote. Inside, the split slabs had started to smoke, and a red flame appeared snaking up through the crevices.

"Open up, please. . . ."

But it is mother—it is alright—may she be happy but for all their short lives my little ones never had one hour's pleasure from her, the poor woman   I had to attend to business, I couldn't

Saw myself squatting down at the north side of no. 6 shaft near edge of shaft or on it saw close to me in front of me a white new baby developing quickly another big white fat baby under it also developing the 2 babies I could see at same time they being newly born & quickly came from no. 6 engine house door a big heavy fat working woman in blue & white gingham & big apron she came quickly to me & put her hand under my arm & she helped me get up very sweet & tenderly   the babies were still developing

Saw a vision of muddy walls under my cabin on east side

From my left I heard my dear Tabor's voice so plain & lovely he said "A house of God struck by lightning go out and watch"

Saw 2 bad wicked men sitting at a table writing something on a piece of paper to harm us here about Matchless Mine followed by vision of two lovely girls lovely baby faces & yellow hair threw their arms around my neck & held on fast & looked in my face held me so strong & loving   their arms never left being around my neck with hands clasped at the back

Saw so much cooked food roast pork & all sorts of things on the floor and Haw said that dog touched the food don't eat it

After I lay down saw myself lying down & thousands of folk come passing close to me just to see me all nations & sizes & all dressed differently all kinds of important folk & common folk girls in dark blue & they walk around my cabin & stare at me & get on my bed & frighten me & I have to light my lamp

I was saying the rosary & little girl spirits filled the room near to me & walking round my cabin

Today this afternoon I was praying for my children & all my loved ones & as I was blessing Jesus for all his mercies he blessed me with a wonderful Vision of his Beautiful Head It was bent down as it is on the cross   His hair dark gold brown beautiful & His face and neck as white as snow

For four days it snowed without stopping. Leadville shut down. No one got in or out. Sue and Mary had no clothes to wash, since they couldn't collect them, nor could folks drop them off. Deke's truck got buried. The Climax Mine had built housing for their employees right at the site, and this became a source of anxiety to the Mobergs, that those who'd chosen to live in Leadville might lose their jobs if they couldn't make their shift.

Deke walked around room to room in a funk. Food wasn't a problem, they had plenty of canned goods, also soup bones in a basket frozen on the cold porch . . . flour, suet, baking powder, dried beans. . . .

Mary sang. Deke said shut up. Every morning, Sue checked outside to make sure smoke was coming out of Baby Doe's stovepipe. She had to climb a ridge behind the house to see it, and each day the snow drifted deeper. It took her half an hour just to go a hundred feet from the house.

"Does she have enough food?"

"Mr. Zaitz sees to that," said Mary.

"In this weather?"

"He makes sure she's stocked up. She says, Put it on my tab."

"Does he?"

"He's been putting it on her tab for twenty years. The town charity fund pays for it." They sat at the kitchen table drinking tea. Deke hadn't come down from bed that morning. The Home Comfort stove poured out warmth, but Sue shivered anyway, the cold was winning.

"Is the winters always this bad around here?"

Mary just shrugged.

"She's got money. I've seen it."

"She spends all her money making interest payments for this or that mortgage on the Matchless Mine."

"She told me her daughter sends her money."

"Which one?"

"Silver Dollar, in Chicago."

"That would be Mrs. Perkins, in Leadville. She sends Mrs. Tabor a check every month and signs it Silver Dollar. Otherwise she wouldn't cash it. Silver's been dead for ten years now."

Upstairs, Deke shouted for Mary. She wiped her hands on a towel—though they weren't wet—and tossed it on the table. From the pot on the stove she poured a cup of coffee and took it up to him.

At the table, Sue sat with legs crossed, fingers wedged between her knees, sinking into herself. She could bust through the snow and take her more hot food. . . . What about the daughter in Wisconsin? Was she dead too? She'd tried several times to clean up the cabin, sweep it out, organize the papers, but Baby wouldn't let her. Did she have enough wood? How could she even make it to the outhouse? The lean-to outside her door always smelled. No, she wouldn't. . . .

This was a new sensation, these dismals. Sue's soul felt like scum. Each wave of emotion curved back like a mirror. Happy people were always hiding something, she realized. They were hiding what she'd discovered, their gloom.

Spirits in blue space flew around the room, stars swung on strings. They spun like tops. Baby Doe lay on the floor, on her back, in the posture of childbirth, knees crooked. She looked down into the ceiling. The cord plugged into the light socket swayed standing up like a bean plant, swinging, it seemed. It balanced the hot plate, the table beside her, the floor, the earth. We're its fruit, she thought. The cold blew right through her. She didn't feel cold. Neither did she feel warm, or wait, she felt a little flushed, she wasn't sure. Six layers of clothes should have had an effect. I'm going to have a baby. A huge toe of white snow scrolled through the open door, and me without a fire. Look what they've done to the Matchless Mine, Horace. They've buried it with sky. The sensation of floating might have been fun if she could veer wherever she wanted, she thought. Until then it felt more like having overflowed. The bucket she used as a chamber pot was brim full. But it hardly mattered since nothing much of consequence was happening to her body. Functions had ceased. No reason for alarm. Breathing was more involuntary than ever, more desultory too. She took a deep breath, yet the sucked-in air wouldn't fill a thimble. Here I come, loons and goons! To inhale nothing deeply was a new sensation. She's not here, she's downtown. She's taking a bath. Being squeezed through a hole. Clogging, unclogging. The rhythm came back. She was breathing again. It felt like a cold rod rammed through her soul. Next she'd climb to her feet and eat a bonbon. Then once more the old round, the daily loop of breath and hash, the weekly grunt, the monthly howl. Breathing out, breathing in. Lack of air made it difficult, though. Bubbles in her chest broke in mid-climb. Her fists unclenched, then she couldn't clench them. Hands unclasped somewhere, dry lips sucked in. Nipples puckered, backs turned away, babies crawled off. Beheaded chickens raced toward immortality. Ships sank in utter silence. She couldn't put things in sequence. Once she'd spotted Horace pawing through her shoes, waistcoat unbuttoned, suspenders unattached. How would she look with a pair of red slippers hanging from her fingers before her squinting eyes? She remembered every shoe she'd ever worn, including her uncle's muck boots in Oshkosh. Whatever happened to the pink satin gown draped with silver lace, and the décolleté bodice made from velvet finished with pink marabou feathers? Lost with the peacocks.

What was he looking for? She gently shut the door.

Or the skirt and bodice profusely decorated with brier roses, the front being trimmed with mousseline de soie caught on the left shoulder with white ostrich tips? Offscum and chaff strewn across the sky, the last rags of daylight. Shreds of Paris fashion enlivened the sunset, like smoke from volcanoes. She'd always wanted to fly. On the Fourth of July, every whore in Leadville raced completely naked down State Street at dusk, displaying bitten fingers. Tough boys strewed broken glass on the street. The thought of Harvey Doe fell open in her mind. Mamma's bosomy hugs. To fly in a plane, to dive and climb. Bread was never enough for human beings, they had to have love, also filled with air. From an aeroplane things below grew huge. One plane in the sky was small as a dump truck, the noise of its engine suspended in a gorge. Shavings of puttering knocks and gasps, random and faraway. The pilot's nose red and sore. What if you died on a plane in flight? Whizzing through sky feet first, but dead. Panic swallowed her heart. Breathless again. Miraculously, a hand thumped her chest. Heartburn, no doubt. This too will pass. Silver Dollar's pony nudged the door open and entered the shack, waiting there to be shooed out. Go buy some Sterno, Honeymaid, quick, put it on my tab. Leadville was jumping!

Civil War veterans hauled up on wagons. Wallpaper at the Clarendon Hotel with misbegotten pitcher plants, inane bluebirds peeking through the branches. Fat cherubs chasing butterflies they'll never catch. Something twitched in her calf. She couldn't shut her eyes. Hurry up, more. Red velvet flock in the hallways of the Clarendon like curtains of blood hung behind the eyes. Haw pulled the curtains down on the landau so they could clench on the way to the Matchless. Their lubricious thighs, hairy and fluked. Then the shaft house filled with squeals and thuds, the comforting sound of buckets descending. All that made sense to Baby Doe's mind was that she'd fallen down number six shaft. She lay at the bottom looking up at the stars. Spirals of light curled and flowed in the air, visions of bright sulphides, bless God. Her mind was a feather. Horace descended large as a bull and covered her body and began pushing down. She pushed up. She pressed. She grew smaller, straining. She became a little girl again, entering Haw, he became a sugar daddy, entering her. Their bodies crossed at belly and hips like a hinged curule. Don't stop now, come on, you monster, push! She was the one pushing out nobody, squeezing darkness, frightened and numb. Help me, don't stop. Please stop! Help. . . . The dry heaves bucked her soul. Impossible to bear down, to stretch, to push harder, to squeeze, to let go, to do much of anything. The more she pushed the smaller she grew. Might as well take it easy. And Haw was enormous! His comforting smile. . . . A fly bit her heart. I'm not here anymore. Mouth wide open. I'm going to have a *baaaaby*. . . .

Nothing came out.

The snow stopped and no smoke came from Mamma's stovepipe. Tom French arrived at the door and offered to help Deke shovel out his car. Down the road from the Mobergs, others were outside surveying the extent of their entombment, pushing snow off their roofs before they caved in. "First help me shovel a path to Mrs. Tabor's house," Sue insisted. He did. Together, she and Tom shoveled all afternoon, digging a tunnel deep as an adit the back way up to Baby Doe's shack. Sue knocked and no one answered. She broke a window with a rock and looked in to see Baby Doe sprawled on her back beside the table. "Oh my God, she's dead."

Services were held in the Church of the Annunciation in Leadville, then her body was removed to Denver and buried next to Haw's. Lily, in Milwaukee, denied to reporters that Baby Doe was her mother. Her father, she said, had been Horace Tabor's brother, John; people had always confused the two families.

Even before spring came and the roads began to clear, Sue had trouble keeping out looters. Rumors flew that Baby had left a fortune behind in coffee cans and cigar boxes, so vandals ransacked the place. Then someone said she'd buried it outside, and holes appeared all around the shack. To save a trip, looters began taking their trash and dumping it in the number six shaft before poking around the grounds and in the shack. Whenever Sue heard cars going up there, she took the back way and chased them off. She became known as the Buffalo Woman for her tendency to charge without notice. One time approaching the door she heard someone inside say, "It stinks in here." A man emerged in long johns, suspenders, and rubbery trousers—needle-nosed and squinting—hauling a peach basket full of stuff, startled to see her. She seized his ear and nearly ripped it off. He dropped the basket. Before he could run, she kicked him in the buttocks so hard it jerked both his feet off the ground.

Inside the shack, the other man, just a teenager really, monkey-faced, scrawny, grabbed an ash scoop from the floor beside the stove and waved it in the air, trying to circle around her. Trash covered the floor, papers lay everywhere. She marched straight up to him, clamped her hand on his neck, and lifted him up while he flailed with the ash scoop as though swatting flies. She threw him so hard against the back wall the whole cabin shook; soot rained down from the disconnected stovepipe. Holding one arm, he picked himself up and ran out the

John Vernon

door. Through the window she watched them jump in their truck and speed off toward Leadville.

Oh Mamma, she thought, I'm doing this for you.

Outside, she inspected the peach basket's contents. A chipped coffee cup with *Tabor Opera House* mostly scratched out and rubbed off. A box of cigars, still wrapped in papers. A silver tray tarnished black. Shoes, a soiled fur collar and cuff. Sue recognized the latter from pictures of Baby's ermine opera coat. An old feather boa, water-stained books, a green wool skirt, a stereo viewer. She carried the basket to the number six shaft and threw the contents in.

It took all day to gather up the rest and dump it as well, saving only a lard box of letters and scrapbooks. Those, and some pictures.

That's it, she thought. The slow explosion of a life. Each load she dumped was a thought broken off or brainstorm hardened, something finished or swept aside or forgotten, the end of a long parade of fine tunings carefully made then spilled into piles. It was order in camouflage till Sue cleaned it up, then it turned back into unsorted waste, one person's tailings. It didn't make sense. It was out of sequence. It became incomplete.

She reconnected the stove and, that night, moved into the shack. She put nice curtains up, from a flowered pattern Mary had given her. She fixed the broken shelves. She swept the floors and scrubbed the corners clean, replaced the table's oilcloth, washed grease off the windows, dusted the mattress, boiled all the dishes, washed all the blankets, Oh Mamma! She sat in Baby's chair. She slept in Baby's bed. She looked out Baby's window. She stood in Baby's door, watching the road. When anyone came she slammed the door and locked it. It might have been pilgrims or scavengers who came. They might have pulled up in a wagon or car. She crouched down and growled, "She's not here, go away." Her fingers plugged her ears. Her eyes squeezed shut. All she could hear through the hiss of her blood was a murmur of thuds sunk in the distance like someone's lost cannon.

Author's Note

Baby Doe Tabor, née Elizabeth Bonduel McCourt, didn't receive the sobriquet "Baby" until she moved with her first husband to Colorado, but for purposes of clarity and continuity I gave it to her while she was still a child in Wisconsin. Otherwise, the events and dates veining this narrative are nearly all factual, more so than those in the other historical fictions I've committed. My characters are uncoincidentally named after and based upon historical persons who lived and died in the manner herein described during the nineteenth and twentieth centuries in America, and my quotes from letters, lectures, and newspaper articles are for the most part verbatim. Oscar Wilde did visit Leadville in 1882, and did sit to a midnight banquet in the Matchless Mine. Silver Dollar did die in the manner described in Chapter 7, and Baby Doe did write down the visions and dreams quoted in italics in my final chapter. Most of them are preserved in the Colorado Historical Society.

Still, my subject is the inner life. To base a novel like this one upon fact is to reserve the purest trespass for oneself. The inner life begins where historical knowledge ends, and utterly transforms that knowledge.

Thanks to Frank Bergon for his helpful suggestions. Thanks to my fourteen-year-old son Patrick for guiding me through the Colorado mine country, and for helping me with my research on the history and technology of gold and silver mining. Thanks to Pat Wilcox for "hurry up your stumps." And special thanks to Stan Oliner of the Colorado Historical Society, who inadvertently suggested this novel to me, and who generously helped with research and materials when I needed them.